BRIAN MATTHEWS, a Melbourne writer and academic, is director of the Europe–Australia Institute at Victoria University. He lives in Little River with his wife, literary agent and editor Jane Arms.

Also By Brian Matthews

Biography

Louisa

Short Fiction

Quickening and Other Stories
Oval Dreams

Fiction

Magpie (*with Peter Goldsworthy*)

Non-Fiction

Federation
Romantics and Mavericks: The Australian Short Story
The Receding Wave: Henry Lawson's Stories

Edited Anthologies

Henry Lawson Best Poems
Henry Lawson Selected Stories

A FINE AND PRIVATE PLACE

Brian Matthews

PICADOR
Pan Macmillan Australia

First published 2000 in Picador by Pan Macmillan Australia Pty Limited
St Martin's Tower, 31 Market Street, Sydney

National Library of Australia
Cataloguing-in-publication data:

Matthews, Brian (Brian Ernest).
A fine and private place.
ISBN 0 330 36225 9.
1. Matthews, Brian (Brian Ernest). 2. Journalists – Australia – Biography.
3. Critics – Australia – Biography. I. Title.
079. 94092

Typeset in 11/15pt Sabon by Midland Typesetters
Printed in Australia by McPherson's Printing Group

Cover and text design by Greendot Design

For Jane

Author's Note

I would like to thank the following people for help of various kinds: Michael Bisits, Jude Bourgignon, Nikki Christer, David Matthews, Vincent O'Sullivan, Jean Paul, Carol Scott, my editor, Judith Lukin-Amundsen, and Jane Arms, of course.

I must also thank the editors of *Scripsi*, *The New Ball*, *The Australian's Review of Books*, *English in Australia*, *Best Stories 1999*, *The Age*, *Overland* and *Kunapipi* for permission to reprint material already published in earlier forms.

The grave's a fine and private place
But none I think do there embrace.

ANDREW MARVELL, *To his Coy Mistress*

Prologue

St Kilda, or Hirta, is an island in the remotest archipelago in Britain. It is 110 howling, storm-tossed miles off the mainland coast of Scotland, forty miles west of North Uist, the westernmost island – the edge of the world. The archipelago, also known collectively as St Kilda, is accessible for only three or four months each year. The rest of the time, the ocean is too rough and the storms too violent to allow of any navigation. Even in the 'good' months, about a quarter of all attempts to reach St Kilda fail. A successful trip, from Tarbert on the Outer Hebridean island of Harris, takes between six and a half and eight hours, and all but the most seasoned sailors spend most of that time racked with seasickness.

St Kilda's inhabitants – before they gave it best and asked to be evacuated in 1930 – had subsisted by hunting various species of the millions of sea birds clustered along its precipitous, rocky headlands, fishing in the treacherous and mostly tumultuous surrounding waters, herding some of the world's hardiest sheep, and crofting.

There is only one anchorage, Village Bay, on the island of Hirta. The title island, so to speak – St Kilda itself – is a frown of massive rock lifting above the spume and crash of ocean, appearing and disappearing in fog and unravelling braids of spray. No one goes to St Kilda for pleasure. It is at best an adventure, at worst an experience of crushing remoteness, of the immense indifference of the natural world and human kind's dwarfed presence in it. And over it all hangs the brood of tragedy and failure.

If there was a saint who provided the original name for this maelstrom scatter of rocks and precipices in a boil of tide and surf, then no one has remembered who it was. It is no use praying to Saint Kilda. He – or she – will not respond, very probably did not ever exist. There is nothing, neither solace nor guidance, to be had from this saint who has no special day in the Columban Calendar, whose monument is a cluster of freezing, ocean-tortured rocks, whose music is the whine of wind or the thrumming roar of gales.

PART ONE

My Story

There are many times in this world when
a healthy boy is happy.

HENRY LAWSON, *Joe Wilson's Courtship*

CHAPTER 1

Cannon Fodder

I was born in the very last days of December 1936. If my mother had been able, or inclined, to hang on just a day or so, I would have made it to 1937 before entering the world – a much preferable year because it somehow sounds younger, more recent. For the historically minded, 1936 conjures up memories of Franco and the start of the Spanish Civil War. For those of a more sporting bent, there were the Berlin Olympic Games, where Hitler previewed monstrosities still to be born in his public and furious disapproval of the great Jesse Owens. In either case, though, the events seem aeons ago, whereas 1937, a more anonymous year, can take its place with all the rest and assume at least temporarily an ambiguous recency. All my friends who were born in 1937, and especially if it was in the later months of that year, have an egregious, arrogant – even if deeply erroneous – conviction that they are significantly younger than I am.

But not only did my mother not 'hang on', she certainly had no interest in doing so. Her labour was long and hard and when I at last appeared it still required the persuasion of forceps to coax me into the dangerous world. This process left me with two black eyes and a broken jaw, although the latter condition went unnoticed until I was eighteen and enduring a medical examination for National Service by an extremely bored, smart-arse Army medic . . .

'Righto mister, drop your daks and let's see your birth defects. Now, I want you to put your right leg up here, that's it. And sit your bum here. Good. Now lean back and put your weight on your left arm – here! Right, now swivel round and straighten your legs . . .'

On and on he goes, commanding me through a baffling series of gyrations which, too late, I realise, is just an absurdly complicated and humiliating way of getting me up on to the examination bed. The whole performance allows him, when eventually finished with me, to say, 'Now I'd like you to get down in a slightly less complicated way than you got up.' This is his party piece and the young man – some sort of army medical student, I suppose – who stands by observing the whole encounter finds this joke fracturingly funny, of course. 'You'll do,' says this khaki-tatty Hippocrates. 'By the way, how'd you break your jaw?'

'I haven't ever broken my jaw,' I tell him, on guard for some new nonsense.

'Look mate, if you haven't broken your jaw, then I'll . . .'

His alternatives are explicit, obscene, physically more or less impossible and increasingly terse. I accept it.

Sometime or other, without even noticing, I had broken my jaw.

A broken jaw did admittedly explain my lifelong lop-sided smile, and the only time it could have happened without being registered either by others or me was at birth. That in turn would illuminate my record as an unmanageable, howling, insomniac infant for about the first twelve months of my life.

The hospital in which this signal birth occurred was called Cambrai. It was run by a stereotypically formidable tyrant named Sister Minogue who, when told that my mother had given birth to a boy, said, 'How sad! Cannon fodder!' Not surprisingly, this reduced my mother, in her already exhausted state, to tears and gloom. But Sister Minogue was wrong, as a matter of fact. Although prescient about the imminent frequency of wars and rumours of wars, she could not have know that to be born in the second half of the thirties was a very strategic act that launched you on a tightrope across the abysses of the twentieth century: too young for the Second World War, which did not last long enough to gather you in; too young again for the Korean War; too old for the Vietnam ballot.

But, as I sit writing these words during the last days of 1999, I know that by far the most important feature of Cambrai and my birth was not the rumbustious Minogue or the jaw-breaking forceps wielded by Dr Bryan (whose less than deft performance was rewarded by having me as more or less a namesake) or the fact that, as my father told me once, I was the answer to a prayer (in later years he would take a much more ironic view both of prayer and the 'gift' it brought). What was significant was where Cambrai and its dramas were to be found. And where the cramped, squinting house was to which my mother and father took their little bundled-up firstborn son to begin his fragile existence. The answer to that, the answer to other questions too, perhaps, is – St Kilda.

Several miles distant from the city and its close-hugging ring of inner suburbs – Fitzroy, Collingwood, Richmond, Carlton, Brunswick, North Melbourne – and favoured in days gone by as a fashionable resort, an escape from the heat and dust of central Melbourne, St Kilda nevertheless retained an inner-city 'feel'. In the network of streets that backed away from Luna Park and the beach, a between-wars malaise had left its mark on the small, jostling houses and the footnote of garden that adorned the better of them. Everything seemed in a state of slow, amiable surrender. And most of the time, this helpless shrug, this concession to entropy, also distinguished one of the other important entities that the words St Kilda communicated to any native Melburnian: the football team.

But first things first.

CHAPTER 2

A Shout in the Street

From the moment I hit the streets – an aspiration constantly interrupted, monitored, truncated and occasionally forbidden by my mother, my grandmother and the army of aunts that constituted my wartime family – I was conscious of the marvellous array of distractions that St Kilda daily offered to its diverse denizens. It was a strange, confused little enclave, the rough bit of it that we inhabited, anyway. Working class mostly, yet without the fierce homogeneity of Collingwood or Fitzroy; grim and dark enough as the smoke from the council depot in Blanche Street mingled with exhaust fumes from the green buses to intensify the winter overcast, yet with Luna Park's mad laugh and the glitter of the bay and the broad curve of the beaches to adjust the balance; bristling with petty crims and with a tradition of more dangerous, gun-wielding gangsters, yet endearing in its polyglot confusion of dinkum

Aussies, orthodox or backsliding Jews, a vanguard of Europeans and a motley, coming-and-going population of drunks, down-and-outs, prostitutes, odd-job men and scroungers.

We lived at 54 Havelock Street where the tiny 'back-yards' jostled with the houses in neighbouring Fawkner Street. Our street struggled for respectability, but Fawkner Street knew exactly where it stood in relation to respectability: it stood nowhere. For me, the grid of streets that were supposed to be imposing reminders of colonial masters, pioneers, deeds and battles – Grey, Inkerman, Fitzroy, Fawkner, Balaclava, Havelock, Clive – became an endless source of fascination, not because I knew anything of their provenance but because these resonant names had been imposed on what became, incongruously, one of the least heroic, sleaziest, most underhand and unpatriotic districts in the whole of Melbourne.

In the years just after the war, when I was nine or so, the most famous resident of Fawkner Street was 'Pretty Dulcie' Markham, a gangster's moll who married one Leonard 'Redda' Lewis in her Fawkner Street house. This was a doubly significant date for 'Redda'. Not only was it the day of his delight, it was also the last of the seven days the local police had given him to get out of St Kilda. The best man was Lesley 'The Butcher' Goodwin who, as he assured the police, was 'in charge of the eighteen and there'd be no blues'. Despite this cast-iron consolation, the occasion was attended by numbers of uniformed and plain-clothes state functionaries who, sensitive to the holiness of the proceedings, remained shadowy in their cars while thoughtfully blocking off both ends of the road.

About a month earlier, Pretty Dulcie's Fawkner Street residence had been the scene of a very different ceremony during which ex-boxer Gavan Walsh was shot dead, his brother, Desmond, was injured and Pretty Dulcie herself copped a bullet in the hip. The matrimonial legacy of this was that the bride was able to set off her outfit with a white cast on one leg. She and 'Redda' were married in the very room where Gavan Walsh got his, which prompted a *Truth* reporter to ask, with the refined punctilio for which that paper was known, if she had any qualms about mixing marriage and violent death.

'Not a fuckin' one,' said the bride.

Pretty Dulcie was not one for the niceties either of language or behaviour. My Aunt Tilly, walking out behind Dulcie from the ladies' toilet of the Middle Park Hotel one afternoon and having no idea at the time who she was dealing with, noticed that Dulcie's dress was accidentally hooked up at the back (a not uncommon hazard for women emerging from public toilets). Helpfully, my aunt flicked the offending bit down for her, whereupon, before a word of explanation could be offered, Pretty Dulcie turned and intimated her gratitude by saying, 'You lay a finger on me again and I'll have the boys break your fuckin' arms.' To which she added a number of other recommendations very difficult to carry out, even if Tilly had had the slightest idea what they meant.

After the shooting, Dulcie used to sit outside the Prince Charles pub on the corner of Grey and Fawkner Streets – not a good place to be around in those days, though my reprobate Uncle Alex would go there in emergencies. She would have her injured leg propped on a stool and her admirers would ferry beers out to her. This was where I first saw her and learned of her fame.

I was at the time an altar boy at the Sacred Heart Church in Grey Street. With a kid named Frank Darmody, a street-wise urchin whose world-weary air of knowingness about gangland mores and aberrant sexuality was equalled only by the unctuous and public piety with which he discharged his duties as senior altar boy, I would do the early morning beat for the small brigade of old ladies, convent school girls and nuns who attended daily mass. Each morning, our duties done and with the priest safely dispatched back to the presbytery, Darmody and I would have a smoke and a swig of altar wine and then repair to Smith's Bakery down the hill in Grey Street where Darmody would buy four custard tarts with cream, which we would consume in scrupulously equal quantities while sitting in the gutter. Darmody always had money and I remember that, even at so tender and, more importantly, thoughtless an age, it was a matter of vague unease for me that I was never able to pay my way. This incipient sensitivity to some notion of fair play was, no doubt, what contributed to a convenient memory lapse and a catastrophic error of judgement on the only occasion when, it seemed, I could genuinely make a contribution. One night, just as I was drifting off to sleep, I became conscious of my grandmother's large figure looming over me in the gloom. She was leaving sixpence on the end of my bed, she told me, so that I could buy a loaf of bread for her on my way home from mass.

When I woke next morning, I had no recollection whatsoever of this half-asleep encounter and regarded the miraculous manifestation of a sixpence on the bedrail as an inexplicable recognition of my due. I spent what seemed to me most of my spare time doing 'messages' for a household of women and I felt greatly put upon as a result. So I was in just the state of mind to find miraculous justice absolutely unremarkable. Triumphantly that morning, I bought Darmody and me more custard tarts than we could handle. Only when my grandmother said, 'Where's the bread?' did I suddenly remember seeing her face like a wrinkled moon rising over me in the sleepy dark and realise that miracles were very unlikely in Havelock Street or anywhere else, for that matter.

It was Darmody who was my original informant about Pretty Dulcie; and, among my juvenile compatriots, it was Darmody who first saw and recognised her outside the Prince Charles. He confidently expected the gunman who had broken her hip to return and finish the job and was determined that we must both be on hand to see the action. I did not know then that Darmody was the source of massive amounts of misinformation. It was he who told me the first version I heard of where babies came from, which was as follows: the bloke buys a special seed from the chemist; he puts the seed in the bottom of a rubber thing called a franger; he puts the franger over his cock and sticks his cock in the woman (Darmody was vague on orifices but since my ignorance far eclipsed his, he was easily able to fudge); after some indeterminate time, the baby emerged from the woman's navel.

But, as it happened, he was right about Dulcie up to a point. There she was outside the pub; and she sure enough had her leg in a cast. But our elaborate and studied show of uninterested loitering was so obvious that Dulcie was on to us in a flash and told us to 'fuck off'.

Darmody was a mysterious character even then. He didn't live in St Kilda but travelled to Sacred Heart School by bus from Richmond or somewhere similar. Since almost everyone who went to the school walked each morning and afternoon, this was a curiosity. Darmody himself claimed that it had occurred because he had been thrown out of several schools in his own district, but most of us in his circle worked out that this was unlikely since his behaviour at Sacred Heart School was more or less impeccable. Which is to say, he did not get caught. Darmody, when I met him and for the duration of our association, was obsessed with sex, fucking, cocks, cunts and tits, words that he pronounced with a relish that was in inverse proportion to his comprehension of them.

He was a source of considerable though frequently inaccurate information on these subjects, both individually and on how they, in some cases literally, fitted together. He was one of those blokes who saw a *double entendre* in practically everything, not that he would have put it that way, of course. When Sister Chanelle, one of the young nuns – probably about eighteen years old, if the truth were known – showed us how to make a face-page for our art exercise books by concocting a mass of embroidery surrounding the word *A R T*, Darmody wrote on a scrap of paper and passed around his variation, which ran, *The beautiful A R T/Of a dirty big FART.* As it circulated clandestinely through the classroom, someone was caught with it, needless to say, but it was not Darmody. Similarly, during a class in which we were examining sayings, like 'A stitch in time saves nine', Darmody embroidered 'A little goes a long way' by sibilantly whispering to me, 'A little goes a long way, said the monkey as he pissed off the bridge.' I laughed, got caught and had to suffer the burning embarrassment of repeating this gem to Sister Ita and then, on her insistence, announcing it to the whole class. My face, given to generous blushing at the most fleeting of provocations, was pink for hours.

Darmody, of course, was not implicated. He was too innocent-looking to get caught in the net that followed such outbreaks of moral or other intransigence and too powerful a figure to risk dobbing in.

For all his prurience, Darmody was a very fine schoolboy cricketer and was genuinely knowledgeable about the game. Some of the best times we had together were discussing the fortunes of Bradman's team in England as they went on their triumphant way during the 1948 Ashes tour. But even here, Darmody managed to be mysterious. He claimed to have a turf wicket at home, in his back garden, which he and his brother and father had built and on which they practised each evening and at weekends. For some reason – probably because I could not imagine such a garden, such parental leisure, such *space* that was domestic and not actually a public park – I always found this terribly difficult to believe.

But Darmody characteristically met challenges not with the bravado and aggression typical of boys our age caught out in falsehood or about to be, but by deepening the mystery, always giving you utterly reasonable and credible rejoinders yet leaving just a chink of a reason to maintain your incredulity. It was maddening. He once claimed to have discovered, in a *National Geographic* magazine in the school library, the pictorial answer to all our puzzles about how women were constructed and what blokes did with them. But he wouldn't tell me in which issue, let alone on what page – and he never did, though he would refer to it often and allow his secret, chubby smile to underline his special knowledge.

When I desperately accused him of making it all up, he would simply assure me there were a lot of 'dirty pictures' in the *National Geographic*. This was easy to check. The school library was a glass-doored case with about twenty *National Geographics*, *Eric or Little by Little*, *Robinson Crusoe* and an undistinguished further assortment of determinedly English sub-literature, but I never managed to track down the erotic truth buried in *National Geographic*.

Even at the time, I recognised vaguely that Darmody was a true, if tricky, original and, while I had no expectations for myself whatsoever, I confidently expected Darmody would make his mark somehow – probably as a Sheffield Shield or even Test cricketer – and that we would all hear about it.

In later years, I would run across one or two of my schoolmates from those days but Darmody was not one of them. After he left school to take up, as I remember, an apprenticeship, I never saw or heard of him again. Unlike Jimmy McNeil, another mate of mine at Sacred Heart. Jimmy was a small, gentle bloke who kept to himself but enjoyed a joke and a laugh. It was laughing together that gave us our particular bond – two boys, on the small side in comparison to the others, pissing themselves laughing over their private jokes in a corner of the school yard or sitting together at the back of the classroom. In 1967 McNeil was arrested for armed robbery and wounding a policeman and spent the next eight years in Parramatta Gaol. During that time, he joined a drama workshop and wrote two fine plays, *The Chocolate Frog* and *The Old Familiar Juice*. Both had successful professional performances and McNeil won an Australia Council for the Arts grant in 1974, a year before his release. Back 'outside', however, he found it difficult to cope. He took to the booze and died an alcoholic in 1982. Some time in the late seventies, I went to see the double bill of *Chocolate Frog* and *Juice* at the Playhouse in Adelaide. I knew Jim McNeil was in town for this production and I decided to seek him out, perhaps backstage or somewhere similar, and say 'Gooday'. But when it came to the point, despite the added incentive of having enjoyed the plays immensely, I did not do it. It all seemed too hard. I felt uneasy in the world of the theatre, was unsure how to go about contacting someone backstage or through an agent and, in any case, I became convinced he would look at me without recognition or suspect me of chasing him for his notoriety. So, in the end, Jimmy McNeil disappeared from my sight as thoroughly as Darmody had. I regretted my failure of nerve ever after. We probably would have had a good laugh together.

Curiously enough, I was to come much closer than ever Darmody did to the real, live violence of the gangs. The quickest way from the middle of Fawkner Street to the middle of ours was to sprint along the drain that intersected both streets and passed beneath each by means of a tunnel. This drain ran right alongside our house, and various Fawkner Street denizens, choosing this expeditious method of escape, could often be heard clattering over our front fence as they emerged from the darkness of the midnight drain on their inexplicable, speedy errands.

One such exodus at about two o'clock one morning late in 1945 was apparently expected and eagerly awaited. As the sprinters emerged from the straight and started tumbling over our fence, they were greeted by what the newspapers called 'a hail of bullets', which took large chunks out of the front of our house and ten years off my grandmother's life as she cowered (a difficult position for one her size) in the front room.

In the ensuing gun battle, Mrs Rose Wajngarten's potted plants were shot off her front verandah like whisky bottles at the back of the bar in a western movie. My grandmother, who could never get her head round a name like Wajngarten and always referred to her as 'Rosie-across-the-road', whisked her away from her shattered eyrie the following morning and installed her in our kitchen where she had loud, continuous and no doubt fully justified hysterics. My Irish grandmother keened (which is a poetic word for a very loud noise), my three-year-old sister screamed in sympathy with the surrounding chaos, my mother made endless pots of tea and my newly returned father walked up and down chain smoking and muttering, 'Christ almighty' and 'It was quieter in bloody New Guinea.'

Though I regaled Darmody with an eye-witness, graphically exaggerated account of these events which, to his chagrin, he knew from the newspapers to be broadly accurate, the truth was that I slept through all the gunfire.

My memory of that stirring night and its aftermath is that my family accepted it all with fair aplomb. Though Celtic to the core, my mother's tribe were already very much alive to the Australian habit of irony. Without ever putting it in so many words, they knew from the example of their Australian friends that irony was a way of coping with life which did not adjust the intensity of the external reaction to the quality of the stimulus. It provided the same reaction, varied only by minuscule gradations of voice and glance, to no matter what crisis. If they ever needed any tutoring on this, they had only to observe my extremely saturnine, Australian father, the antipodean intruder into the shamrock, mist and thistle romanticism of the clan.

I was reminded of this ironic habit years later when, forced by a temporarily strangled cash flow and an empty petrol tank to ask a service station attendant for 'Two bobs worth of super', I evoked the utterly deadpan, monotone reply, 'Whaddya tryin' to do, mate, wean the bastard?'

But irony was not the mode of Rose and Ernie Wajngarten – 'Rosie-across-the-road' – and her husband. They needed the ministrations of my grandmother and her entourage on that morning after the shooting, and Ernie was grateful to be able to leave Rose in good hands as he hurried to work in a high state of nervous excitement himself. And so, over many cups of tea in the comforting if chaotic surrounds of my grandmother's kitchen, the sensation was discussed over and over and made manageable. My grandmother said that 'villains' were pouring into St Kilda and soon there would be no room for decent people. Doreen Wajngarten and I chucked a ball around and the old man, still at a loose end because he had returned so recently from the war, went for another smoke and a moody walk along the beach.

I don't think anyone knew from this pleasant, friendly but impenetrably self-enclosed Jewish couple just what horrors they had fled in Europe. They had arrived in the later years of the war and at first lived in a kind of barricaded privacy. Their house encouraged reclusiveness. It had the only real verandah down our end of the street – a long, high-walled, fortress-like space further shaded and made mysterious by the prolific fronds, vines and languorous blooms of Rose's ill-fated potplants. But gradually Rose and Ernie opened out to friendly advances, greetings and visits. Their one child, Doreen, had already, in the manner of children, introduced herself to the rabble of the street.

We junior philistines had no idea of the resonance of the name 'Doreen' in the Australian literary culture, but it sounded funny anyway and Doreen thus became the bearer of many burdens. She was a late-arriver, a little older than the rest of us, the lone girl in a street full of boys, and she had an unconventional name. Unabashed by derision and insult, she threw herself so relentlessly into the street cricket and football that she became an honorary. Her campaign for acceptance would never have gone far on the strength of her bowling or batting, which exhibited a truly European impatience with the subtleties of the longest game. But the stories she told us of another life before Havelock Street invariably captured our unwilling attention. When rain brought cricket or football or just general mucking about to a temporary close, we would all sit on the famous verandah and yarn and boast and bicker. But above all, we would listen to Doreen's stories, which we derided as lies but which somehow broached the breezy ramparts of even that most daunting of defences – small-boy skepticism.

Among Doreen's fragmented European memories were

sudden, inexplicable night-time abandonments of one house for another; days spent in gloomy rooms; door-knockings in the dark, and hushed, nervous comings and goings and streets full of shouting people and the splutter of gunfire. No doubt it was actually all a vague blur to Doreen. She embroidered the wisps of memory, anecdotes overheard, the splinter of a scene revealed then hidden as a remembered curtain flapped across an alien window, because it was the one way she could impress us. But there was, of course, awful truth behind it all. Even we recognised an urgency to her anecdotes once she got going on them and we never tired of the climax – a scrambling, half-dragged race down a country road as the strafing planes began their run, a dive into the high, thick waving cover of a wheat field beneath the chatter of machine guns, Ernie's trembling arms as he tried to cover Rose and Doreen, the wild truck ride which, in Doreen's recall, seemed to have brought them all the way to Havelock Street. Probably gunfire in the night was the very last thing Ernie and Rose could tolerate.

Years later, a young woman in her late teens, Doreen committed suicide in the grip of schizophrenia. And not long after, Ernie Wajngarten, a non-swimmer clad in winter clothes, heavy overcoat and solid working boots, walked to the end of the cold and deserted St Kilda pier and threw himself in. His body was found the following morning drifting and rolling gently just off the shore he had so often walked with his wife and daughter in their newfound freedom. Rose left the district and was never seen or heard of again by any of those who had known her. An entire family had died.

CHAPTER 3

Annie

Annie Carroll was a dark, striking Irish immigrant of twenty-one when she married Glaswegian Alexander Murray, who was thin and serious-looking but with soft blue eyes and a mouth used to smiling. They were, it seems, in love, optimistic and broke and had little choice after their marriage but to return to Glasgow's grim slum, the Gorbals, where Alex had grown up. On the marriage certificate Alex is described as a Flesher's Assistant. Annie did domestic work when she could get it and took in sewing.

The world into which, over the next ten years, their children were born (James, Elizabeth – my mother – Alex and Jean) was grey and tough. In the foreground, the bleak Gorbals streets streaming with damp and darkness that seemed somehow unrelieved even by the brief summer; nearby, ugly, industrial Glasgow; and, more distantly – probably so distantly as to seem not worth worrying about – Europe heading for the brink.

Undaunted by his surroundings and the apparently imprisoning nature of his foreseeable daily existence, Alex was planning to take his increasingly beleaguered but close and happy family to Canada or Australia to start a new life when matters were abruptly taken out of his hands and he became Private Alexander Murray, Driver, Army Service Corps. Thereafter, their marriage was conducted through letters when he was able to write from France and, finally, in official documents.

> ... I shall try to write as often as can I hope this settles your mind a bit your prayers are being well answered my dearest Ann ... I am glad to hear that Jim is keeping all right, this war is at its worst. My Dear Ann, I am sorry to hear about David once they are reported missing you may say good bye. My dearest Ann, leave is still stopped, but when it starts I shall get away on leave, it is hard lines My Dearest Ann, if it is not too much trouble you might send me on a small parcel and when I do come home I shall give you as much money as I can. I wish this war was finished for I am fed up. My dear Ann, you and the children try to be as cheery as you can I feel all buggered up but I shall just have to carry on the best way I can ... I hope David turns up all right – try and keep cheery and keep on praying for me your prayers are being answered and I am glad to hear that the children are keeping all right. We are not on the same front now, we are on another front and it is actually hell. I could tell you more but this letter might get opened. We are out for two or three days. I shall try to write as often as I can, try and keep cheery I will now close hoping this letter finds you and the children keeping well. I am keeping not so bad at present.

I remain your ever loving husband,
Alex.

*

Madam

I regret to have to inform you that your husband 17051 Pte. A. Murray 1/6 Duke of Wellington's was admitted to No. 10 Casualty Clearing Station last week suffering from shell wounds to head and chest, and that he died on the 28th April. He received the sacraments during his illness, and was very resigned and patient. He desired me to say that he sent his love to you and the children. He was interred on the 29th April in the local military cemetery according to the rites of the Catholic Church. I beg to offer you and family my sincere sympathy in your sad bereavement.

Yours faithfully
Rev. P.J. Kilduff

*

Madam

I am directed to acquaint you that the Command Paymaster, eastern Command, Science Museum, Exhibition Road, South Kensington, London SW7, is being authorised to issue to you the sum of Sixteen Pounds being the amount that is due to the estate of the late No. 17051 Private Alexander Murray, 6th Battalion, West Riding Regiment on account of War Gratuity.

Should no communication on this subject be received from the Paymaster within the next few days, application for payment should be made to him by letter.

Of the above amount, two thirds is the property of the

deceased's children and must be used for their equal and exclusive benefit.

I am, Madam,

Your Obedient servant

*

P&O

Australia via the Cape Service

32 Lime Street London EC3

Third Class (Steerage) Passengers' Contract Ticket

The P&O Steam Ship Balranald of 13,100 tons register, to take in Passengers at the Port of London for Australia on the Twenty-first day of August 1924.

I engage that the person(s) named in the margin (Mrs Annie Murray, 39, Miss Elizabeth do, 14, Miss Jean do, 7, Mr James Murray, 17, Mr Alexander do, 12) shall be provided with a Third Class (Steerage) Passage to, and shall be landed at, the Port of Melbourne in Australia in the Steam Ship Balranald, with not less than Fifteen Cubic Feet for Luggage for each Statute Adult, and shall be victualled during the voyage and the time of detention at any place before its termination, according to the subjoined scale, for the sum of 148-10-0 including Government dues before embarkation, and Head Money, if any, at the place of landing, and every other charge, except Freight for excess of Luggage beyond the quantity above specified.

*

On arrival at Port Melbourne late in October 1924, Annie disappeared into the labyrinthine streets of St Kilda, beginning with Clive Street, where she was reunited with her old friend Molly Bradley, chasing cheap rents through adjoining lanes and byways. During their first year in Melbourne, she moved house six or seven times, assisted by Mr O'Brien whom Molly Bradley introduced to her and who became so used to her nomadic ways that he would move their few sticks of furniture and other gear during the day while Annie was working and the younger children were at the Sacred Heart Primary school just up the hill in Grey Street. (Jim was beginning what would be a long association with the Collingwood boot factory.) They would farewell her at one house in the morning and greet her that afternoon at a different one.

They fetched up at last, though, at 54 Havelock Street, that same little squinty place to which my mother would a dozen years later return, bringing her screaming, broken-jawed scrap of cannon fodder. They would have been far too preoccupied to notice – even supposing they had the slightest interest – that in settling at last for Havelock Street, they had adopted not just a neighbourhood, not just a highly cosmopolitan milieu, not just a distinctive, rough-and-ready street full of people doing the best they could with always stoic and often insouciant bravado – but also a football team. During their first full year in Australia, bouncing from street to street and house to house, the Murrays, like it or not, would have had their attention drawn by neighbours and casual acquaintances to one of the more unusual and noteworthy local phenomena: the Saints were having a pretty good year – eight wins, nine losses, sixth on the ladder at the end of the season and the Brownlow Medal winner in Col Watson.

What they would not have known or even begun to

comprehend was that 1925 was an epochal year for the Victorian Football League. A meeting of the VFL in January of that year laboriously reached the decision to admit three more clubs to the League, making a total of twelve contenders and eliminating the much criticised bye which had been necessary for the previous six years in a nine-club competition. The three new clubs were North Melbourne, Footscray and Hawthorn, which marked their elevation to the VFL by finishing tenth, eleventh and twelfth respectively. But it took the heat off St Kilda, whose sixth position overall looked better out of twelve than out of nine. In the following year, 1926, the three new clubs maintained their monopoly of the three bottom positions – but the Saints, reverting to type, were ninth.

Settled at last, my grandmother Annie ensconced her little clan – Jean and Elizabeth, Alex and Jim – in the Havelock Street house and began to run it, as she had been accustomed to do for years, with a grappling discipline and a heart full of purpose and controversy. Her courage and determination would at times decay into doggedness and wilful refusals. Her stern, sometimes rather un-Irish mien would soften with memories and Seppelts Purple Para Port; and her view of things then was dominated by hardships and loss, by that grave somewhere in Europe that she had never seen and never would see. But she marched into 54 Havelock Street intent on two main purposes: to settle her family and bring them all through – in which she succeeded splendidly; and never to leave there till she was carried out. And she never did.

*

As I grew up during the war in a house which, from where I stood, seemed to be full of and surrounded by women, I saw a great deal of Annie, my grandmother, and – oblivious to the matriarchal bullying of which I later realised she was an accomplished and canny exponent – I grew to love her. She looked after my baby sister and me at nights and weekends and during school holidays. She was stern and affectionate, lovable and brusque, generous and puritanical, entertaining and gloomy, funny and indecipherable. She would say, 'Whisht!' which meant 'Be quiet', and 'We'll get w'dinner' – not 'our dinner' but 'w'dinner'. She spent a great deal of each morning energetically going about her domestic tasks in dressing gown and slippers. The slippers were ancient and indestructible but broken down at the heels, which caused them to make the *shush-shush* rhythm that drove my father crazy after he had been home half of one morning. Always hard of hearing, she had miraculous aural remissions when she would hear a whisper from the other end of the house during a thunderstorm, whereas her normal response to almost any remark, question and especially rebuke was, 'What's that?' She relaxed with a few glasses of Purple Para Port and *really* relaxed with several, after which she would sing Scots songs in the thick accent which she let out several notches for the occasion but which always remained in her very strong. Her speech was speckled with dialect words from both Ireland and Glasgow.

Of all her children, Jim retained the strongest accent, but my mother seemed to pick up the rhythms and some of the phrases that she had grown up with, and she carried them into her normal speech ever after. Once, when I had been explaining to her a particularly heavy schedule of meetings, classes and appointments that I was facing on the following day, she exclaimed, 'My God, you're full o' functions.'

My grandmother called the chimney in the sitting room the 'lum'. This chimney was the bane of her life because it refused to *draw* and only my father seemed to be able to get it under control. When he was not around, the standard method my grandmother employed was to hold sheets of newspaper across the opening of the fireplace, sealing it off. The draft generated by the fire would suck the newspaper inwards, the fire would spring into life, the newspaper would catch with an explosive *whump* and the whole chimney would burn like a blowlamp, spitting flame and sparks into the cold St Kilda darkness, betraying our position during the war to the ever-vigilant Japanese and leading my father to remark, when he heard about this practice long afterwards, that that must have explained why St Kilda had become strategically known as 'the soft underbelly of Australia'.

'Lang may your lum reek' is an unlovely Scottish blessing which I think roughly means that if your chimney continues to emit smoke then things must be going not too badly. In the case of Annie's chimney, it reeked back into the sitting room and thence through the house, and it went on reeking immoderately until brought under a stronger regime. As an omen, it was not up to much.

CHAPTER 4

No. 17051 Private Alexander Murray

He gazes out at me from an ornate, scrolled, oval frame – a gentle, slightly bemused look to him, a thin boyish face overshadowed by the military cap. On either side of the portrait, his medals, still with their faded ribbons; and between them, a citation in which futility grapples with dignity:

> He whom this scroll commemorates was numbered among those who, at the call of King and Country, left all that was dear to them, endured hardness, faced danger, and finally passed out of the sight of men by the path of self sacrifice, giving up their own lives that others might live in freedom. Let those who come after see to it that his name be not forgotten.

Annie never saw her husband's grave and neither did

any of her family. And since Alex's letter, perforce, mentions no location and Kilduff is likewise silent on the whereabouts of that 'local military cemetery', no one ever knew in any detail where Alex was buried. By the time my grandmother Annie had settled in St Kilda and, still young, begun her long life of widowhood, Alex's memory had broken loose from its moorings in the earth he trod as surely as his spirit had flown the shattered body when the shells knocked him over. In Annie's head he lived on – but only there, and, in the nature of grief and loss, ever fading.

Where had he been all these years?

Working in London in the early nineties, I decided to track him down. I read a lot of military history, talked often to historians of the Great War, pored over maps of the barely shifting front and of the big push of 1918, took a few punts and scarcely justifiable imaginative leaps and came at last to the conclusion that when Alex moved to 'another front' he must have been part of that intense concentration near Ypres where the fighting in those last months was 'actually hell'.

I then landed the fruits of this flawed research on the Commonwealth War Graves Commission in Buckinghamshire and – they found him! In a small British war cemetery just outside the village of Arnèke near the Belgian border and a few kilometres from Ieper, as Ypres is now called . . .

Fields of corn, crowding up to the low stone walls on two sides, briskly rattled in the same breeze that tuned the cypresses to a pensive sigh. 17051 Private Alexander Murray's meticulously tended grave was over near one of the walls: bees lazed through the lavender nodding across his engraved name; summer sun radiated from surrounding stone.

It had been a nightmare getting there from our rented holiday house in Normandy and it would be worse going back when darkness overtook us on the mad autoroutes. Time and again on the way up we – my wife, my two stepsons and I – had come close to abandoning the whole journey. And as if to underline our folly, things went wrong. We took a wrong turn and bogged down in provincial lunchtime traffic. Later, after a stop by the roadside, we drove off forgetting our coffee cups and picnic plates incautiously left on the roof of the car – until we heard them smashing along the road as we resumed the journey. What after all was the point? Black cypress shade; a moulding of earth; a name cut in stone . . .

But of course it was worth it. It was as if we knew him at last, as if he had struggled home (*My dearest Ann . . . I shall get away on leave*) years too late, with no one to meet him, but home nevertheless. Such thoughts were enough to spring tears for this young man who never saw thirty and whose grandson was twice his age when finally they 'met'.

Beyond all that, though, was the sense that this small meeting contained something of what history itself is about, the long, faltering, half-muffled conversation of humankind. We could not talk to him but, one way and another, we had talked of nothing else for days, and we would talk often thereafter of the experience of finding that grave, the look of it at last securely in our memories and imaginations.

In a nondescript bar back in the village of Arnèke, the boys and my wife and I held a small and long overdue wake for Alexander Murray. With some fairly rough red and a couple of lemonades, we saluted him, welcomed him back from his long exile, reclaimed him from the indeterminate and unyielding past and returned him ceremonially to the grey halls of memory.

My Aunt Jean was overwhelmed to see at last, in our photos, the grave of the father she could not remember, and my sister wept for her grandfather – it was as if he had at last come to visit, she said. But my mother, curiously, showed only a spare and withholding interest in the photographs of her father's grave and the story of our 'find'. Perhaps she did not want the distress of re-opening those imaginary doors, of looking again on the vibrant lives of Alexander Murray and his beloved Anne and their large plans and their four kids and the lamp-lighter sparking the murky dusk of Glasgow long long ago, before wars and wounds and disappearances.

Despite my mother's aloofness, the family was enriched by knowing that two of us at least had seen the grave, placed flowers on it, photographed it, signed the cemetery's memorial book. It was a lesson in history. Why history – detecting, listening to, making sense of the alien voices of the past – matters.

CHAPTER 5

Alex

Nobody famous lived in Havelock Street, although it was intermittently home to several outstandingly public drunks, one of whom was my Uncle Alex. Alex was in the Tank Corps and what must be one of my first memories of him was when he came home on leave. He paid a great deal of attention to his mother, Private Alexander Murray's beloved Anne, who ran our crowded home with an iron fist but who melted at Alex's merest glance. This enabled him to wheedle some money from her with which he financed a spectacular, day-long spree that ended late that night in the 'side path' of our place. There he brawled with his elder brother, my Uncle Jim, until both were exhausted and staggered to bed in the room I shared with them. Next morning, spruced up, unrepentant, irresistibly charming and witty, Alex would hit the trail again, making every pub a winner until his leave was over and he went back to camp.

On his return to civilian life, Alex became a brilliant chef who had a succession of high-class appointments each of which he would eventually lose after some spectacular binge threw the kitchen into confusion and put the establishment's reputation on the line. He was well known round St Kilda – to which he would return after each sudden termination of employment from Sydney or Hobart or somewhere up the bush – as a good bloke, a fierce drinker, a fighter of threshing-machine quality, a friend who would give you his last penny and who was destined inevitably for disaster.

Behind this lamentable descent lay the disruptions of wartime and, in the late forties, a doomed marriage. Like many another returned soldier, Alex could cope with neither. In his own inadequate way, he desperately tried to rescue his marriage in the disintegration of which, for all his alcoholic and larrikin excesses, he was by no means the wholly guilty party. For a while he and his wife, Gwen, and their one child, my cousin Margaret, lived in an extraordinary, ramshackle house on the corner of Havelock and Carlyle streets. It was the wonder of the district because it was actually on a large, though weedy, block and the house itself was sprawling and spacious. Moving there after a succession of unsuitable flats and rented rooms was Alex's last throw in the marriage, his last attempt to settle. Gwen soon tired of it and took off to Sydney. I did not see my cousin again for thirty-five years.

To the very end, Alex was a reprobate. Once, years later, when I was assiduously courting a young woman of whom I had high hopes of some kind or another, I returned to my FX Holden, which I had parked and left unlocked near her house not far from Havelock Street, to find Alex curled up in the back seat. He was drunk, of course, but woke with a beatific smile, as eager to meet my 'young friend', as I was to ensure he did not.

My father always felt a sort of special bond with Alex. They had met around 1930, when my father was twenty and Alex eighteen, as members of a bicycle road racing team and hit it off together. Alex in those days was fit, teetotal, full of cheek, a foil to my father who was quieter, diffident. As their friendship grew, my father was invited to 54 Havelock Street where he met Jim and Jean and the indomitable Annie but above all Alex's older sister, Betty, a vivacious redhead who loved to sing and dance. My father, who had doggedly battled through Pianoforte and Theory Grade V under the tutelage of Miss M. Hendry but who had, even in his own estimation, a tin ear, was not given to singing and dancing. But he took them up with gusto because he knew, very early, that Alex's sister Betty was the girl for him. And so, my father, Owen Thomas Matthews, married my mother, Elizabeth Ann Murray, on 27 October 1934 with a beaming and ebullient Alex as master of ceremonies at the wedding reception.

But a decade later, no bond could withstand Alex's growing, booze-fuelled urge to self-destruction. He would turn up at the Havelock Street house, often after long and unexplained absences, drunk and looking for trouble. Even after his marriage to Gwen, he would still arrive on the doorstep, forlorn or raging, looking for help or sympathy or money. I remember one winter evening, probably around 1946, Alex rampaged down the long passage and burst into the lounge room where my father was sitting reading the paper, having just returned from work at Fishermans Bend on his bike.

Alex bumped the back of the chair and the old man said, 'Don't do that, Alex, if you don't mind.' Alex bumped it again, announcing that some people were too high and mighty for the likes of him, and the old man said, 'If you do that again, Alex, I'll punch your nose.' So Alex bumped the chair again and, in what seemed like the one continuous movement, the old man was on his feet, the newspaper flying to pieces around him as he stood, and nailing Alex with what I remember as an uppercut rather than a straight punch to the nose.

What is it about blokes like Alex? He had terrorised that household off and on for a few years, yet, when the old man took some action, all the women – my grandmother (understandably, I suppose), my mother and whatever bevy of aunts happened to be present at the time, all flocked round the recumbent drunk and treated the old man like a pariah.

My father strode out to the walled-in back verandah where he had his tiny workbench, collected a handline and assorted other gear, and walked down to St Kilda pier. He came back about midnight. I was in bed but awake, Alex was in bed and comatose and everybody else was still up, goaded by anxiety and sensation, when my father walked in with the biggest flathead any of them had ever seen. Years later, he would tell me the fish must have 'collided with the hook' because nobody ever caught anything like that off the pier at St Kilda. 'I'll clean it now and you can stick it on the ice for tomorrow,' he said to my grandmother.

He neither mentioned nor asked after Alex and soon everyone went to bed.

I watched the moonbeams slanting slowly across the skylight in the passage outside the bedroom door as my

Uncle Jim breathed evenly, Alex snored his way into yet another spectacular hangover, the old troubled house creaked into silence and St Kilda's dangerous streets and byways subsided to the uneasy state of rippling disturbance that was as quiet as they ever managed.

Alex was a St Kilda man and my father was not. This meant that Alex and, for that matter, my mother and all her family, felt at home in the bustle and grime, the smoky air and the shady comings and goings. My old man was never comfortable as a St Kilda denizen despite being a stalwart of the Saints. The mix of pace, sleaze, gaudiness, and slackness did not suit him. He made this clear by planning endlessly and publicly to escape it: by transforming our minuscule bit of it with vegetation and by taking us on modest picnics to distant bay beaches as soon as he had the means to do so.

But my mother was at home in St Kilda, like all the women in our extended family, and I see now that my father's constant and explicit rejection of it was a cause of important disagreement between them. Acland Street and Balaclava and, only a little further afield, the market in Prahran were her stamping grounds. She was a diminutive, pretty woman with great musical talent and a quick, incisive mind. She was my father's inferior in education, yet she brought an intuitive intelligence to the partnership. She had a severe, practical line on life that no doubt she both learned and inherited from her mother and that would occasionally drive my father crazy when he was launched on, or about to announce, one of his more amazing lateral leaps.

My mother certainly regarded his plans to escape from

St Kilda as being among his more lunatic schemes. She could not see how it would be done and, perhaps more importantly, she did not see the necessity. Of course, if it came to a stand-off, my mother, though incredibly stubborn and tough-minded, would in the end concede. She had promised to love, honour and obey, and that was what she did even if she ran a very good and sometimes spectacular line in equivocation, blunt objection and sudden, infuriating inability to understand the simplest propositions.

Following the footy team did not make you a St Kilda denizen in the mould of my mother or Alex. The true St Kilda people tended not to be true St Kilda Football Club supporters. The two conditions involved very different temperaments and views of existence. Among the inhabitants of St Kilda in the years immediately after the war there was a tough, slam-bang sort of optimism that was not deterred by realistic appraisal of the way things shaped up every day when you stepped on to the streets. There was not much going for you, but life seemed to consist of an endless parade of minor sensations, some of which would beam a temporary and wavering light into the literally grey atmosphere. Somehow, the mixture in St Kilda threw up constant departures from the calm, the everyday, the settled.

Overall, postwar Melbourne was a ritualised, smug place, its profound sense of self-satisfaction, its addiction to the predictable and the unsurprising, being reflected in the pages of the *Herald* each evening. This was why St Kilda, the western side anyway – ragged, unpredictable, below-the-belt – was regarded as exotic and, in the end, reprehensible, somehow letting the side down.

St Kilda Football Club supporters, conversely, were, in

the nature of things, given to gloom and, above all, bullied by predictability. They had none of the knock-about, take-it-or-leave-it philosophy of the men and women you would bump into any day in Acland Street, or Balaclava or Fitzroy streets. If there was one thing you knew about the St Kilda footy team in those days, it was that they would lose and that they would continue to lose, but that 'next year' would be 'the year'.

What I have styled the gloomy, stoic sort of Saints supporter probably more often lived in Brighton, or Elwood or Caulfield. Their predilection for the sweet taste of self-indulgent defeat was honed and polished amid the pressing conventions of standard Melbourne suburbia. In the depths of St Kilda, though, nothing was standard. So when a true St Kilda denizen became also a true Saints addict (and there were some who combined these two contradictory traits), he or she was less likely to be bludgeoned by fate and history, more prone to a kind of optimism that was shorter term than 'next year', and often drove the stoics mad.

In general, however, St Kilda supporters came from East St Kilda and environs. In the part of St Kilda I am talking about, booze, sex, deals, crime, making do, playing it a day at a time – all took precedence over the team and its fortunes. As a true Saints supporter, knowledgeable, loyal, committed, and yet at the same time a denizen of deepest, direst west St Kilda, my father was something of a rarity.

CHAPTER 6

Down Among the Women

Talk about down among the women. Truly, I grew up among droves of them. My mother and grandmother were in the bustling foreground of a large, volatile group which in later life I would characterise as my 'innumerable aunts'. They were not really aunts, not all of them anyway. There was my Aunty Jean – slim, dark and flighty – who was a real aunt, being my mother's younger sister. But then there was Aunt Bet and Aunt Tilly and Aunt Vina and Aunty Anne and Aunty Pat and Aunt Kitty and Aunty Letty, and several others.

Most of these women were under the iron rule of two formidable matriarchs: Annie Murray, my maternal grandmother, and Molly Bradley, her long-time best friend. They had all grown up in Glasgow's infamous Gorbals, where Annie and Molly were left to fend off the dangerous world after losing their husbands in the trenches. With a resilience that is humbling to contemplate, they had established their little enclave in the gangster-ridden, smoky and furtive purlieus where I grew up. When they arrived, hit-man Squizzy Taylor was the kingpin of the district. He would be succeeded by 'Redda' Lewis, 'Butcher' Goodwin and their mates.

I was a small boy when all the males in this Caledonian corner were suddenly drawn back, in one capacity or another, into that troubled Europe that Annie and Molly had fled. Along with them went my dinky-di Aussie father – north in Beaufighters. And there I was, among the women – a feather boa of aunts.

They cleaned offices, pulled beer, worked in the Collingwood boot factory, sewed, mended, served behind counters, polished and scrubbed in the late nights or early mornings, and went to mass on Sundays flanking their large, stern mothers. They would gather for a drink and a smoke together in Annie's Havelock Street house or at Molly's in nearby Clive Street. They laughed a lot and alternated between spoiling me and treating me, unwittingly, like a flunkey. I remember once, when I was about six or seven, confiding to O'Gorman, who lived next door but one, that 'I was born to run messages'.

At least, if you were a messenger boy, the shops were close by. Up Grey Street way: Rollason's for milk, bread, smokes and a bet on the SP and Armstrong's (the 'wee grocer', as my grandmother called him, in delicate reference to his dwarfish, hunchbacked stature) for just about everything else.

One time my Uncle Jim, home on leave, took me to Rollason's for a milk shake.

'What flavour,' asked Mrs Rollason ('a sour old bitch', my grandmother had called her).

When I vacillated about that delicious decision, torn hopelessly between strawberry and vanilla and chocolate, she said, 'Make up your mind, boy! You'll get nowhere in the world dithering like that.'

My Uncle Jim turned on her and said, 'Leave the kid alone! For God's sake, woman, he'll be soon enough making decisions and regretting them. Let him enjoy his youth.'

Up the other way, to Acland Street, were the butchers and the market. This whole area was called 'the Village Belle'. The women would describe themselves as having been 'on the Belle' or 'down the Belle' if they had just shopped there. At one end of Acland Street was Luna Park, behind it the footy ground known as the Peanut Farm, and pretty well opposite the big laughing mouth was the Candy Corner – haunt and gathering point for prostitutes and other interesting sub-legal life. All magnetically attractive but forbidden to me.

My grandmother loved a punt on the horses and would send Aunty Jean up to Rollason's to put her bets on the SP. Once I went with Jean and her 'beau', Mannie, while she put on the bets. (There was always the chance of chocolate or ice cream if you went to Rollason's with Jean and Mannie or Jim. If you went with Alex, he would try to buy you the shop.) My grandmother would risk two shillings and her bets would go like this: threepence each way Mighty Prince, if any, each way Matador, if any, each way Savoy's Pride, if any . . . It prompted Mr Rollason, only marginally less sour than his disgruntled spouse, to observe, one no doubt particularly bad day, to my aunt, 'Y'mother gets a bloody good run out of two bob.'

CHAPTER 7

Mr Armstrong and Uncle Mannie

I didn't like the Rollasons, but because I ran so many errands, I got to know the 'wee grocer', Mr Armstrong, very well. He was a great supporter, in theory at least, of the Victorian Football Association. I would linger in his shop, nibbling broken biscuits and talking about the sad misfortunes of the St Kilda Football Club in the past, how different and more successful they would be after the war, and how Mr Armstrong would take me to see Brighton in the Association one weekend when his mother was not feeling so ill.

We never went, though he arranged this outing with my mother several times. I think his theory was that watching Brighton, who were becoming a powerful team, would give me some experience of success.

But I was less imbued with the St Kilda Football Club variety of accepted failure than he thought. I did not see a game until the day I saw Carlton beat St Kilda with O'Gorman. New to it all, I cravenly slapped some Carlton champ on the back for helping crush our team. My father was still far away and not able to guide me.

I never again saw our team play until my father returned home. I knew they lost a lot, but their losses were at a distance from me. And, because for several of the war years they played their home games at the Prahran Oval, they were even distanced physically.

From the start of the season in 1940 through to and including that great Saturday in 1945 when my father took me, aged eight (remember – my age clicked over each year at the very end) to see them play Fitzroy in round six (they lost by four goals), the 'mighty Saints' played eighty-four games, of which they won twenty-two, lost fifty-nine and drew three. Mr Armstrong was undoubtedly oppressed by this record, but he seemed to explain a lot of things in life by deciding they were the result of conspiracies, and perhaps that lightened the burden of defeat. He gradually became convinced that the game was 'rigged' and therefore not worth watching. The Association, being by far the lesser of the two competitions – less glamorous, less skilful, poorer – seemed to him therefore somehow purer.

No doubt disappointment, enforced bachelorhood and a generally tough lot had slowly formed the ground in which these rather mad ideas found sustenance. Nothing was 'fair dinkum' in a life that had so few winners and seemed to confine its handing out of rewards and favours to people who already had plenty of endowment. The only way you could explain why some people prospered while you did not was to suspect conspiracy and that readiness to see conspiracy at the heart of existence easily washed over into sport.

As I grew up, I saw my Uncle Mannie go the same way. After a long courtship, which necessitated his frequent visits to 54 Havelock Street, he married Auntie Jean at the Sacred Heart Church and Jean asked me to be the altar boy. As they had the simple wedding ceremony and not a nuptial mass, there was actually no need for an altar boy. I was pretty well redundant, a fact that the priest – the curate of the day, whose name I forget – made abundantly clear when I walked on to the altar.

'What are *you* doing here?' he said. It was a pinch-gutted, nasty slant on things on such a happy day. Why shouldn't this impoverished, wide-eyed pair, embarking on a path the church so stridently and repeatedly recommended, do so with their ten-year-old nephew in his altar-boy robes lending some – however phony and needless – vestige of ceremony?

Perhaps this spare occasion with its testy celebrant was an omen. Mannie loved children and had a wonderful way with them. When he arrived at a house where there were little kids, he would invariably squat down on his haunches – putting himself at child level – rather than take a chair, and all the children would flock to him. Anxious friends would feel the need to 'rescue' him at some stage from the little people so that he could rejoin the adults. Somehow kids seemed to recognise that he was intuitively in tune with them, and they adored him.

In the years following that cold and uneasy wedding, however, Mannie and Jean were childless and they remained so. In the manner of those days, it was simply assumed that Jean was infertile – 'barren', as my grandmother put it in whispers to Molly Bradley. The idea of adopting either did not occur to them or they for some reason rejected it. Slowly, relentlessly, their lives contracted. They lived for the next forty years in the Havelock Street house, clubbing together with Jim, a lifelong bachelor, to buy it after Annie died in 1961, getting on each other's nerves, having a few too many beers, backing the horses (with, in Jean's canny case, spectacular and fairly frequent success).

Mannie had another very powerful reason for the gloom that enveloped him in his middle years and deepened as time passed. Beginning in his young manhood and thereafter for the rest of his life, he suffered from asthma. This, fatally, became emphysema as he aged and as he continued to smoke with the dedication the tobacco firms were able to encourage in those years almost as if they were doing a public duty.

Not many years after he married Jean, Mannie was forced out of his job in a dry cleaning plant because the steamy, chemical atmosphere exacerbated his asthma. Desperate not only for work but for conditions that would not make his life a misery, he accepted an offer from Jack House, who ran a crash repair shop in South Melbourne.

Jack was a rough, philistine, self-made, small businessman who had married Jessie Gow – a close friend of the Bradley clan – and was therefore 'family'. In accepting Jack House's offer of help, Mannie, a smart, self-taught mechanic, had ideas of moving on eventually to his own business or perhaps making a jump to something entirely new. Jack House's enterprise would be just a stage. But none of this ever happened.

Mannie was by nature easygoing to the point of inertia, and day after day was sapped of strength and resolve as he coughed and hacked and wheezed in the draughty, cavernous South Melbourne shed that was the headquarters of J. House Crash Repairs. His natural inclination to prevaricate, intensified by his failing health, became a kind of syndrome: the longer he failed to act the more supine he became, and the more he contemplated his own inaction the more the prospect embittered and depressed him.

In my early twenties I had plenty of opportunities to observe Mannie's working conditions as the owner of a succession of ailing, tired rustbuckets that were kept operational by his improvisatory talents and Jack House's generosity in letting him repair my cars on the boss's time. Not that I didn't pay for these jobs, but I was never charged what Jack called 'the full tote odds'.

As options closed and the days and months and years succeeded each other with not the slightest promise of change, new starts, travel, or diversion, Mannie – lacking the inner resources and broad literary interests that he so often derided in his brother-in-law, Jim – became bitter and silent.

It was in these years that he began to construe the world he inhabited as being riddled with conspiracy. Conspiracy explained everything: the perfidy of politicians, the failure of the horses he backed, the deteriorating record of the South Melbourne Football Club (Mannie followed the 'Blood Stained Angels' from afar), the solidly hopeless performance of the St Kilda Football Club, the lack of employment openings for someone like him ... It was all a 'put-up job', in which the rich and corrupt and the leaders were productively complicit and the rest, the mugs, were there so it could all happen.

Like Mr Armstrong, who accounted for his deformity and his enslavement to a perpetually ailing but very durable mother by proposing life as conspiracy, Mannie explained his entrapment in a hated job and, through a vague process of displacement, his childless and unfulfilling life, by seeing himself at the centre of a web of conspiracies, all incredibly and intricately interconnected. Nothing escaped this mordant net of circumstance in Mannie's world view.

One of Mannie's many endless arguments with Jim was over Shakespeare. For Jim, Shakespeare was solace and marvel and wonder and delight. For Mannie, who never read a word of the Bard after about Grade 8, Shakespeare was a 'put-up job'. No one man could have written all that on his own and in any case it wasn't as good as it was cracked up to be. Who said it was great literature? What right did they have to say it? Jim, moderately inarticulate to start with (he began every riposte with the phrase, 'By the same token is'), would be reduced to spluttering and red-faced rage at this heretical idea, but Manny never tired of it and Jim never failed to take the bait.

Long after my family had left St Kilda, I would get sucked into these debates when the Havelock Street clan visited us in East Brighton. As a young teenager, becoming intensely excited and passionate about the works of literature I was encountering during an otherwise excruciatingly boring and gloomy education, I would willingly come to Jim's aid, arraying my books and quoting with a liberality and above all an intensity which embarrasses me to remember.

I discovered poetry when I was about sixteen in an

anthology so nondescript I cannot remember its title. But when I read T.S. Eliot's 'Preludes' – *A lonely cab-horse steams and stamps. And then the lighting of the lamps* – I was so excited I didn't know how to cope with my feelings. In the same book were extracts from Keats' abandoned 'Hyperion', the first lines of which – *Deep in the shady sadness of a vale / Far sunken from the healthy breath of morn* – suddenly revealed to me, or at least so I fancied, what was meant by blank verse. Then, in my first week at university, we first-year English students were given a question to do in class under examination conditions so that our tutors could get a line on our critical abilities. When I instantly recognised the untitled poem on which the question was based as 'Preludes I', I felt so lucky it was almost as if I had been caught cheating. It turned out to be no advantage. My answer was hopeless, full of half-articulated enthusiasms, passionate declarations of admiration, but not much criticism of the kind envisaged by the Melbourne University English Department.

It was this sort of overblown, half comprehended and above all inarticulate championship that I brought to Jim's side of the arguments with Mannie whenever I happened to be present at them and my support was enlisted. Against Mannie's imperturbable cynicism, his certain knowledge of conspiracy, his profound unburdened ignorance of the actual works in dispute, my flailings were like trying to face fast bowling with a baguette, and they passed Mannie by, to paraphrase his *bête noire*, like the idle winds which he respected not.

CHAPTER 8

Jim

Jim was the eldest of Annie's four children. He was a short, chunky bloke with a ready, self-deprecating grin and a look to him that was very much like the one forever caught on the mild face of 17051 Private Alexander Murray – quietly humorous, amiable, yet with a depth to the gaze which suggested an understanding, even an expectation, of pain. Of all the Murrays, Jim was the one who gave you a glimpse of what his father must have been like – that loving man of the unpunctuated, wrenching letters, whose ambitions for his family and his beloved Anne dwindled away to a chest full of shrapnel, a requiem murmur of prayers, and thereafter, pain, a mouth full of spit and a last inane glimpse of the receding world: the tent canvas of the casualty station whipping and cracking in the chill wind. Annie was tough and persistent. Alex was flamboyant, superficially carefree, weak. My mother combined Annie's iron will with an imaginative flair and an inherent capacity for laughter and enjoyment.

But Jim was the most gentle, humane and tolerant of them all, desperate to capture with his inner eye some bigger picture he knew must be visible somewhere, yet without the education, the mentors, the range of reference to get the focus right. Jean was his female equivalent in gentleness, but she lacked Jim's aspiration, even if in the end it was a bitterly exhausted one, for something beyond the work-a-day. Jean settled very early for a kind of mild hedonism held in check by lack of money and an enduring religious faith.

One of the reasons Jim used to become so agitated with Mannie's implacable attacks on Shakespeare, Shaw, Keats, Scott, and all his pantheon of literary heroes, was that these monuments of enduring intellect and creativity were central to whatever meaning Jim saw in life. Literature and beauty replaced the church and its teachings for Jim, though, in deference to his mother's wishes, he accompanied her and the rest of the tribe to mass on Sundays and holy days of obligation and was a loyal if unconvinced member of the Men's Sodality.

But long before Annie died in 1961, Jim was merely going through the ecclesiastical motions. The only time I ever saw him talk with animation about anything to do with the church and church-going was when someone apparently interjected during the parish priest's sermon at a packed Sunday mass. Jim recounted this event to everyone who would listen, quoting the interjector who had shouted out, 'Like angels without wings!' As a boy I heard this incident often re-told, without ever understanding what the point was. What tickled Jim, though, was the amazingly out-of-order nature of it. No one had ever done such a thing in that church or, probably, in any Catholic church in those times.

Because of a serious tropical ear infection that put him out of active service, Jim came home from the war a bit earlier than the others. He remained in camp and in uniform for a while, but then he simply went back to his civvy job at the Collingwood boot factory, where he remained until he retired on the pension. He became for a short time the only man in my life and, though he had little enough time from his shift work, he tried when he could to be a father to me.

In particular, Jim set out to show me a world he himself had missed out on until it was effectively too late. But, for all his already somewhat entrenched bachelor life, he was too instinctively attuned to the world of a small boy not to get the balance right. We saw Shakespeare on the stage, but we also saw the Marx Brothers' *Night at the Opera*. We spent hours in the gallery and the museum and more hours fishing fruitlessly from St Kilda pier. He read to me from his favourite poets – Burns, Keats and Browning – and we went to the circus and Luna Park. One afternoon, we saw *Macbeth* performed in some rundown theatre in Elsternwick by a fairly disorganised repertory company. The place was filled with school kids who were no doubt studying *Macbeth* for some exam or other. They gave the whole thing the razz from the start, so much so that the actor playing Macbeth – the one accomplished player in the whole troupe – advanced to the footlights at one stage and told them to shut up or get out. They did neither. Jim was bitterly disappointed with all this. As if it wasn't enough to have Mannie bucketing the Bard at home . . .

But I was entranced by the blackness of a story I did not fully understand and above all by the spectacle – which I had never before seen – of people acting out a story on a stage, live, and remembering lines! Men and women (the same three or four men and women, it must be said – the company was short on cast) telling a story *not their own* with their bodies and their actions and their words, without embarrassment, with great passion. A passion that moved several of the players to spit visibly with the intensity of their utterances.

Long before I had much of an idea what he was talking about, Jim impressed upon me the arguments for Shakespeare's genius (and Shaw's if it came to that. Jim had a vast admiration for Shaw and the question of Shakespeare versus Shaw was actually a great worry to Jim, a chink in his Shakespearean armour, though this was not a possibility he allowed Mannie to glimpse). I was wide-eyed and eminently persuadable, a much easier, infinitely more sympathetic and attentive interlocutor than Mannie.

These outings and conversations and readings were amazing experiences for me. My mother, working alternate day and night shifts and caring for my baby sister, had little time for such indulgence, though she never missed reading to me at every opportunity and she would often play Annie's pianola and sing tunes she knew I liked. Everyone else was similarly inaccessible: the 'aunts' were all working, the men were all still away. But for just the year and a half or so that he was back home first and demobbed, Jim helped to shape my ideas, my incipient intellectual tendencies, my awareness of literary and artistic possibilities and how they bobbed up not as oddities or interventions but as a natural part of 'real life'. He could never have actually phrased any of this, but he demonstrated it, embodied it, by tramping all over St Kilda and Melbourne with me, pointing out buildings and skies and the fall of light on the bay and by taking me to films and the odd play (there were not many to choose from) and standing in front of paintings with me, the two of us calmly and silently looking; even by lecturing me to the point of destruction on the relative merits of Shakespeare and Shaw, and Shakespeare and everybody who had ever lived.

What Jim helped to release in me above all and almost in passing, were a reverence for books – as physical objects, as sources of great entertainment, as repositories of knowledge and wisdom – and a capacity to enjoy paintings and through them, partly because of his choice and preferences in art, to understand that history mattered.

For the art, we did not rely on the gallery alone. On 27 July 1936, exactly five months to the day before I struggled into the light at Cambrai, Jim had taken a deep breath and made what must have been for him an extravagant purchase – the three-volume set of *The World's Greatest Paintings* arranged and edited by T. Leman Hare. The volumes were substantial and impressive looking, but the paintings themselves were magnificently reproduced on paper of the finest quality, pasted by their top edge onto backing pages and protected by a tissue film. I remember especially from those books Holman Hunt's *The Light of the World*, mainly because I was fascinated by the idea of the secret, half-hidden doorway. And Sir John Everett Millais' *The Boyhood of Raleigh* because even if you knew nothing of the context, and I did not till Jim explained it to me, something about the excitement in the boys' faces, the extravagant sweep of the sailor's arm, and the broad, seductive horizon made the hair stand up on the back of my boyish neck. Jim's small library, including *The World's Greatest Paintings*, was locked up in a double-doored bookcase in the room he shared with Alex and me. For me, he opened the glass doors.

Jim would come home each day from the Collingwood boot factory at about half past six, have tea (we never called it 'dinner') and then retreat to his room for an hour or two. After his retirement, he changed this time of reclusion to the morning – usually between about ten and midday, after he returned from his morning walk along St Kilda beach. What he did during these hours of withdrawal was to indulge in a process he described as 'working on his papers'. This meant many things. He had a betting system to which he devoted depths of concentration and spans of time that seemed well out of proportion to the ratio of his successes on the track.

As well, he wrote poetry and plays and he was a craftsman builder of exquisitely turned and polished ukuleles. Jim had a mate named Harry McCausland who was a good ukulele player and the two of them would entertain themselves playing and singing on Jim's latest productions, though Jim's playing of the instruments did not anywhere near equal his mastery of their construction. Jim also wrote some of the songs for which Harry did the musical notation.

There were few women in Jim's life outside the family and I think this was because he had simply decided that he was not much of a prospect, being diminutive, not especially good looking and in any case, at almost any given time, financially and materially unable to contemplate matrimony. The degree of loneliness that this entailed was scarcely glimpsed by Jean or Mannie, who lived with him for forty-odd years, because Jim was not a whinger and he took genuine pleasure in the compensations of being a bachelor – freedom to come and go and apportion his time as he chose.

Like Mannie, Jim was a great favourite of children, although he made his impression on them in an almost offhand way, and he was wonderfully generous with gifts, surprises, treats and casual largesse. When Jim won on the horses, an occurrence that was certainly not unusual but should have been more frequent given the time he devoted to theorising it, everyone benefited.

The deaths of Mannie and Jim would be suffused with an irony that neither deserved and that could not credibly be passed off in fiction. Mannie, the childless favourite and lover of children, died on Father's Day, 1982. The emphysema had finally killed him, well before he was seventy. And Jim, after a resurgence of the old ear problems that had never left him, became seriously ill just over a year later in November and died aged 76 on Melbourne Cup Day – a cruel last twitch of fate for a failed punter.

I flew from Adelaide to help my mother and Jean organise and run their brother Jim's funeral. Most of his mates were dead or had gone up north, and the funeral was a pitifully small gathering. The brief ceremony took place, as so many of our important family moments had, in Sacred Heart Church, St Kilda, and was in some ways a re-enactment of Mannie's funeral of the previous year, except that the mourners were dwindling with each gathering and the atmosphere seemed resigned and defeated, as if more than a particular life was ending.

The altar at which I had been a redundant assistant years before at Mannie and Jean's wedding seemed not much changed. Mannie, who had long since given away any connection with religion – the Catholic Church, he said, was a put-up job – had nevertheless been buried according to the rites of the church and the same was true for Jim, a less public but probably more profound unbeliever. Most of the small congregation, which included three venerable representatives from the Collingwood boot factory days, returned to 54 Havelock Street while two of the Bradley clan – John Bradley and Ray Walsh (who was the husband of 'Aunty' Tilly) – made the long journey with me to the crematorium.

No one, least of all me, regrettably, seemed to have given any thought to the structure or content of Jim's funeral, so the church part of it consisted of what a couple of elderly pillars of the parish thought should adorn the exequies of a backslider. It was only when we were on the way to the crematorium that I realised we should have had readings from his poets and something from *The Stones of Venice* and a proper valedictory. Death in Havelock Street, so many years after the old days, was still spare and done hard. Even the weather was terrible.

Two days after Jim's funeral, I had one of those encounters that make you feel you are acting out the chapters of someone's novel. I met my old friend, mentor and teacher, Vincent Buckley, by arrangement, in a Lygon Street restaurant. He was with his friend and namesake Brian Buckley, whom I had never met, despite having been roughly contemporary with him at

Melbourne University. They had lunched well but not too well and were in good form.

Brian Buckley suggested we go to the house of some friend of his in Carlton. There we had a drink and were joined by several others whom to this day I cannot recall, for reasons that may become clear. Some Irish songs were sung and some more drinking ensued. The atmosphere was pleasant and, if not sober, certainly not out of control. But the register changed when someone mentioned the name of a Melbourne writer who had recently published a novel. The writer, who was a good friend of mine (and, incidentally, of Vincent Buckley), had apparently been reading from his latest novel on the ABC the previous day, and Brian Buckley had heard the program. He described the reading as embarrassing and the novel as trash and launched into a violent personal attack on the writer.

The novel was trash, he said, if for no other reason than that the writer pretended to know about poverty and working-class hardship but did not know anything about that world at all. I objected to this, partly because I wished to defend my friend, partly because the accusation was most certainly untrue, but also because I thought the novel was good and certainly did not fail in that way, whatever else might have been its shortcomings.

Brian Buckley became extremely agitated to hear this and attacked me with a barrage of sneers and insults mainly to do with my total ignorance of the working class, of working-class life and mores and what he saw as my lifelong protection within the walls of academe – in 'the Ivory Tower', as he termed it with a venom in inverse proportion to his originality – where, incidentally, he said I belonged because I could scarcely make any contribution 'out here' – that is, he meant, in the good old 'real world'.

I was forty-seven years old at the time of this onslaught, yet it all burst upon me as a huge surprise. Nobody had ever spoken to me before with such apparent detestation, such free-ranging capacity for insult, such strenuous determination to take me thoroughly apart not on intellectual but on unashamedly personal grounds. I had spent my whole life till then being, as I thought, reasonable and pleasant. It was not possible to accuse me like this with any conviction. I couldn't believe it.

This was not hubris, even if it sounds like it. My temperament had been moulded by those years with the aunts and then by the example of my father who, for all his many virtues and talents, was diffident to a fault and all his life lacked confidence in himself despite great and accumulating evidence to the contrary. I was the same. I so much admired my father that, when I was old enough to think such thoughts, I construed his obvious diffidence as a virtue. My enlistment in this way of thinking and acting was re-enforced by the, presumably, biological fact that I was a late maturer, a late starter at everything. It had taken me two full years before I understood what university was about, but then I came top in everything in the third year. And this has been repeated over and over in many different spheres of my existence. Like my old man, I tended to avoid confrontations if I could. Unlike him, I was not all that bad at defusing them, as I grew older and notionally wiser. But also unlike him, I made the grievous mistake of trying to make everybody happy, to see to it that everyone 'got on well'. The fate of such shallow peace-makers is to be crushed between the opposing sides, which, in any case, are probably not even opposing if viewed by less anxious, less confrontation-sensitive eyes. As far as sturdy self-confidence was concerned, I was well over fifty before I saw that there was a difference between big-noting and calm, accurate recognition of your own abilities. As for wanting everyone to be happy – that doomed urge is now so much a part of me a doctor could probably activate it with a rubber hammer, like the patellar-tendon reflex. The pity of it is that there is no surgery that would remove it.

All of which constitutes only some of the reasons, no doubt, why, when Brian Buckley launched his tirade – something, it must be said, that he would not have regarded as particularly out of order, being accustomed to fierce and continuous disputation and argument in the circles he inhabited – I didn't handle it very well. For one thing, I blushed. Not as brilliantly as that day in front of Sister Ita, but Darmody would have recognised it. In the end I said, 'Two days ago, I buried my Uncle Jim who spent a lifetime in the Collingwood boot factory except for when he was in the fucking Infantry as a private, where he picked up the ear infection that became a tumour and eventually killed him. You wouldn't know the Collingwood boot factory if it dropped on you. As for the Ivory Tower, I'm sorry you didn't get in, since you obviously envy it so much.' I then said goodbye to Vincent Buckley, who had attempted unsuccessfully to intervene in Brian Buckley's tirade, and left.

At the front door, I was ushered out by a woman who, I presumed, was the owner of the house. She said, 'Don't worry, they're always like that.'

But I did worry. I was absolutely shattered and brooded on the incident for days. Years.

*

Jim left me his 'papers' and a box of books, including T. Leman Hare's *The World's Greatest Paintings*. I could not understand the betting system; but, given its undistinguished record, this was probably just as well. I could see only too clearly, though, the picture of profound loneliness that emerged from the fragments and fugitive observations that, scribbled in margins, between paragraphs and in notebooks, constituted as much of a diary as Jim ever kept. In his last months, all the entries were about the pain that began in his head as soon as he raised himself from the pillow and gradually took over his whole being. *The pain*, he wrote, in his very last entry, *the pain*, in what was almost certainly a deliberate echo of Conrad's *The horror, the horror* and was probably intended for me, above all others, to notice.

CHAPTER 9

The Endlessness of 1944

As the years of war lengthened, I distinctly remember seriously considering the possibility that 1944 might not ever end, that perhaps the war had somehow shut us in to that year forever. I carved the figures 1944 on the gate to underline my conviction that this was as far as we were going and then lived in fear that my grandmother would notice it and punish me for disfiguring the house and surrounds. It was always vaguely surprising to me that, encircled as we were by houses, streets and people all in advanced stages of decay or disarray, my grandmother should nevertheless be always on the lookout for the slightest sign of dysfunction, flaw or breakage in her little domain at number 54.

The endlessness of 1944 emphasised one of the puzzles of my life. I could never work out why some fathers were home from the war and mine was not. My mother explained that some men were kept at home in 'reserved occupations', such as teachers. Since I was taught exclusively by nuns, I had no experience of male teachers except for Mr McDonald, who came once a week and took us for 'Exercises' in the school yard.

Mr McDonald always wore a grey suit and a tie. He would stand out in front of the group and demonstrate various physical manoeuvres, threatening always to burst out of his straining pants and buttoned coat. The likelihood that a seam would split and expose some part of Mr McDonald other than his round, sweating and rubicund head and his freckled, sinewy hands, injected a growing tension into these sessions as the year wore on. But his sartorial integrity remained intact, as far as I ever saw at least, and no one dared even giggle as he knee-bent and toe-touched and arm-stretched his way through our weekly session. Mr McDonald's only concession to the weather was to remove his suit coat in the heat and this would reveal an immaculately ironed white shirt buttoned to the wrists.

Mr McDonald conducted Exercises in the 'big yard'. The school had a 'small yard', reserved for the girls, which you entered as soon as you passed through the Grey Street gate, and a big yard where the boys played cricket and football. In the bottom corner of the big yard was 'the burner' where the caretaker, Joe, disposed of the rubbish beneath stupefying clouds of noisome smoke and behind which little kids established a 'hideout' when Joe wasn't going about his incendiary business. The tallest boy in the school, Ray McManus, could drop-kick the entire length of the big yard and occasionally could put the footy right over the high mesh wire at the Grey Street end and into the backyard of whoever lived there – a very irate bloke, as I remember, who was constantly threatening to keep the ball and constantly complaining to the nuns.

Having no brothers and, apart from my interlude with Jim, effectively no father or uncles during the war, I saw few men. Many of those I did see – the drunks around the Prince Charles on the corner of Fawkner Street, for example – scared me witless with their shouting, swearing and random violence. On one of my forays to Rollason's, a hairy, ragged, dirty-looking bloke actually leapt at me as I turned from Havelock Street into Barkly Street. He roared and shouted and waved his arms and I nearly fainted on the spot. Once I had got some strength back into my legs, I ran home and incoherently attempted to tell my grandmother what had happened. She calmed me down – and then sent me back to Rollason's.

Another time, I was called away from a game of footy in the street to go right up Grey Street, nearly as far as the school, for messages at the delicatessen. There were a lot of women waiting, I remember, and I was standing right up against the counter, which was like a long bench sheathed in metal, when a strange thing happened. I was thinking about the footy we had been playing and I was itching to get back and furious that I had been taken out of it. I was fantasising how I would return and take a high mark over Carter or Waller (I wouldn't be able to reach over O'Gorman) and how I would land on my feet, play on and kick . . . and that is just what I did.

There and then, in the delicatessen, in the grip of my heated imaginings, given a powerful edge no doubt by resentment that I had to be there at all, I lashed out and kicked, striking the metal covering below the counter. It was entirely involuntary – as if my whole leg had become reactive instead of just the knee – and as big a surprise to me as to everyone else. Well, perhaps not quite so big. The noise was sudden and booming. Several of the women jumped and two of them screamed. They all looked at me and one said, 'Little wretch, they're all the same at that Sacred Heart,' though I had nothing of my school uniform on.

Even in my shocked state this struck me as both unjust and very odd and I had a sudden imagining of all the kids at my school filing down to the delicatessen and lining up to kick the counter. I was inarticulate with embarrassment and blushed like a stormy dawn, but I was too young to know what else to do or say, so I just looked down at my chunky black boots. I was served immediately, even though it was not my turn. I suppose they thought I would wreck the joint if I had to wait a minute longer.

I felt different, hard done by and – because I was a loudly reluctant messenger boy frequently chastised for carelessness – I accepted I was irredeemably 'bad'. I was embarrassed by the swarms of women who seemed to be always buzzing round me. Other kids of my immediate acquaintance had their fathers more or less at home. Dennis O'Gorman's father was in a 'reserved occupation', Keith Carter's was a drunk, Ray Waller's was in and out of gaol, and the Flaherty boys' father was a journalist. There was not much cachet in having a father and uncles at the war because you didn't know where they were or what they were doing. Mail was infrequent and the thud of a battered, much-travelled letter into the tin letterbox on the gate was an occasion not for joy but tense anxiety followed by tearful relief.

These misanthropies were exacerbated by my growing

conviction that, because I had temporarily no father, or anyone who could possibly stand in for him (Mr Armstrong would never have done, he was too small and too strange-looking), I was somehow not as tough as the other kids. When we played footy in the street with a 'ball' made of old socks or tightly rolled newspaper held together by elastic bands, I seemed to be more easily hurt than the others. I would crash to the ground or reel into the cobbled gutter or become espaliered on the Millers' front fence as the momentum of various ill-judged lunges, dashes and leaps carried me on to disaster.

In summer, when our activities switched from kicking up and down the road to bowling as fast as we could across it, I would get hit in the testicles or on the nose – the latter producing merely lots of blood, the former an agony undreamt of in our philosophies. Worse, I would often *cry* after such encounters. My father witnessed one of these crises while home on leave. I had got whacked somewhere or other, probably in the balls, and was crying. My father, standing at our front gate, called out, 'You've got to be tougher than that, mate.' One of the kids echoed him. 'Tougher,' he said. 'He's tougher,' said another. Undoubtedly they were having a go at me, but the name, applied at first with the kind of exultantly laid-on irony that kids essay when they have got one of their number at their mercy, began to stick. 'Tougher' I became and 'Tougher' I stayed, until the exigencies of hurried speech, shouting and exhortation corrupted it among my knockabout friends and acquaintances to 'Tough' and that in turn to 'Tupper' and then to 'Tup'. The discovery years later in *Othello* that 'tup' had a quite different and unattractive meaning (*Even now, now, very now, an old black ram / Is tupping your white ewe*), scarcely impinged on the durability of my nickname. In any case, such knowledge was arcane and belonged to few. Through one long line of friendships the name survived and I am still 'Tup' to two or three old friends, much to the amusement of my children.

I see now that some of my more bizarre juvenile exploits were efforts to assert in some other, more manageable way, the emotionless grittiness the street required. One day when the great Joe Louis was in the news, I boasted to Ray Waller, as we dawdled outside Mrs Murphy's Penny Library in Grey Street, that I was strong enough to take any blow anyone could dish out. Wasn't I 'Tougher', after all?

'Go on,' I said, 'hit me on the jaw. It won't hurt *me*. Go on!'

Waller, who was as hard as a jumps jockey's bum, obliged with a smashing thump that knocked me over and relieved my lopsided jaw of several baby teeth. (Though not all. Having a check-up with an Irish dentist in London in 1995, I was puzzled when he stepped back from the chair and said, 'It's a miracle of nature, and I wouldn't dare to touch it.' 'It' was one surviving baby tooth. I was fifty-nine years old at the time.)

Another time, discovering that to jump off the high balcony into the small yard at school was something even Waller jibbed at, I sauntered casually up to the rail and leapt over it. When I hit the ground with both feet, my legs doubled like lorry springs bottoming out and rebounded me into a spiral of continuous somersaults that seemed to go on forever. I should have broken both ankles at least, but I came eventually to sprawling rest and had the presence of mind to dust myself off with a great show of nonchalance, sensing as I did so the shrill note of sensation rising through the schoolyard babble.

In the shelter shed, opposite the burner in the big yard, I fought O'Gorman. He was rangy and formidable looking, but I knew intuitively that he was all talk and bluster, partly because I employed some of the same line in talk and bluster myself. This fixture was precipitated by a clash in the yard at playtime and arranged during the day's lessons by means of clandestine notes, significant glances and sibilant whispers. Ray Waller shaped up to such encounters, which were much more numerous in his way of life, with a genuine insouciance that I envied, aspired to but would never attain. As always, I went into the contest with such exaggerated determination and displays of force and will that I was beating the shit out of O'Gorman before his superior reach could avail him anything. Being basically a crybaby (it took one to know one), O'Gorman, bloodied and grazed, was capitulating early in the contest. He did, though, land two blows that split my lip and blacked my eye. In the end, his seconds, with a mastery of bureaucratic authoritarianism which I resent every time I think of it, had the fight stopped and a draw declared before my more plebeian backers realised what was happening. This all sounds very sturdy, but I was crying at the end and shaking before it started.

'Why do you always cry?' This more or less unfair, leading question was addressed to me by a girl in my class at Sacred Heart who even then I could see was rather hard and tartish. I cannot remember her name and I have no idea what became of her, but it was a good question. She asked it just after I had been hit square in the right eye by a rock-hard, ink-soaked paper pellet fired from a shanghai across the classroom, so maybe even she would not have been so stoic if hers had been the eye in question. The pellet was not actually intended for me, but I had turned round in my front desk to survey the pandemonium induced by the temporary absence of nuns and was characteristically just in time to cop the winging missile at the height of its velocity. It hurt like hell and I felt surely blinded. Possibly a glass eye looming. Nothing I could do – leaping publicly from no matter what heights, pounding no matter which better-equipped opponents, jumping from no matter what speeding trams – could apparently obscure the truth unerringly apparent to the tactless and precocious eye of youth: I was a crybaby. There was something suspiciously, well, *soft* in there.

About that tram. One day, Sister Mary Burkman deputed me to take a large, round biscuit tin full of unconsecrated hosts over to the convent on the Esplanade in Middle Park. She gave me the tram fare and off I went. On the tram, the conductor and one of his mates started teasing me. I was wearing my school blazer the breast pocket of which proclaimed, in heraldic mode, SHS, for Sacred Heart School.

'What's that stand for?' asked the conductor – 'Sheila's High School?'

I employed my usual physically exhibitionist method of countering reflections on my toughness. When the tram was approaching the convent stop, I jumped off with great bravado before it stopped. Long before it stopped, as it turned out, so that I went cartwheeling along the road while the biscuit tin, having survived a ricochet off the footplate, hit the tarmac and burst open like a grenade.

Unconsecrated hosts, their original explosive momentum added to by a slick sea breeze, blew and wheeled and rolled over most of Middle Park. The conductor laughed and laughed and his mate, fascinated by my now revealed burden, said, 'Those little buggers'd be bloody handy for cards, wouldn't they, Bert.'

I picked every last one of them up. The tram driver, though equally convulsed, graciously refrained from moving until I had levered fifty or so out of the tramlines, thus avoiding blasphemy and eternal damnation.

But these events – the leap from the balcony, the fight (one of many), the tram incident – were what might be called highlights. I did not like primary school (I am specifying here, because I hated secondary school) and my memories of it, excluding a few of the nuns who were good teachers or fine human beings or both, are not fond. This might have been partly because I got off to a bad start.

If Australian children of my vintage were to be fortunate in the matter of war service, they were a good deal less so when it came to virulent and deadly disease. I have a vivid memory of being carried into an ambulance by my father, shouting, 'Don't let them take me away, Dad.' Months of throat trouble, fluctuating temperatures and failed remedies had resulted in a diagnosis of diphtheria, at that time an eager and efficient killer of children. For a while, I used to think this must be my earliest memory, though I don't suppose it is, since I could apparently talk well enough to shout for help. I can recall my mother singing, 'Off to bed, said Sleepy-head' to me in my cot. That must have been earlier.

My shouts and struggles had no effect, other than no doubt to upset even more my mother and father helplessly watching, and I was taken to Fairfield Infectious Diseases Hospital where I was kept in isolation. Even my parents had to talk to me from a distance and through some kind of screen.

This was until I was diagnosed as *not* having diphtheria after all but acute tonsillitis. So I 'had my tonsils out', as the saying then was. This was no simple operation either in those days and thought to be rather dicey for very young kids like me. I had swollen glands and a split mouth for a week or so afterwards and, on my grandmother's insistence, wore fire-warmed wrapping things round my neck. One way and another, my mouth and jaws took a hell of a pasting in those early years.

In 1942, when I was about six, my mother, who was worried about the omissions in my war-time diet, took me to the dentist for what must have been my first ever check-up. The dentist's name was Mr Mackenzie King and his surgery was in Acland Street. Mackenzie King may have made jokes about his being the namesake of a famous Canadian prime minister, but by the time I came into his orbit he was beyond jokes. He was portly, frowning and smelt of something or other which I could never identify but which I certainly found unpleasant. Obviously it was only evident when one was in that intimate embrace that the dentist has with his patient, because my mother professed never to smell it and scolded me when I complained. All retrospective evidence would suggest it was the smell of a swift whisky, a heart-starter for a man whose loathing of teeth, mouths and all to do with them had reached such a thorough, uncompromising and wholly unforgiving pitch that only a good slug of how's-your-father could induce him to face up to yet another day of molars and gums. This profound ennui must also have affected his professional judgement. He recoiled in horror at the spectacle of my boyish fangs and predicted forcefully that I would not have my own teeth beyond the age of eighteen (they are still intact). He then set about helping to ensure the truth of his prophecy by making an appointment for me to have six of them out. With gas.

Mr Mackenzie King probably had a few bad days and my encounter with his gas machine was surely one of them. My mouth and jaws ballooned, I couldn't eat, I couldn't sleep. The only consolation was that, yet again, I couldn't go to school. I became a professional cot case. I would sit outside in the sun, wrapped in tartan blankets, and chat feebly to anyone around.

In autumn or spring, I would watch our neighbours, the Miller boys – Don and Eric – play very good tennis in the middle of the street. In winter, I would languish on the couch in the lounge room while my grandmother battled with the non-drawing 'lum', in order to ensure my warmth and comfort. I sustained headaches, stomach upsets, vague uneases, constipation and achy joints to go with the indubitably serious whooping cough, suspected diphtheria, tonsillitis, teeth troubles, swollen glands and the routine battery of childhood ills – chicken pox, mumps and measles.

The hard-pressed women who surrounded me were consumed with concern and sympathy, to the extent that they had the time and energy to be consumed by much outside the business of making a wartime living, and I settled into a routine of sybaritic ill health punctuated by inevitable encounters with early schooling. Until my father, coming home on leave and witnessing these shenanigans at first hand, pronounced the whole business 'bloody nonsense', personally conducted me to school and said, 'This is where you go each week day for quite a few years to come, my boy. And you go even if you're on crutches or your head's in a sling!' He then went back north, but the spell was broken. Much as my grandmother, mother and aunts were open to reinstitution of the old regime, neither they nor I were quite game enough to give it a go. I scarcely had another 'sicky' in my entire school career – or afterwards, if it comes to that.

Havelock Street was geographically ill-favoured, quite apart from all the other ways in which it was ill-favoured, because it was a short cut between busy Barkly Street and the big square into which ran Acland and Carlyle streets at one end and the Esplanade at the other, and round which were distributed the Palais, the Palais de Dance, Luna Park and the Candy Corner – the very hub of St Kilda's more tawdry profile.

In my boyhood, you couldn't really say traffic was a problem in the street. There were some cars, but they were not the nuisance they later became. Today, Havelock Street's unfortunate strategic position has been negated for the benefit of the residents by a succession of speed humps and a one-way system running from Carlyle to Barkly Street, that is, away from the magnetic Luna Park end.

But if there was little noticeable vehicular traffic, the street's role as a short cut was very visible in the form of innumerable pedestrians and quite a few cyclists. This meant that you saw some odd people now and then, sometimes to your cost. One day during the endless 1944, a new kid turned up on his bike. He rode slowly towards where we were kicking our sock-footy end to end, then, leaning his arms on the handlebars and with both feet touching the ground, he watched us. His scrutiny naturally spurred us on to unusual heights of achievement. A succession of spectacular marks and fast breakaways from the pack followed by raking pinpoint passes would have impressed the most critical eye. But eventually, as if recognising that we could not possibly sustain this brilliant and uncharacteristic routine for another minute, O'Gorman said, 'Gooday, do you want to have a kick?' The kid said no he didn't and then, released from our charade, we clustered round his bike to question him. Any adult watching this encounter, it must be remembered, would have seen a number of small boys and one coltish girl – all in the age range seven to ten years (if 1944 ever ended, I would be eight just before the year turned) – milling round a slightly older small boy of perhaps ten or eleven. If such a senior observer had bothered to continue looking, he or she would undoubtedly have recognised that the interloper was vastly more worldly-wise, more 'aged' and wearied than any of his wide-eyed listeners.

He had a round, rather fat face and seemed quite fleshy in build. He did not look like a footballer to me and I was not surprised by his lack of interest in having a kick. He had a sardonic way with him, a dismissive, confident air of knowing he was our superior and didn't have to prove it by kicking a football or by any other means, although he did use ostentatious and frequent resort to a packet of Craven As to bolster his authority. Before very long, I decided I didn't like him much and began to toss the sock-footy in the air and catch it, sometimes overhead, sometimes on the chest, now one-handed, now within inches of the ground . . . Recognising no doubt that I was demonstrating my lack of interest in him and all to do with him, he looked at me several times, interrupting himself telling O'Gorman and the others how he'd 'seen a girl's cunt', when he was at the beach one time. She was changing out of her togs behind some ti-tree and as she stepped out of one leg and then the other, *he saw it*, saw what it looked like. I was as a matter of fact extremely interested in these details, but my need to maintain my nonchalance, to resist his desire for total attention, was stronger for the moment than my fascination with what the poet Rochester would later easily convince me was that 'soft anvil' on which 'all mankind was made'.

We only ever knew him by one name, which I think was Roberts or something like that, but privately I called him Fish Face because of his fleshy, almost expressionless pasty visage and his cold eyes.

A couple of the other kids were gradually becoming converts to my view of Roberts after he had made several more visitations. But then, on about his fifth appearance, he brought with him something truly wondrous, which suborned the waverers and captured me as easily as any of the others. It was a small movie projector. Set up in O'Gorman's bedroom and projecting a compact moving picture on to flowery patterns of the wallpaper, it proved a great marvel. I watched a Mickey Mouse cartoon and the start of Donald Duck when my mother's call crossed the intervening fences and easily rang through the O'Gorman house. I had to do some messages. I missed the rest of the show which, naturally, was by far the best according to those who saw it. This was another one of those times when I walked up to Rollason's or Armstrong's burning with resentment and feeling doomed in a way those other kids did not seem to be.

Fish Face returned a week or so later with a mate called Ocker, who was muscularly squat, neckless, foulmouthed and radiating aggravation. I somehow knew when they arrived that I was going to be in trouble. I had never been the kind of acolyte Fish Face required. My deliberate aloofness, for reasons I scarcely understood myself, and my apparently precipitate and scornful defection from his grand film demonstration when Fate and my mother called me to Armstrong's, put me in bad odour. Because Roberts himself was intensely political in his dealings with us, using his greater maturity, experience and native cunning to divide our ranks – to set O'Gorman against me, for example, recognising us as incipient antagonists; and isolating Doreen as, derisively, my only ally – he understood and resented what looked to him like a naked challenge to his leadership over this new and utterly naïve constituency. So, like all his kind, he brought in a 'heavy'.

This bloke, Ocker, a bit older again than Roberts, after a few preliminary obscenities, suddenly turned on me, grabbed me round the neck and said, 'You're a fuckin' little weed, okay?'

There didn't seem to be a lot of point in disputing this, especially with his ham-like arm wrapped round my wind pipe, so I said, 'Righto.'

'You don't say "Righto" to me,' he said, 'you say "okay".'

'Righto,' I answered, seeing where we were headed and digging in.

He belted me round the ear with his free hand.

'Okay.'

'Righto.' Another whack.

The kids shuffled nervously and someone said, 'Leave him alone.'

'Okay?' said Ocker.

'Righto,' said I, flinching under another thump.

This went on for quite a while and I would like to say that I outlasted him and was the hero of the whole group, but eventually, with my head ringing, tears barely squeezed back and my ear feeling three times its normal size (which, in due course, it was), I gave in.

Ocker and Fish Face swaggered off, vowing to return and 'fuckin' do anyone of you little cunts' who stepped out of some line they had in their heads but which they omitted to detail. But we never saw them again and I believe we were no more than the victims of geography. Havelock Street led either way to terrain that people like them felt at home in. We just happened to fall foul of them on their way through and became for a short time part of their mindless rite of passage.

While it was true that we never saw Ocker or Roberts again, there were many who felt sure that Ocker *did* return at least once more. A little further up the street, towards the Barkly Street end, there was a rather beautiful girl, a couple of years older than us, who lived a secluded and protected existence with people who rumour said were her adopted parents or special guardians. No one really knew, so speculation, gossip and rumour abounded. She was by no means aloof, often chatted with one or other of us, especially Doreen, but she was kept under a visibly tight rein and attended not Sacred Heart School like the rest of us, except for Doreen, but St Fintan's Girls' Convent, further up Grey Street towards the church.

A month or so after Ocker had worked me over, there were suddenly police in the street and the word quickly spread that there had been an attack on this girl. I overheard my mother say she was raped. The police circulated a description of her assailant to neighbours and, when this seeped through to the lower ranks, we all realised that it was almost certainly a description of Ocker. The police talked to us about Ocker and other blow-ins and a few days later he was arrested. I never did find out what happened to him but for the sake of his victim and, being honest with myself, for my own satisfaction, I hoped he was tortured, gaoled, starved and tormented until he begged for mercy. Preferably by having to answer, 'Righto!'

The group of kids in the street who existed in a constant state of forming, disintegrating and re-forming flux, depending on ever shifting patterns of favours, acrimonies, vendettas and revenge, and who formed the audience for my stand-off with Fish Face, were O'Gorman, Keith Carter, Ray Waller, Doreen, Pat and Dennis Flaherty and Dougie Brand. O'Gorman, Waller, the Flahertys and I all went to Sacred Heart School. Carter and Doreen were Proddies and went to the state school. Dougie Brand was a Proddy too, but he went to Sacred Heart for some reason.

Dougie was the runt of that litter, scapegoated in a way that now makes me cringe. He was a bit slow, Dougie, and for a lot of reasons he did not have a chance. He was a carrot top, unlike me – I was 'sandy' – and therefore immediately noticeable and somehow inviting satire and insult. He was unprepossessing, with an ever-so-slightly wandering eye and an accumulation of white spit in the corners of his mouth when he spoke. He was ungainly, occasionally silly, often annoying and on some days unpredictably aggressive. Though not tall, he was thick set and muscular and could have pulverised any one of us, even Waller, but there was a soft, fearful streak in him. Like me, he would cry at times and hate himself for it. Unlike me, he was probably having a fairly hard time at home. You did not see much of Dougie's parents. They existed, but they were rarely visible. My grandmother said Mrs Brand was a 'wee moos', meaning mouse, but she did not deliver this judgement with unkindness. According to Dougie, his father gave him a 'bloody good belting' pretty regularly.

But Dougie had one distinction at least. He lived at the top of Havelock Street, on the Barkly Street corner, right next to the woodyard, which was a magnet for all of us. Dougie's father worked there for a while. The woodyard sang with the spin and bite of the saws, which were turned by long, bucking belts connected to a central motor. The belts broke often and the woodyard men repaired them by overlapping the ends with a replacement section and smashing chunky metal staples through them. As these whipped over the pulleys, they added a mad, metallic *ping ping ping* to the flapping of the belts, the bass rhythms of the motor and the insane screams of the saws. As well as the saws, there was a metal axe blade fixed to a long shaft which, driven by its own slow chugging motor, went up and down, up and down. The trick was to balance a log under the blade while it was on its upswing so that when it descended it split the log in two. This routine was carried out with effortless nonchalance by one of the 'woodmen', as my grandmother called them. The idea of feeding in the logs, collecting the halves, poising the new one on the spot – while the blade rose, paused, then began its murderous descent – fascinated, attracted and appalled me all at once. This relentless and metronomic chopper was the machine everyone watched whenever we walked slowly past.

The woodyard was a cacophonous, chaotic, exciting place, a kind of hell to our eyes, where one false move or lapse of attention would see you fingerless or scalped or split in half. Needless to say, none of us was allowed to go near it, but we all managed at one time or another to loiter at the sagging double gates and watch and listen to the fury of the yard. It was inside the closed gates of the woodyard that Dougie took refuge during a stone fight we had one grey, miserable Sunday afternoon. Somehow, he had climbed into the woodyard, perhaps over his back fence. Provocations I no longer remember sparked an exchange of insults and, soon, of 'yonnies'. There was a pile of them, as it happened, left over from some footpath work by the council, so that was ammunition for me and O'Gorman and Carter. Dougie, inside the yard, had lumps of wood and a few rocks lying round, for some reason or other. Not much harm was done until one of my missiles flew, by monstrous fluke, through the wide lurch of an opening, where the gates were supposed to fit together, and whacked Dougie over the eye. There was much blood followed by stitches, parental meetings, accusations, apologies and trouble, shame and admonition for me. I could scarcely meet my mother's gaze for days after. Strangely, though, it made Dougie and me friends. I came to know this odd, loyal, ugly-duckling kid, and I look back on him now with affection. You couldn't be a close mate of Dougie because he was too much tyrannised by rules, regulations and obscure fears and threats that seemed to dominate his home front and would see him disappear for days on end. But in so far as it was possible, we became friends after we had tried to kill each other, and we remained so until, inevitably, we disappeared forever from each other's sight almost overnight.

O'Gorman was and was not my best friend in those times. We seemed to suffer from an intensely exaggerated version of the serial jealousies, acrimonies, passionate commitments and savage fallings out that distinguish the relationships of small kids who are too much together. O'Gorman was a great conspirator, constantly hinting at pacts and arrangements and assignations that would exclude someone or other, usually me. For my part, though, I think I infuriated him with my, for want of a better phrase, social strategies. These knew no moderate middle ground between an apparently aloof reclusiveness (more often explained by my being forbidden to go out or being haunted by message deadlines) and an attitude to friendship that owed much to the habits and characteristics of the limpet. So we stumbled on for years, fighting, laughing, teaming up and dropping apart, creating and destroying alliances around us until at last we went our separate ways.

Dennis O'Gorman's lanky figure and unfathomable

temperament dominated my life from my first memories of St Kilda and the street, perhaps around 1942, until I left the Sacred Heart School at the end of 1948. We would finally part, I remember, good but ever more distant friends – and would never set eyes on each other again.

O'Gorman's father – Leo was his name, which of course we all found comical – was a gentle, quietly spoken man who ran his cabinet making and wood-turning business from the backyard of their Havelock Street house. Some quirk of geography or surveying had endowed the O'Gorman block with a much bigger back yard than most others – bigger than those that I saw, anyway. Mr O'Gorman had built a shed that ran right across the back fence, the full width of the block. In this refuge, he sawed and planed and morticed and glued and produced his artefacts.

Two dramatic incidents happened on the patch of lawn that separated the O'Gorman back verandah from the workshop. The first occurred when I went round to O'Gorman's place one hot summer day to play under the hose. I was barefoot and, as I arrived, I saw on the grass the broken, jagged bottom of a glass jar. I suppose it had fallen from a rubbish bin. Mrs O'Gorman ran a tight and pristine domestic ship, so it could only have been rare chance or extreme misfortune that explained the presence of such a squalid and dangerous item squatting in the green shade of the summer grass. I remember being overcome with fascination as I stared at the upright jags and points of glass from which the light of the hot sun beamed and winked as if it were a jewel. What if you stepped right on it? It made me shiver with an exquisite horror. It gave me, as we kids used to say, that funny feeling you get in your bum when you imagine some awful pain or hurt, or when you think of teetering on a huge cliff. Experimentally, I poised my right foot above this circle of glassy stalagmites, overbalanced slightly and – true to my fantasy – stepped right on it.

The inside of my right foot was slashed from the middle of the sole in a sweeping arc heading up to the anklebone. My father had to be called home from Fishermans Bend, so it must have been late 1945 or early 1946, making me about nine or ten at the time. I had fifteen stitches and bear the scar to this day. I told everyone that I did not see the glass, was unaware of it until my weight fell on its murderous teeth. Almost everyone reading these lines can remember cuts and stitches from childhood; it is such a standard experience that it would not be worth mentioning were it not for the fact that, being as honest as I can about my recollections, I think it was more than half deliberate, a mad testing of a reality I had heard about – severe injury – but could not quite believe in. It was a strange business.

The other incident in the O'Gormans' backyard was more dire and potentially fatal. It happened probably in 1947, when my sister, Carol, was five. Like all younger siblings in that span of their lives, when their attainment of mobility and unquenchable inquisitiveness have not been matched by any sense of responsibility, awareness of danger or social judgement, she was getting on my nerves. But from time to time I had to include her in my activities by parental decree, or cancel the activities. On this occasion, I had been sent to the O'Gormans' by my mother to borrow something, perhaps sugar or butter, and had taken Carol along with me, by the hand. Naturally, I was distracted once I arrived, and Carol began exploring the O'Gorman backyard. Mr O'Gorman's success at cabinet making had no doubt led to expansion and improvement. At this time, anyway, he was becoming mechanised. He had an electric saw and other labour savers in his shed, which were plugged into a chain of two extension cords. The first connection was close to the machinery in the shed, but the second occurred half way across the grass where the cord snaked its way to the house, and consisted of the requisite two plugs snugging together in a kind of fur of frayed insulation. My sister, wandering free and unnoticed, picked this up to examine it and screamed. Her small hand tightened on the cord as 240 volts jolted her thin body. In the same moment, Dennis O'Gorman dived at her and dragged her to the ground, breaking her grip. Without question he saved her life and, incidentally, endangered his own.

A new cord slung high on two poles replaced the half-baked arrangement of extensions – almost too late. And life went on its minor sensational way.

Not all of the incursions into Havelock Street's tight community were unfortunate. There were, of course, routine arrivals and departures. During school holidays, we would see the dynamics of the street from morning to night, so familiar to our parents but mostly not available to us (though during my ailing phase, I saw more of these mysteries unfold than most of my peers could claim). Cumberland's bread cart was one of these regulars.

Painted a rich, chocolaty brown, it had the name spelt out in elaborate curlicues: *Cumberland's Bakery*. Mr

Cumberland would fill his basket with bread, while the horse plodded the cart slowly on, and run up to each front door announcing his arrival with a melodious yodel that went 'O-de-leddy-dee.' During the holidays, kids would cluster round the back of the cart where two doors opened on to his cornucopia of bread. Occasionally, we would be rewarded with a roll or a bun.

Once he had finished a street or a section, Mr Cumberland would sit up the front, on a high seat with the reins ready to be taken up and a whip stuck vertically in a holder beside him. His pozzie was protected by a little awning and his 'rear window' was an oval of glass through which he could see not the following traffic but his load of bread in its dark haven as the eccentric carriage faltered along to the next delivery run.

The horse was called 'Lion' though there were variations on this, including, 'You bloody animal', 'Lion, you old bastard', and an exhortation which extreme exasperation left unfinished, 'Lion, for Christ sake . . .' Lion had one pace and it was distinguishable from no movement at all only by very close attention. As he traversed Havelock Street, Lion would evacuate two or three large offerings of steaming golden manure, which Mrs Lynch would collect with a beach bucket and a child's spade for her flowers.

To my profound chagrin, my father ordered me to join this feculent trade once he was back home for good and had got his vegetable garden thriving. And so I would have to beat Mrs Lynch to the punch – or rather the scrape – and, in front of my highly satirical offsiders, gather in Lion's largesse. This was the most repellent of my many domestic chores, not because I was especially sensitive to the noisome nature of the task but because it laid me open to such ridicule. You could not do the job early or in the dark: its timing was tightly tied to Lion's arrival and the operation of his capacious bowels. 'Here comes the shit cart,' the kids would shout at me when Cumberland's outfit loomed at the faraway Luna Park end of the street. And I would be on the rack for the next half-hour or more, while Lion ambled towards us and Mr Cumberland's 'O-de-leddy-dee', many gateways distant at first, gradually became louder as nemesis approached.

Then there was the council cart. Pulled by two huge, shaggy horses that look like Clydesdales in memory but were probably much less distinguished, the cart ambled slowly the length of the street twice a week, accompanied by two council men who swept the gutters, shovelled up the accumulated rubbish and heaved it into the cart. When I was indulging in my innumerable sick days, I would often sit up on the gatepost and watch their decorous broom-and-shovel procession. The younger of the two men would always say, 'Gooday, Snow, how're y'goin' today?' The older, cigarette sticking out invariably from beneath a luxuriant moustache whose natural straw colour was deepened by decades of nicotine, uttered never a word but could not be called silent because his progress along the gutter was often marked by the emission of a firecracker fusillade of stupendous farts.

Because I had discovered this performance during one of my sick days and had related it, as the *onlie true begetter*, to the usual unbelieving circle – O'Gorman, Waller, Doreen, the two Flaherty boys – the man with the moustache became the object of intense scrutiny when next the school holidays made it possible for us all to assemble and observe. We loitered in his increasingly irritable wake, making elaborate shows of boredom and distraction while listening, doubting, conducting *sotto voce* commentary. This was empiricism at its best.

I don't know what that man had for breakfast each morning but, after an anxious hiatus and just when the doubters and cynics were beginning to assail me with triumphant abuse, he delivered. The result was stunning and established me in a position of authority for some days until, recounting this interlude to Darmody at school, I was eclipsed by his assurance that the true exponent of serial farts would strike a match and light them, a phenomenon which, naturally, he had personally witnessed. Like all Darmody's claims and stances, this one teetered on the edge of easily dismissed outlandishness yet took tenacious life from his knowing and mysterious smile, the sage and world-weary manner with which he imparted his shifty truths. And so my moment passed, as always.

Schoolboy stuff – farting and behind-the-hand giggling. But we were, after all, schoolboys, and small ones at that, even if we sought to assign to the 'school' part of that designation the least momentum and recognition possible. It was an aspiration made feasible by the chronic preoccupation of our parents with war, work and silent loved ones at the front.

Another locally famous visitation to Havelock Street occurred in 1946. Living as I did in a household full of dedicated punters, I developed an incipient grasp of the romance of the turf. When, week after week, the form guides began to flower all over the kitchen table on Friday night and Saturday morning, it was difficult not to pick up at least a sketchy sense of what was hot and what was not. Just as it would become apparent, as Saturday afternoon reverberated with footy scores punctuated by the rhythmic, nasal litanies of famous race-caller, Eric 'Never bet on anything that can talk' Welch, that some canny wagers and well-informed plunges had yet again come unstuck. I always knew, for example, when my grandmother's idol, jockey Jack Purtell, had 'booted one home', because she had invariably backed whatever he was riding. Family anecdote recorded her perspicacious investment in Velocity when Purtell rode it to victory in the 1941 Caulfield Cup. Without a doubt, the Purple Para Port took a beating that Saturday night. And I knew of her implacable opposition to another champion jockey, 'Scobie' Breasley, an irrational prejudice that reduced Jim to worse than normal tortures of incoherence and seemed to have originated in Breasley's 1942 Caulfield Cup victory on Tranquil Star. As I was only five and six at the time of these two triumphs of the turf, I do not remember them in any detail, but within a few years I had inherited the knowledge and a sense of the emotions that went with them.

It was from this background noise – the imagined drumbeat of hooves, the whine of the wireless as they 'tighten on the turn and head for home', my grandmother's half-whispered incantation, 'C'mon now, c'mon now' – that I gleaned the first inkling of a brewing turf sensation.

The amazing Bernborough, ridden by Athol Mulley, came to Melbourne in 1946 with a hat trick of wins behind him in Sydney and won the Futurity Stakes by five lengths carrying an 'impost' of 64.5 kilograms. In his next race, the Newmarket, he beat twenty-seven other horses and set a weight-carrying record of 63 kilograms for the dash down the straight six at Flemington. Back in Sydney, he kept on winning – the Rawson, Chipping Norton and All-Aged Stakes fell to his mighty finishes and apparently limitless strength as a bearer of ever greater burdens. Finally, in what would soon be known as the Doomben 10,000, he lugged 65.5 kilograms to come from last on the turn gathering up twenty-seven other runners and winning by two lengths in record time. With a penalising 68.5 kilograms on his back in the Doomben Cup, he spread-eagled the field and won again from last at the turn. No horse had ever achieved that double and no horse has done so since.

Havelock Street was a long way from these stirring scenes, but on the day that Bernborough won the Futurity we became enrolled in the fortunes of this amazing horse when a woman came wandering down the street at about five o'clock, singing and laughing and punctuating her performance with the incantation, 'Bernborough! Bernborough!' I was 'mucking round' out in the street and at first I thought this approaching woman was Mrs Lynch. It was this misconception, much more than the impact of Bernborough's record, which drew my attention. I knew very well, even if only in my boyish way, how alien it was to Mrs Lynch's stern, Calvinist regime to be tipsy, staggering and shouting along the very street in which she regarded herself a moral arbiter and exemplar among backsliders and reprobates of monumental persistence and misguided dedication.

It was not Mrs Lynch of course. This ebullient woman, stylish in black and swinging a shiny black handbag in extravagant arcs, rolled on past Mrs Lynch's gate and continued down the length of the street towards Luna Park. But she returned. After each of Bernborough's

Melbourne wins and a couple of times during his Sydney campaign, she did her victory waltz down our street. We began to wait for her. Other Bernborough exponents, who included inevitably my grandmother, would greet her across their fences and gates and cheer as she passed. They would wish her good luck, ask her for tips and especially for inside knowledge on when Bernborough might at last find the weights and the expectations too burdensome. She, for her part, would laugh and conduct their applause and greetings as if she were directing an orchestra.

The speculation was that she must have been going to the track when Bernborough was in town and that she was punting on the SP for the Sydney races. It was generally agreed in our house that she was a bigger than average punter used to more than average success, in which case, wondered Aunty Jean, why did she not take a cab? This was mildly mysterious and was given delicious tension by being tied to Bernborough's winning streak. It became even more mysterious when the newspapers reported the activities of someone they called 'The Woman in Black'. With her sombre but stylish outfit set off by a matching black bag, from which she extracted large amounts of cash to bet on Bernborough, she became a familiar figure at the track, following the big bay's triumphant trail. For one heady moment, when this story broke, we all thought that our lady in black was the exotic stranger, only to realise immediately that we were dealing with a copy-cat. Nevertheless, the Havelock Street version did appear to be a genuine punter whose loyalty to Bernborough was filling her own black bag.

Meanwhile, the cause of these odd manifestations was still winning. Ten in a row. Eleven. Twelve. The whole of south-eastern Australia was enthralled by the gallant bay thoroughbred's phenomenal fortunes, and even people who had never placed a bet in their lives knew that when Bernborough returned to Melbourne for the 1946 Spring Carnival he had won fifteen races straight and the Caulfield Cup was to be his sixteenth. But Bernborough's run had ended. Despite carrying 68 kilograms, he started as a seven to four favourite and dazzled the huge crowd with a characteristic, electrifying finish. This time, though, he made his charge too late and finished fifth. The real 'Woman in Black' bet 6000 pounds on him, left the course in silence after the race and was never seen at the track again. 'Our' woman in black did not arrive that Saturday and completely disappeared from our lives.

Bernborough, unabashed, was cruising home a couple of weeks later in the L.K.S. Mackinnon Stakes, when he shied and cracked a sesamoid bone. His *annus mirabilis* had ended. He never raced again.

Mannie said he was not at all surprised that Bernborough had failed in the Caulfield Cup. The amazing fifteen-win run had obviously been a put-up job and they (it was always 'they') had to bring it to an end some time or they would have been rumbled.

CHAPTER 10

Hydraulics

After the war, my father worked in the Government Aircraft Factory at Fishermans Bend. He was a very smart, memorable bloke, my father, whose ironic humour, temperamental inclination to gloom, and stoic philosophy were all born of his perception that a sort of doggedly pursuing adversity – nothing so grand as the hand of fate – simply had to be coped with at every one of life's significant turns. This made him, among other things, an absolutely archetypal candidate for supporting the St Kilda football team. Educated at Christian Brothers College, St Kilda, he was a high jumper of note, a handy footballer and cricketer, a canny handballer and a brilliant sketcher and designer.

With the latter talents in mind, he set out to be an architect, but early in his studies, following a rain-sodden fishing trip along the Murray, he came down with pleurisy and was eventually found to have 'a spot on the lung'. This meant probable tuberculosis, so he had to leave the drawing office. After rest, recuperation and, luckily for him in those days, recovery, he joined his father, Thomas Ernest Matthews and his brother, Eric, in the small but respected firm, Matthews and Sons Builders. My father did the plans and specifications for the business as well as playing his part in the physical building work, and Matthews and Sons designed and built many of the wide-verandah'd, splendid houses still to be seen in quiet streets through Caulfield and East St Kilda. As a result, my father's drawing and design capacities were nurtured and what turned out to be his brilliant aptitude for all kinds of working with wood was discovered and developed.

Allowing for the setback with his health, life was looking promising when the crash came and wiped out Matthews and Sons Builders. My father spent long hours looking unsuccessfully for work and other long hours sitting in the garden of his parents' house – the only thing they had saved from the ruins – reading the complete Charles Dickens.

Tom – Pop Matthews, as he was known – was a Devon man, born in Totnes. He looked like Thomas Hardy, with a slightly hooked nose, large forehead and a pipe, sometimes glowing, sometimes cold, more or less grafted to his lips. He was universally liked – a genuine man of peace, with humorous eyes and a wry look to him. His shed, on the front of which I remember the sign, *Matthews and Sons Builders*, was a marvel of gadgetry, machinery, abandoned knick-knacks and shadowy corners and half-stuck drawers that invariably rewarded curious inquiry.

Especially I remember a huge grindstone that whined

louder and louder the faster you turned it, and the sparks that would fly from it when Pop sharpened the axe or a carving knife, or the pen knife he carried everywhere. When I was very small, Pop made me a pedal car – a bright red dasher with white trim and black mudguards. I kept it long after I could even fit in it. Somehow, I don't think Pop knew much about Australian Rules. I suspect he might have just amiably gone along with it as his sons became more and more involved. In any case, it was probably good business to declare for the local team if you were building in Caulfield and St Kilda. And he knew enough to paint my pedal car in the Saints' club colours.

Another thing I remember about him was his shooting. Somewhere near Rosebud, I accompanied my father and Pop Matthews as they tramped across wide, seaspray-smelling paddocks near the back beach, shooting the odd rabbit. This would have been before the war, or before my father's part in it, anyway, and their interest in getting a few rabbits would not have been entirely recreational. My father was a good shot and he bagged several. Pop, however, was deadly and, as if to underline his special status, one of the rabbits he shot was black and white.

At Fishermans Bend, my father turned his draughting ability to new account. He would bring home books on aircraft hydraulics and sample sketch plans based on contemporary aviation systems, and spend evenings teaching himself their intricacies and how to represent them. Among his papers I found two letters from the 'Office of the Suggestions Board' at Fishermans Bend Aircraft Factory, each one commending him on his suggestion 'relative to' a specified 'Revised Assembly

Sequence' and awarding him, as a consequence of the decision to adopt his suggestion, the sum of two guineas. His demonstrated and growing mastery of the systems resulted in his transfer on probation to the drawing office where he stayed, never permanent, always about to be dismissed if Menzies closed down the plant, which he was constantly threatening to do.

As far as work was concerned, my father lived his life in a state of chronic insecurity. I remember him throwing the *Herald* across the room one night in frustrated outrage at the journalist, E.W. Tipping, who had referred in his column to public servants *scurrying around in panic* as their jobs were axed by the government.

'He's got no bloody idea,' the old man said, 'no bloody idea what it's like to be out of a job, or what it's like to go each day and wonder if they'll hand you your cards. The bastard.'

This was probably hard on Tipping, for all I know, but it was only in the last few years of his working life – which, as it happened, were also the last years of his life – that my old man was given job security. These insecurities were to have huge ramifications for me.

Work was an overwhelming preoccupation with my old man. This was partly because of the acute day-to-day unpredictability of his working life and partly because he was a worker – not a workaholic (terminology uncoined then), but someone who saw that work was inevitably part of the fabric of living, part of the rationale, the reason, for living, and not something to be avoided as much as possible or to be regretted or simply borne.

In the ten years or so between his return home and the mid-fifties there was scarcely a weekend when my father did not work. During the week, he would attend to hydraulics at Fishermans Bend. On Saturdays and Sundays (interrupted by only one serious season of football on Saturday), he built the new house in East Brighton to which we would 'escape' from St Kilda. He was consumed by this project – planning, looking at land, trying to borrow money, organising licences and permissions, scrounging materials and, finally, building the place pretty much on his own – from 1945 to about mid-1948, when we moved in. After that great day, he continued to work entire weekends and most evenings painting, plastering, making cupboards, starting the garden, and so on. If ever he stepped back from these tasks, it would be to help a mate plan and build *his* house. Or, later, after the death of his brother, Eric, in 1955, to help his widowed sister-in-law, Annette – who, in the possibly uncharitable view of some, including my mother, did not deserve it – maintain and renovate her family home, that same handsome house that had been the headquarters of Matthews and Sons Builders.

When all these tasks and calls upon his time finally began to peter out in the second half of the fifties, he was enormously grateful and relieved. Yet, if he endorsed the dictum that 'you wouldn't be dead for quids' – and he did – the fleeting pleasures that made sense of that mildly hedonistic philosophy amid such a relentless existence must have been few and often hard to identify.

One of the pleasures was to go to the pictures at the Palais, next to Luna Park. And another was to roll and smoke his own cigarettes. These two pleasures clashed in an elimination round sometime in 1948 when the Palais became a non-smoking cinema.

My mother and father went to the 'Palais pictures' most Friday nights. Although Hoyts Victory was marginally closer, my father scorned it on the theory that it screened inferior films. This theory was almost certainly wrong but was sustained every time he tested it. I will never forget a film called *The Girl on the Bridge* at the Victory. Even I detected quite early that this was gold-medal garbage, but I was not prepared for the old man's reaction; neither, it scarcely need be added, was my mother. We left early – an extraordinary occurrence in itself. My father almost always sat them out, no matter how grimly. As we attained the top of the aisle in the flickering darkness and were about to go through the exit door, my father turned to face the screen and the backs of the audience and called out, 'This is an insult to anyone's intelligence.' We were on the move before the usher got to us but, undaunted, my father then confronted the manager, holed up in his minuscule den behind the box office, and told him the same thing, adding that in a just world we would have our ticket price refunded. Then we walked home in an uncomfortable silence broken only by sounds of the distant revelries of Acland Street and Luna Park and a tram clanking over points somewhere.

But the night the Palais went non-smoking was an even more resounding event. Going to the Palais pictures on a Friday night was a matter of stately and unswerving ritual. To begin with, we had to be striding along Havelock Street with a good forty-five minutes up our sleeve. My father could not afford the back stalls so the aim was to get in to the very back seat of the front stalls.

This took speed, organisation, a certain amount of steely determination and a capacity to tough it out when your better feelings were being appealed to by apparently feeble competitors either for a place in the queue or, once inside, one of the last three seats in the row.

Once ensconced, the old man would light up the first of his six going-to-the-pictures cigarettes. The next would be during the newsreel and 'shorts'; then one at interval, two during the main feature and one walking home. On this fatal night he had to forgo the first because there were notices everywhere forbidding it and, when the lights dimmed in preparation for the Val Morgan advertisements, a notice on the screen spelt out the ban. When he saw this, my old man hissed, booed and stamped his feet, to the exquisite embarrassment of my mother and me. We then settled down for the next three hours or so in the close presence of people who had identified us beyond dispute as a family of loonies. Not that the old man cared what they thought.

Another of my father's small pleasures in those immediate postwar days – which were undoubtedly much harder for my parents than I ever realised or can now establish – was to follow the 'fortunes' of the St Kilda Football Club. He enjoyed their games, though 'enjoyed' was rarely the appropriate word, vicariously through the pages of the *Sporting Globe* – the 'pink comic'. He had no time much for any other team but, no doubt remembering serial drubbings of astronomical proportions and mindful of the way in which the press was totally mesmerised by them, he especially loathed Collingwood. Alf Brown was the gun writer on football for the *Herald* and the *Sporting Globe*. He would give a quarter-by-quarter – sometimes it seemed almost kick-by-kick – account of one of the games.

In the early edition you might get only the first quarter. Later editions would enlarge on the saga as the game unfolded, and the whole story, told with Alf Brown's invariable slants, biases and sometimes barely suppressed testiness, would be available in the final edition. Brown was unconsciously but thoroughly a slave to Victorian Football League culture. He expected Collingwood, Carlton, Essendon and, in those days, Richmond to dominate the scene and the other clubs – lesser, struggling to one degree or another – were really only there to make up the numbers. St Kilda therefore scarcely ever detained him for an instant but when his reports occasionally took in the Saints they were invariably patronising, dismissive or silly.

The old man hated Alf Brown almost as much as he detested Brown's *Herald* colleague E.W. Tipping. When Brown reported on a match between Geelong and St Kilda – in which the Saints had got out to a huge lead but, of course, lost by a few points in the last minutes – under the heading, *Cats Delete Saints Lead*, the old man raged about the misuse of 'delete'. No doubt the only satisfaction and outlet he could come by after the crushing disappointment of an after-the-siren loss was to bag Alf Brown. He didn't know, and neither did I, that the sub-editors would have given the piece its illiterate headline and poor old Alf was guiltless that time.

CHAPTER 11

Not One of Your Prime Sites

When all the men were back by 1945, number 54 Havelock Street was crammed full of extended family. It was a sort of sawn-in-half house. All the rooms on the western side should have had mirror images on the other side of the long passage, but instead there was a long, redbrick wall unbroken by window or doorway, dropping down into the wide stormwater drainage channel. So, as you walked down the long passage the bedrooms (three of them), the sitting room and finally the kitchen, all opened off to your left.

When you stepped on to the front porch, which was a mere two or three paces long and only slightly wider than the doorway, you passed a brass plaque bearing the name of the house, *Orcades*. No one knew what this name meant or what was its provenance and its inherent inanity somehow caused it to become the focus of all my father's loathing of the house, the street and the atmosphere. But my grandmother polished the plaque furiously with Brasso every Monday as part of a ritual domestic turnover that included the washing and general house cleaning.

The first bedroom, immediately inside the front door, was occupied before the war by my mother and father and me in a cot, then later in a fold-down bed. When my sister was born in April 1942, she took over the cot and shared the room with my mother – and my father when he returned. My grandmother and Aunty Jean shared the second bedroom and Alex and Jim were in the third. I joined them when my sister arrived, my bed being squeezed into a spot along the wall just inside the doorway of this room.

Because this arrangement made it very difficult to close the door (though Jim managed to occasionally when he wanted some privacy to read or contemplate), I could see out into the passage from my pillow. This was how I became at first terrified of but eventually mysteriously bonded to the ever-changing luminescence of the skylight – the only source of light in the long, windowless passageway.

The next port of call after my room was the lounge, in which a sofa and armchairs surrounded the fireplace. The pianola stood along the wall opposite the fireplace. To get to the kitchen, you just walked straight through the lounge as if the passage was still there. The kitchen was divided into three parts. The main area was taken up by the table, where all meals were served, and the ice chest and a dresser. A door over in one corner opened into the bathroom, where there was a chip heater. Alongside the bathroom was a doorless opening into what everyone called the kitchenette, where there was the stove, the sink and a bench and cupboards.

The back door opened from here onto a cramped closed-in verandah. To the left was the toilet where there was a fixed, wooden seat scrubbed almost white over years of Mondays and, hanging within reach, neatly cut squares of the *Truth* and the *Sun* and the *Herald*, that you tore one by one from a wire hook. At the opposite end of the verandah, my father had built himself a neat, necessarily narrow bench, on which were bolted his vice and small grindstone and above which in organised rows hung various tools – different sizes and species of hammers and screwdrivers and saws. On shelves fixed to the end wall were jars and tins and wooden boxes of screws, nails, nuts, bolts and knick-knacks. There was not much room to wield a hammer or ply a saw, let alone swing a cat, but it was a workshop of a kind and utterly necessary to my father's equanimity.

When you left the verandah, you entered the impossibly tiny backyard, made even smaller by the luxuriant climbing, encroaching, creeping, rambling, towering or leaning ubiquity of my father's vegetable garden in vats. In summer, Aunty Jean would sunbake in the tiny square of hot light that visited from mid-morning before surrounding roofs and sagging, ruptured paling fences brought about an early dusk. There was a ball game that, incredibly, O'Gorman and I used to play on this ludicrous arena, but it was called off after our ball flew three times over the fence, across the drain, and point blank through Millers' kitchen window. After he had gone next door for the third time to replace the window, the old man lowered the boom. So the 'yard' was abandoned to Jean and the burgeoning plants. The latter, attracting, as is their nature, droning squadrons of interested bees, finally won the space from Jean as well, but neither she nor anyone else complained. The vegies were too abundant and too good and the square of backyard concrete too insignificant to warrant a shootout.

Regular visitors added their numbers to this already crowded establishment. My uncle-to-be, Mannie, when courting Jean, was an almost constant visitor in the evenings and at weekends, and my paternal grandparents and a mysterious, bald family friend named Reg would visit every Sunday for tea and to play cards. I ascribe my life-long detestation of cards to those evenings when my father, so recently returned, would spend hours of his time over the green baize.

It was a roller-coaster ride at 54 Havelock Street in those days just after the war, as if affairs within the house were somehow incurably infected by the maelstrom outside it. The inimitable clank and clatter of Luna Park's literal Big Dipper was clearly audible at our place on summer days, mimicking the plunging and peaking lives of the street. And in the larger district – a sort of polyglot principality bounded by Acland Street, Robe Street (the place of prostitutes), Grey and Barkly streets and Carlyle Street, but spilling over at all perimeters – the different enclaves, stratas and incipient ghettos clamoured through their daily (and nightly) negotiations, driftings and confrontations at a frantic and chaotic pace.

My main memory of my father in those days after his return to civvy life (somewhere round the middle of 1945, in his case), was that he stood as a solid and reliable bulwark in all this rush and excess. Yet, in another way, he was easily the most adventurous, the least impressed by boundaries, in our extended family and by far the most interesting. Alex looked more amazing – rampaging, irresponsible, amiably drunken as he was – but his was a shallow bohemianism that wore thin very quickly. The old man was much less spectacular but quietly in tune with the heady times, with the sense of possibility. Although he never spoke of his experiences (except to recount one hair-raising incident involving an aircraft shot to pieces, leaking oil, flying 'at nought feet' and almost certainly incapable of getting over the pine trees on the coast at Darwin if it got that far at all), I think he was quite surprised to be alive, healthy, in love and with a little family. The next move was to make life as good and as absorbing as he could for them and himself. It was all bonus really.

I see now that his almost immediate aim on returning was to leave St Kilda, which he found mean and constricting, not to mention violent in a way that appalled him as a father and husband. As a 'returned man', he found St Kilda somehow disappointing, not up to some ideal he had of what they had all been fighting for. But in the meantime, he was not going to be repressed by his straitened finances and a glimpsed quality of deep disorder in the world he had come back to, which he, at least, disliked.

Very early on, he acquired a job lot of metal vats from some redundant war industry or other, deployed them all round the edges of our postage-stamp backyard, filled them with soil delivered by a mate and grew magnificent tomatoes, pumpkins, cauliflowers, lettuce, cucumber . . . On summer evenings, ours was the only backyard, in that tatty and mean conglomeration of leaning fences and rusted galvo, from which rose the epiphany-making scent of tomato plants exhaling in the luxury of a sprinkler after the hundred-degree heat of the day. Our salads were the envy and wonder of the street. He pulled out the drooping, smelly geraniums and the funereal lilies choking a narrow strip of soil running the length of the side path, dug it all up (encountering old cans, coins and other detritus of the years), and grew onions along the front edge and trained beans and peas on to a lattice that he fixed to the fence. Mrs Lynch, on the other side of that fence, complained, of course – water seeped through, she said – but he shut her up by giving her produce.

He rode a bike to and from Fishermans Bend each day, rolled his own, had a bet and a beer and, for a while, went to the footy. But his weekends soon became unavailable as he worked on through his plan of escape. And anyway, the Saints won two and lost eighteen in 1945 so there was not a great deal of distraction there.

At the end of that year, though, as a treat, he took me to the Grand Final between Carlton and South Melbourne. My father must have thought he was somehow cursed in his efforts to bond with his small son in a peaceful postwar world when the game, at Princes Park, turned into the most notorious Grand Final ever – the 'fighting final', a bloodbath of king hits, elbows, shirtfronts and score settling. I thought it was marvellous, but the old man devoted a good deal of time on the way home, and later, to insisting that the game was nobler and more skilful than that and, anyway, what would you expect from 'bloody Carlton'. This was probably unjust as far as I can tell from very sketchy memories and reading later accounts of the game, but St Kilda and South were neighbours, their grounds at either end of Albert Park Lake turning all their encounters into

'Lake Premierships', and, with their more or less working-class constituencies, were the only League teams south of the Yarra.

A few years later, in a similar spirit, he took me to see Don Bradman's Testimonial Game at the Melbourne Cricket Ground. Throughout the winter, we had listened to 'Rickety Kate' and the relayed 'description' of the triumphant 1948 team's invincible progress through the Tests in England (I would hear only the start of the broadcast on the Thursday but was allowed to listen a bit later on Friday and Saturday).

When the conquering team returned and Bradman had announced his retirement, my old man, despite frequently proposing that Archie Jackson would have been better had he lived, felt I should see the great man in the flesh. The experience turned out to be a marvel for me but was agony for him. He wanted me to see a Bradman century, but he did not want me to expect it.

'He doesn't make a hundred every time he bats, you know,' he cautioned me as we walked across the footbridge to the ground. 'You've got to remember he's human. Hollies got him, for one thing. Just when he should have turned it on for the last time. You can't expect miracles. They reckon his eyes are pretty much gone now. If he gets a really good thirty or so, I'll be happy.'

The unspoken message was, so will you and that's an order. But nothing could undermine my certainty that I was about to have the privilege of seeing the great man triumph. The old man had shown me a photograph of that billboard which simply announced, *He's Out*. I reckoned it could easily go that way again.

Well, there were all kinds of shenanigans, including

Sid Barnes bowling a tennis ball and Ron Hamence coming in at number three to a huge and continuous standing ovation. He was much the same stature as Bradman and he had his cap well pulled down. Only slowly did the crowd realise that the Don had played a last trick on them. But eventually, in he came and swept stylishly into the nineties. The crowd became more and more tense. My old man was beside himself, chain smoking and assuring me that even if Bradman didn't get a hundred we had still seen a wonderful innings. There was no point in getting anxious about it, he told me, his voice straining with anxiety and his brow knit with concentration.

Within a few runs of the hundred, Bradman mis-hit. The ball ballooned out over mid-off where Colin McCool, one of the 'ground staff bowlers' of the '48 Tour rumoured to have good reason to bear Bradman ill, positioned himself under it for the catch. A long distraught gasp gusted out from the stands and terraces and my old man grabbed me so hard by the arm that it hurt and said, 'Christ, if he catches it they'll lynch him,' and McCool expertly dropped the ball and so I saw Don Bradman make a hundred.

These were signal events at either end of the years between my father's return and our move, which he planned, led and masterminded, out of St Kilda to East Brighton in 1948. But the intervening years were equally packed and diverting once he got into his civilian stride.

One day in the mid-winter of 1946, an extraordinary thing happened: my father came home in a car – a Baby Austin. His car. He had bought it from someone at Fishermans Bend. Everyone was stunned. It was an extremely radical thing to do, almost out of order.

My grandmother in particular regarded this development with unconcealed suspicion and disapproval. She had welcomed my father home with relief and affection, but the party was soon over because she recognised that, unlike her sons Jim and Alex, and Mannie, who in that same year became her son-in-law, my father would not knuckle under to her iron dominion. He went his own maddening way, complicating matters by being not only willing to do repair and maintenance on the house but also proving brilliantly efficient and innovative at all these practical tasks. He could – and did at one time or another – fix the electrics, the plumbing, the fireplace that wouldn't draw and the odd broken lock, sagging hinge and recalcitrant 'wire door', which was what my grandmother always called a screen door.

Home on leave one time, he had made and fitted black-out frames for all the windows; his garden had transformed the backyard and our diet; he was not to be treated lightly. On the other hand, my grandmother's scuffing slippers drove him mad. What he regarded as the Murray clan's impenetrable Caledonian logic reduced him to speechless frustration. The cramped conditions and (I guess) the lack of privacy depressed him, as well as never being secure in his job, despite constantly being, and being seen to be, outstanding at it.

In short, my grandmother, much as my father basically liked and respected her, often loomed as one of the forces which he was damned if he was going to be constrained or bullied by after spending years copping it from 'the Japs' and fate generally.

The Baby Austin was an obscure threat to my grandmother because of the wild independence it might endow, I suppose. It made her uneasy. She had been used to having her daughter and grandchildren close to hand and under control. My father's return, with the best will in the world, had represented a subversion of that certainty. The car compounded this by making manifest and physical a hankering for movement, for horizons, for escape.

Much of the unease and suspicion was no doubt unspoken and only half conscious. But the Baby Austin became an utterly palpable and graspable problem when my father built two wooden ramps so it could be driven up over the kerb, and announced a plan to widen the side gate to allow for off-street parking. Annie was outraged. The landlord would not put up with it. *She* would not put up with it.

Nevertheless, beginning on the following Sunday and concluding a couple of weekends later, my father stripped the pickets from the fence, built and hung splendid new double gates (there was nothing like them anywhere else in the street except at the Millers' and theirs were falling over), sawed, sanded, shaped, nailed on and painted new pickets. He replaced the sad and now trampled straggle of dispirited geranium and phallic lilies with three rose bushes, which he formally handed over to my grandmother's care as he unveiled the new fence. It was a rout. She capitulated thoroughly and without a vestige of embarrassment and was even heard instructing the insufferable Mrs Lynch on the virtues of getting the car off the road lest it fall foul of 'villains'. Mrs Lynch, who was certainly pondering which one of several complaints she would formally lodge, about the car's being near her side fence, or infringing the footpath or posing some other form of nuisance, was overwhelmed by Annie's conviction. And so the Baby Austin found a safe and in the end undisputed home.

Characteristically, my father also began almost immediately to take the car apart and improve its looks and performance. Soon, it was ready for a family outing and off we went, my mother in the tiny passenger seat clutching my baby sister, the old man dwarfing the wheel, stooping a bit under the low roof, and me in the back. Annie, Jean, Jim, Mannie and regular Sunday visitor, Reg, waved us away, as if we were setting out for Darwin or Perth (Alex was away on a bender in Sydney, where he had gone to be interviewed for a job).

We cruised round East St Kilda and Caulfield, took a turn down the Esplanade and circled back through quiet Sunday afternoon streets towards Balaclava. It was a revelation to me to see the life going on around us – the games and strollings in parks; the benign couples bent over their front garden plots and flower beds, weeding, digging, planting; the skidding and darting ecstasy of dogs on the winter beach. And, closer to home in narrow, smoky streets, boys playing footy end-to-end only reluctantly yielding room for us to pass; young men squatting beside disreputable looking motor bikes amid a litter of oily sprockets, coils of cable, spanners, screwdrivers, rags.

Some of these activities took place in Havelock Street too – the footy certainly, and the occasional dismantling of recalcitrant motor bikes – but somehow it had never occurred to me what a maelstrom of life was going on around us.

People took a great interest in us as we passed, staring,

pointing and occasionally calling out something indistinguishable. I thought this was because of the wonder of our car and, at first, so did the old man and he was rather touched by it. After a while, though, he must have felt something odd in the sensation we seemed to be causing, which reached its climax in Blanche Street, only a matter of a few hundred yards from home. My father had been grim and tense for the past fifteen minutes or so, refusing to stop. He nursed the Baby Austin along at embarrassingly slow speeds – even for those days – until finally we inched up the new wooden ramps over the gutter and came to a halt in the small 'driveway'.

Immediately, my father was out of the car, which he quickly jacked up at the front, watched by Annie, Jean, Jim, Mannie and Reg who had all come out to greet the returning heroes. When the Baby Austin was safely upheld, he touched the off-side front wheel and it fell off. Its last line of defence in emergency was a large, ordinary split pin. This had bent and finally snapped. It was a miracle we hadn't lost the wheel out on the road. No wonder onlookers were fascinated and disturbed. The wheel had been wobbling drunkenly on its axle for the last quarter mile or so.

'So much for my new toy,' the old man said gloomily. He was always one to see the dark side, the potential for real catastrophe, but he always bounced back quickly.

The necessary parts were soon acquired – those he could afford were bought, those that were too dear or unavailable he 'scrounged' – the wheel was soon fixed, and the Baby Austin rolled back on to the road.

It had an important job to do far transcending anything so frivolous as touring or Sunday driving. At every opportunity, he would drive out into the suburban margins to look at land. He was determined to buy a block and build a house on it himself. As far as he was concerned, we were leaving St Kilda just as soon as he could organise it.

His advisers in those days were his elder brother, Eric, and two old mates of his father's – Hughie Paine and Bert Stiggants. Eric was a lovely, quietly spoken man with a marvellously wry wit and a great humanity. He was about as good as the old man at practical things – building and renovating – but didn't have the drawing skills. On the other hand, he was a self-taught, highly successful amateur mechanic and my father would always seek his guidance when, as he often did, he acquired an old car that needed to be torn down and reinvented.

Eric drove a 1928 Essex, which he had completely overhauled and brought to a pitch of excellence that it had scarcely known in its heyday. It had a polished wood dashboard, leather seats and a bonnet that seemed to stretch out of sight. During the war he spoiled its lines but kept it going by fitting a huge, bulky gas producer on the back.

Eric's easy smile, chubby features and rotund shape all proclaimed humour and tolerance, but he was an intensely anxious man within and his repressed tensions were exacerbated by his attempts to mollify a truly awful wife. Watching my Aunt Annette hector and harass Eric was how I came quite spontaneously to the pejorative, domestic meaning of the word 'nag'. 'Bellyaching' was one I learnt from Eric, used in the same context but always in Annette's absence.

Hughie was a plasterer, a formidable autodidact and a communist. He was always on for a yarn or a political debate and, though I did not discover this till some years later, he was a fount of dirty jokes. Like his mate, my grandfather Tom Matthews, he drove a 1928 Chev, though not all that often and not with much conviction. My father and Eric would stand chatting to him while he went through the ritual of starting this splendid machine after one of his regular visits to Matthews and Sons Builders in Ash Grove, Caulfield. 'I reckon she's a bit rich, Hughie,' they would say, 'a bit too much choke there, mate,' as Hughie's Chev alternately gasped and roared. Eventually, he would go leaping and halting down the road with the motor backfiring like all the cars did in Laurel and Hardy films. He was much more comfortable with the battered and paint-splattered truck in which he transported his tools of trade and went to and from jobs.

Hughie was thoroughly versed in Marx, Lenin and other political theorists. He called Dr Evatt, whom he admired, 'Doc Ee-vart' and he was always on for a discussion about the Labor Party and the commos with my father. He had read and re-read Dostoievsky, Tolstoy, Chekhov and Shakespeare, but had little time for the English novelists or the English themselves, for that matter. His great love was classical music, especially opera and ballet. He had hundreds of 78 rpm records and when I was older I would go to his house, squeeze past the gleaming Chev in the narrow driveway and sprawl on his lounge-room floor listening to the whole of *Swan Lake* or *Giselle* or *Sleeping Beauty*, or any number of his huge traditional jazz collection scratchily rationed out on endless black platters. To this day I think of Hughie when I hear or see *Swan Lake*. Not that he would ever actually go to the ballet, though his wife constantly begged him to accompany her.

'Bit bloody embarrassin' actually,' I overheard him explaining to my father. 'The blokes, y'know, wearin' these tights. Their balls and tackle stickin' out all over the bloody place. I did go once with the missus. Sittin' right up in the front row, too, we were. Well, y'd think they'd put tennis balls or somethin' in their strides. I spent half the night duckin' in case I copped an eyeful. Never again. I like to listen though.'

Hughie lived in East St Kilda and was a loyal St Kilda supporter, though many years of working at least six days a week had put him out of the habit of going to the games. His first wife had died in her forties and he had married again. I once heard him say to my father that he had 'picked another dud'. He was a saturnine, witty bloke but even when I was quite young I remember assuming that his life had been in some way tragically blighted, and probably it had – by the relentless requirement to work long and hard and by the Depression, which made nonsense of all his diligence.

Bert Stiggants was anathema to Hughie, even though both were mates of Tom Matthews. Stiggants was a tough, puritanical, self-made man who had backed Matthews and Sons Builders before the collapse. I scarcely met him, but vaguely remember a large, grim sort of bloke and I recall conversations between my mother and father in which Stiggants seemed to emerge as necessary but unlovely.

When my father found the block of land in East Brighton – one that seemed a good proposition and that he could possibly afford – all three advisers took a look and counselled against it. Stiggants's opinion ('a corrugated-iron fence in front and a drain at the back – not one of y' prime sites is it?') was especially disheartening, though, because the price of the block was a hundred pounds and the old man was hoping to borrow the hundred from Stiggants.

My father had what is these days called 'spatial ability'. He could look at an overgrown paddock bounded on the east by the corrugated iron rear fence of the Army Drill Hall, on the west by the unlovely Elster Canal (which did not know if it was a canal or a creek); and to north and south by flat anonymous tracts of looping and collapsing weeds; and he could envisage how it might be. Trees and shrubs and vegetable rows sprouted before his squinting eyes; the 'street' (the route of which absolutely nobody either in the vicinity or in the local council could understand or imagine) wound its neat S shape between nature strips and painted front fences; his car – whatever model it might turn out to be in that built-up future – sat in a flower-lined driveway and through the double doors of the garage he could glimpse his bench and tools ... My mother, seeing only a straggling, nondescript paddock dominated by *that* fence, was apprehensive. Eric thought there would be better chances 'further out'. Stiggants was deeply disapproving in his most sombre ecclesiastical manner – but he came up with the hundred pounds and the old man bought the block. With characteristic foresight, he remarked to my mother that if he had been game enough to ask Stiggants for 300, or if he could have got that much from somewhere else, he would have bought the entire paddock. Thirty years later, with the iron fence gone, the parade ground turned into a park-like expanse and a dozen or so houses adorning the leafy, S-shaped street and its cul-de-sac offshoot where the orchard had been, it represented riches even he had not dreamed of.

Never one to prevaricate, my father had already drawn up the plans and typed out, on his father's venerable Remington, specifications for the modest, pleasant weatherboard house he intended to build. As soon as he became officially owner of the land, he bought a City of Brighton Building Licence for three pounds fifteen shillings and sixpence. On the licence, the builders are named as Eric Ernest and Owen Thomas Matthews so that, though Eric played little physical part in the project, the old firm came partly back to life. My father then turned his mind to the seemingly imponderable problem of getting building materials less than a year after the end of the war. Reviving old friendships, he approached David Provan and Sons and D & H Bunny, who had been suppliers to his father in the palmy days of Matthews and Sons Builders. Though sceptical about his chances of getting anywhere near enough material to keep the job going, they were delighted to renew their association with the 'Matthews boys' and vowed to do their best.

All these exciting developments signalled the end for the Baby Austin. It was useless for carting timber, bags of cement, pipes, tools and the other bits and pieces that would be going up and down between St Kilda and East Brighton. Ideally, he needed a small truck of some kind.

At just this time, Tom Matthews died. He had been in a sad decline for about a year. I remember him bent over, gaunt and yellowed in the face – a frailness, almost a delicacy, replacing the squat, tough muscularity of him, his voice ghosting into whispers where once he would speak with gentle, firm huskiness through the smoke of his pipe. He was a splendid, much loved old man and of all the people on both sides of our family, he and my Uncle Jim were the two of whom no ill was spoken – either then or later.

Amid great acrimony, most of which originated from Eric's acquisitive, peasant cunning wife, Annette, the spoils were divided. My father, I know, stepped back from these confrontations – a diffidence admirable in its way but contributing significantly to the creation of family power vacuums which were duly filled with misconceptions, wrong decisions and territorial coups. Much pain would result from all this in later years. When the dust temporarily settled, Eric, Annette and Ma Matthews, my paternal grandmother, began a doomed sharing of the large and elegant family home in Ash Grove. And my father inherited the Chev.

It was a splendid antique even then, with its round ogling headlights, sweeping, dark no-nonsense mudguards, long bonnet and the black hood so drum-tight that its metal supports were outlined under the fabric like bones showing through the hide of a starving cow. On the steering column were long, knobbed levers – hand throttle and choke; the dashboard was a tight cluster of small, clock-like instruments with indicators continually and unreadably aquiver.

My father could afford neither to indulge this stately luxury nor to buy something more practical to replace it. Besides, for all the grief attending this bequest – and there was great grief because both men had been very close to Tom – its timeliness could not be ignored. My father and Eric overhauled and re-bored the Chev motor, took out the rear seats and rebuilt the back of the car, turning it into – a ute.

And so he had his truck, as he saddled up to build more or less single-handedly the three-bedroom, weatherboard house between the canal and the corrugated iron fence, on the street that nobody believed was there, in East Brighton. Not that he wouldn't have loved to keep the Chev in its pristine state and chug ceremoniously through the streets of old Brighton. That motor really did chug and the Chev went nowhere without radiating ceremony and panache: you couldn't move as slowly as that and still seem inconsequential. Even more sensationally, he fancied himself propped up behind the wooden-rimmed steering wheel that looked as big as a ship's helm, navigating the smoky and sinister byways of St Kilda. But style gave way to pragmatism, the Chev became a ute and I spent several years jolting around in the back of it amid sliding flurries of bent or discarded nails, random bits of timber and the powdery swirl of cement. It was an alfresco novelty that I quickly tired of.

I'm sure my father must have regretted the hard necessity that forced him to insult the old Chev with a conversion. Hughie Paine's own spotless and authentic Chev would have been a constant reminder that some sort of betrayal had been perpetrated. Hughie himself was sad but understanding about it. 'Well,' he would say in one of his many variations on the theme, 'I s'pose y'had to do it. Y'know, I can understand the necessity. I dunno what y'r old man would'a said. We bought our Chevs on the same day, did I ever tell y' that? Yeah, well. But there y'are. There's necessities, no doubt about that. For blokes like us and y'r old man. We gotta make do. Do the best we can.'

CHAPTER 12

Upstream

Despite the benign tyranny of the women, once my father was back on the scene I successfully aspired to greater freedom. I was allowed to go on my own to the Peanut Farm on Saturday afternoons to kick a football round. The Peanut Farm was a sports oval in the swooping shadow of Luna Park's Big Dipper, where the West St Kilda Catholic Young Men's Society played their home games. The CYMS played a notoriously rough, merciless brand of Australian Rules Football and their loud blasphemies and obscenities were an education to a ten-year-old boy of curious mind such as myself.

Standing on the boundary on a Saturday afternoon when the West St Kilda CYMS were playing at home, I would hear the Catholic young men shouting 'fuck' and 'bastard' and 'cunt' and 'Jesus Christ' and other shocking expressions that I was certain at the time must surely have damned them beyond even the most liberal dream of forgiveness. It was not that I gave a great deal of thought to the spiritual, but at my school, Sacred Heart, where many of these Catholic young men had gone as small boys, there was much talk of sin and its punishments. It was hard not to be aware of sins when people like the Catholic young men seemed to commit a whole range of them at the top of their voices.

I would stand on the boundary clutching my footy and watching and listening. The official story was that I would meet and have a kick with two of the kids from Havelock Street, Keith Carter and Dennis O'Gorman. The reality was, though, that both Carter and O'Gorman went almost every Saturday with O'Gorman's father to see Brighton play in the Association. Sometimes they even went to watch Essendon in the League. They rarely invited me; in fact O'Gorman mostly seemed to take obvious pleasure in excluding me. I didn't ever reveal this to my mother because I had a vague fear it would result in bad blood between the O'Gormans and the Matthews.

Only one house – the Millers' – separated us in Havelock Street and the adults had a casual, friendly relationship. This must have been one of my very earliest attempts to engineer the keeping of the peace in a lifetime that would be studded with such dogged attempts. Even then I could obscurely glimpse the truth that amateur peacekeepers like me were invariably better described as the meat in the sandwich. So, most Saturdays when the West St Kilda CYMS were playing at home, I would stand on the boundary watching the game, and listening to the yelling of the players and the barracking of the fifty or sixty supporters who usually turned up. At half time and after the final bell, I would kick my ball and chase it alone. I didn't know any of the boys who flooded onto the ground at each interval to continue interminable games on mysteriously demarcated sections of the ground according to impenetrable rules local to each group. As the light faded and the sound of boots thudding on leather had become isolated and echoing, I would wander off home, past Luna Park, round by the Candy Corner which, when I was with my mother, we would always cross over to avoid, and then on across the exotic upper reaches of Acland Street to the ill-lit gateway into Havelock Street.

These solitary sorties were directly connected to the converted Chev ute and the East Brighton house (consisting at this stage of freshly sunk foundation stumps and flooring joists) between the Elster Canal and the Drill Hall fence. My father was embarking on what would be a prolonged routine of spending weekends and holidays building the house. And so, after his years away at the war, he became again something of an absentee, working 'at the block', which meant that he couldn't go to the League or Association football or even come to watch the West St Kilda CYMS.

Every now and then, depending on the weather and what stage of the work my father was up to, my mother and baby sister and I would walk down Inkerman Street to High Street and take the Number 64 tram to join him 'at the block' in East Brighton. We would watch him sawing and hammering and digging and wheelbarrowing until it was too dark to see. Then we would all go home together in the Chev ute, with me in the back.

One Saturday afternoon, when the West St Kilda CYMS were twelve goals behind at half time, I decided to walk down to St Kilda beach. I had never done such a thing before and, according to the strict letter of my mother's law governing these excursions, the beach and its environs were forbidden territory. I comforted my conscience with the speculation that no one would worry much when swimming was out of the question, the beaches were empty, and 'strange men', drawn there by the crowds and the warmth of summer, were off hibernating in whatever havens they favoured during Melbourne's grandstand-roaring winter.

When I arrived at the Esplanade, it seemed much wider than I remembered from previous occasions in the company of aunts or my mother. I squinted into the teary wind at the winter sands and the dark jut of the pier over the cold, white-capped waters of Port Phillip Bay. The broad expanses of beach and lawn, the cool sweep of the roadway and the immensity of the bay were somehow a little frightening after the secure narrowness of Havelock Street and familiar figures and voices of the Peanut Farm. On the Esplanade, there were a few couples, wrapped round each other in the sharp air. There were solitary figures here and there on benches, coat-collared against the slicing wind, and dogs darting and snuffling in a sea-sprayed ecstasy of wild smells and trailing leashes, torn asunder from their masters and mistresses by the sheer joy of it all. The probing cold and spray stung my eyes, but I pushed on, leaving the beach-front shops behind. Sometimes I walked on the beach itself, sometimes on the footpath and, experimentally for a while, I teetered along the sea wall until I found myself staring down not at sand but at a jag of toothy rocks. Then I returned to the path.

It was just when I knew I should go back, when I was beginning to feel a bit scared by my own daring and by the total unfamiliarity of everything around me, that I saw something amazing. I arrived at a bridge over what looked to me like a broad shallow river. A sign on the bridge said *Elster Canal.* For a moment I couldn't take this in. The canal at the bottom of 'the block' where my father was building our house was called the Elster Canal. I was certain this was what he had told me. Only slowly was I able to accept that this canal was that canal. This was where it ran into the sea. I felt like an explorer – like Sturt at the Murray mouth or Phillip gazing for the first time on Port Jackson. And I was contemplating the preliminary vestiges of a plan so daring that it made me gasp and feel the excited thud of the blood through my body.

I ran home. I said nothing about my adventures to anyone. I was bursting to tell my father, but the sheer daring of what I was planning might be spoiled if I prefigured it. Also, he might forbid it.

For one reason and another, it was months before I could put my plan, reviewed over and over and rendered into sketch form at the back of one of my school exercise books, into action. It must have been a Saturday late in September that I set off after lunch as usual for the Peanut Farm. My mother accepted without suspicion my decision not to take the footy because, as I truthfully reported, one of the finals in the CYMS competition was being held at the ground that day (not featuring West St Kilda, however). There would not be the usual latitude available for a kick.

But of course I didn't go near the Peanut Farm (it would be just my luck for O'Gorman and Carter to turn up for once and spoil everything by being nosy and feeling morally obliged to report my activities). In the shadow of the Luna Park scaffolding, I ducked through the bushes and dropped down on to the Esplanade. A swift and confident progress took me along the beachfront to the bridge over the Elster Canal. Where the bridge railings started, there was a path leading down the bank to a rough trail running along beside the water. I set off. Upstream.

After I had been walking only five or six minutes, the first bend in the canal seemed to close behind me and the bridge disappeared from sight. The occasional sound of traffic was suddenly muffled and soon silenced. The waterway narrowed. Wooden paling back fences of houses rose on each side at the top of the banks in long, ragged crenellations like mouldering castle walls looming over their moat. It was a warm, sunny day and along the fenced-in, steeply banked course of the canal an unusual heat seemed to be trapped and shimmering. I began to have misgivings. A couple more bends of the channel cut me off completely from all sound, sight or memory of roads, people and cars. The track became no more than a thin line of hardened earth on either side of which rose reeds and high, looping weeds. I passed into this abyss of unfathomable grass with a growing irrational terror censoring any decision to return or even simply to stop and give in to paralysis: so I plunged on.

I walked along the bottom of the canal for a long time. Lonely bridges with small roads or footpaths on their backs would leap the canal every now and then. And I would have to go through long caves of reaching and aggressive echo, the huge gape of drain pipes, walking sometimes in the shallow wash of water, because high fences and barbed wire prevented any escape back into the world above.

The first time I did this, I fully expected a wave to rush through and drown me, but soon I became accustomed to seeing the cylindrical, gloomy entrance under each looming bridge and I would march into the dark and booming tunnel with at least a fair show of bravado.

I met nobody, though occasionally voices would drift from the hidden backyards – shouted orders to children, someone being called to have a cuppa, a shrill 'Goal! It was a goal!' – until, rounding yet another bend, I saw a gate open in the fence up to my left. This gate was made of palings like the fence and was invisible until it actually opened. Through this sudden aperture came a boy about my age and a large Alsatian. I waved uncertainly and called 'Gooday' to the boy, but, in total silence, he released the Alsatian from its lead and said, 'Sic 'im Bo.' The insignificant width of the waterway lay between me and the dog as he arrowed down his bank while I stumbled raggedly up mine. At the water, he stopped and growled and the boy screamed 'Sic 'im' with a frustrated edge to his voice. I saw two stones in the grass as I retreated and I scooped both of them up. The dog seemed still to be reluctant to cross the water, to the intensifying fury of his young master who now slid down to the bottom of the channel the better to cajole him. The dog let out a truly manic growl and advanced into the water. I threw both my stones in quick succession. The first splashed uselessly to one side of the Alsatian, but the second, by a remarkable and star-crossed stroke of fate, hit the boy on the side of the head. He screamed, Bo hesitated and, after one horrified glance to confirm that there was blood pouring from somewhere near the boy's ear, I bolted. Three bends later, scarcely able to breathe, I stopped, splashed canal water over my face and hair and tried to work out how long it would take the police to find me.

With legs like jelly and my heart thumping so hard it hurt in my chest, I plodded on. There was, obviously, no going back – and no hint of what lay ahead. I was a sitting duck for any pursuers while I stuck to the water-course, but I didn't know what else to do and, if it came to trying to return home, the canal was the only way I knew. My grand plan was in ruins and I was wishing I had never thought of it.

For a long time again I followed the channel. The warm sunlight slanted across my squinting gaze, my legs ached, my shoes had let in canal water under one of the bridges. When I suddenly arrived at a small clearing where the bank flattened out and the leisurely current warbled over a broad sweep of rocks and sandy ridges, I dropped down into the wildflowers and grass, lay on my back with my joined hands as pillow and stared into the uninterested blue sky. Almost certainly I would have fallen asleep had it not been for the low moaning and staccato gasping sounds that immediately had me sitting up and peering from the half-cover of the tall grass. A few yards away, a man was lying on top of a woman, rhythmically bouncing on her. He had a shirt on but she was naked and I saw her breast under his embracing arm. A tartan rug rising and falling with his thrusts covered their bottom halves. I knew very well what was going on here. This was 'fucking' and I felt an excitement that seemed both intimate and yet alien – to be expected yet incomprehensible. What I didn't know, though, was the precise mechanics of the business. This seemed such a good opportunity to find out, especially as the increasing tempo of their ardent negotiations was gradually shaking them clear of the rug. Already, I could see the top of her thigh; already I was in my imagination explaining to Darmody just what fitted where and who did what to whom – when, leaning too far out above the screen of vegetation, I must have momentarily caught the man's eye in its fine-frenzied rolling. Without stopping, and shouting to be heard above her moans which were now becoming small, obscurely word-shaped cries, he said, 'Fuck off, son, or I'll tell y'father.'

Looked back on from this distance, it was an odd thing to say, its eccentricity probably engendered by the urgency of his situation at the time. But, as his luck would have it, he could not have chanced on a more potent threat. Knowing with one part of my mind that he could not possibly 'tell my father', I nevertheless was instantly convinced that I was sprung, that my father would appear at the top of the bank wanting to know what I was doing there. For the second time in my increasingly ignominious long march, I ran.

Before I stopped jumping, hurdling and scrambling to get out of sight, the banks had resumed their precipitous angles, the waterway had curved and zigged and zagged several times and, up ahead, another bridge loomed.

I was beaten. There was no way up the bank on either side and the only way to negotiate this one was to go into the tunnel. Though I had been through a number of previous tunnels, I knew that, for some reason, I was not going into this one. It seemed darker than the others, it was certainly bigger, more echoing and cavernous, and you couldn't see daylight at the other end because it was long and slightly curving. I stood at the bottom of the channel, almost in the water, dwarfed by the banks, exhausted and on the edge of panic. I was too scared to climb to the top because I knew this would reveal to me only street names and houses I had never before set eyes on. I slumped into the long grass and the sounds of the afternoon washed over me – the ripple of the water, occasionally a bird whistling or warning, someone hammering somewhere. It was the hammering that began to blot out everything else and, after I had listened to it for minutes as if it were a piece of music, I climbed indecisively up the bank, more to be doing something than with any hope that this would be helpful or revelatory. At the rim, I ascended through the screen of tall grass to see the frame of a house surrounded by stacks of timber, heaps of earth, various bits of equipment – ladders, a wheelbarrow, spades, a shovel – and a man in the middle of the labyrinthine framework hammering: my father!

He couldn't work out whether to be delighted or appalled. He said it was quite dangerous to walk alone along the canal channel.

'You don't know what types are in those backyards. And there are some strange people who drink under the bridges, and so on. Your mother's going to have a fit when she finds out. How the hell will she know where you are?'

I hadn't thought of that. And I didn't reveal that I had seen people fucking, had been threatened by a dog and had probably killed a boy about my age and would hope at best for a manslaughter verdict. I just said, 'Sorry, Dad – it was a sort of a, sort of an adventure.'

The smile that had never been far from his lips, even when he was being very serious about my mad journey, now broke through without constraint.

'Well, I'm pleased to see you, mate. That goes without saying. I'll knock off a bit early and we'll keep Mum sweet. It'll be all right. In the meantime, feel the weight of this.'

He gave me a shovel, showed me what he wanted done, and we got down to some hard work – he resuming with the hammer, me making what were no doubt token assaults on the hard weed-stringy earth. For weeks after my great journey, the woman's cries ('Don't stop, aaah don't stop') would surface through the maelstrom of voices in my imaginative worlds with a peculiar, undifferentiated excitement that always disturbed me; and the blood streaming down the boy's face surreally invaded my dreams. But just for that moment, as I struggled with the long-handled shovel while the sound of my father's hammer beat out its rhythm nearby, it had all been worth it. I felt as if I was the first that ever burst into that silent world of the canal and there I was at voyage's end, triumphantly able to tell my father the tale. Though neither then nor at any time after did he hear the whole story.

We moved into the house at 11 Noel Street, East Brighton, early in 1948. The wrench of leaving Havelock Street – a wrench for me at least and possibly for my mother but certainly not my father – was temporarily ameliorated by the necessity for me to continue attending the Sacred Heart School. It was an important year. At the end of it, I would sit for a diocesan scholarship that would entitle me to a year at one of the 'central schools', so called, attached to Catholic Colleges like Christian Brothers, St Kilda, Xavier College and De La Salle,

Malvern. My father was desperate for me to win a diocesan scholarship because it was the only way he could afford to send me to what he regarded as a decent secondary Catholic school. He couldn't afford the fees or anything else much as the house, in its raw, even if now inhabited state, was chewing up every penny he and my mother could make.

The timing could not therefore have been worse for my father's plans. I was about to enter a world of potentially steep education costs just as the burdens of house payments and continued building were becoming entrenched for the foreseeable future. But he was absolutely adamant that I should aspire to and achieve full secondary schooling.

'From now on,' he said to me some time during 1948, 'you have to keep getting scholarships or it's the tomato-canning factory.'

The tomato-canning factory was in Nepean Road, Brighton, near the much-abused statue of Sir Thomas Bent. ('Tommy Bent', as he was known round the district, would be adorned with a St Kilda Football Club guernsey on the portentous night of 24 September 1966 to mark the Saints' first – and still *only* – VFL Premiership.) I had never heard of or set eyes on this noisome and rackety suburban enterprise until we moved to those parts and the first time I saw it I was half convinced that, given one false move, there lay my destiny.

But only half convinced. My father's threat to consign me to the factory was tongue-in-cheek but it masked a real anxiety. Like so many of his generation, he was scarred by his experiences of the Depression – and he did not suffer as badly as some. Still, he had endured both the tedium and more importantly the ignominy of having no work for long periods. His marvellous talents and promise had been pushed relentlessly into the background by conditions and contingencies over which he had no control. One by one he'd abandoned the aspirations that had so excited him when, as an eighteen-year-old in 1928, he seemed on the brink of a career in architecture. The shape of his ensuing life was moulded for him, as it was for innumerable other Australian men and women, by the events of the decade that began in 1929.

He was determined that his own children would, as far as possible, have the shaping of their lives in their own hands. The shaping tool, or, to change the metaphor, the key, as he saw it, was what he constantly referred to as the 'piece of paper'. You had to have that 'piece of paper' – whether certificate, diploma or degree did not matter, so long as you could produce a qualification. This was his insurance against a repetition in the lives of his children of his own and his wife's tribulations, their life-long battle with work – work sought, work achieved, work lost, work promised, work unpaid for; work petering out, work incessant, work unpalatable, work repugnant; work suddenly withdrawn, work back-breaking, working till you wept, working at night, at weekends, through holidays . . .

That was what the 'respectable working class' meant by 'work'. Not necessarily endless toil or a life without leisure or bereft totally of amenity, but continuous encounters with work, nothing that could be called a career, nothing that was ever secure, just constant negotiation with work, with jobs, with bosses; serial jousts with labour. Even if you spent your entire working life in the Collingwood boot factory, with time out only to be patriotic in war, you did not escape this process. You were never secure, you were rarely encouraged to take pride in your work, you rarely glimpsed the bosses. You left each day with relief, arrived each morning in doggedness or dread, backed the horses to escape, took tickets in Tatts and prepared to tell them to stick their job up their arse, then back to work when your number didn't come up. Being unemployed is a demeaning, debilitating experience. But only those who have never done any speak with approval and longing of 'good hard yakka', 'honest daily toil', 'the sweat of the brow' and the 'dignity of [hard] labour'.

My father was a self-deprecatory, diffident but intelligent and insightful man, broader of mind and vision than my friends' fathers in general, lateral-thinking in a way that was unusual then. He was pretty much on the left politically, strongly approved of Ben Chifley's Labor government and supported the nationalisation of the banks. I remember standing alongside him while he talked to the father of a friend of mine in Alexandra Street one Saturday evening in the winter of 1949. I think we were returning from the newsagents on the corner of North and Hawthorn roads, where we had bought the *Herald* and the *Sporting Globe* (the news would not have been good: St Kilda did not win a game for the first twelve weeks).

My friend's name was Peter Rule. Mr Rule was a stubby, reticent North Country man, who told my father, 'Chifley's not gettin' my little bit o' money.' We stood there, as the winter dark gathered along the street and the cold started to nip our cheeks and ankles, while my father quietly but unsuccessfully tried to demonstrate how Mr Chifley was not after Mr Rule's or anybody else's little bit of money. On the contrary, he ... But Mr Rule remained strenuously unconvinced and when we got home my father had things to say about 'bloody poms' and how we might 'lose the Labor government on this one' if too many people were thinking like Rule.

When I managed to win a diocesan scholarship at the end of 1948, my choices of school, allowing for geographical constraints, were St Leo's, attached to De La Salle College in Malvern; St Thomas Aquinas, part of Christian Brothers College, St Kilda; or Kostka Hall at Xavier College, a bit further away in the very pukka suburb of Kew.

At each of these, diocesan-scholarship winners from the network of primary schools in the Catholic system would do the equivalent of Grade 8 while being prepared for an assault on the junior government scholarship. The latter was critical to my father's plans for my education, because it paid for all fees and books right through to matriculation. Because I would be only thirteen at the end of 1949, I was actually young enough to have two shots at this scholarship. But this was not to be much considered because, if I failed, my second shot would have to be as a full fee-paying student in 'sub-intermediate' (Year 9) at whatever college I was attached to. It would be touch-and-go whether my parents could run to this, together with the cost of uniforms, sport and other extras. So the simple answer was to make sure I triumphed first time up.

Because he had gone to CBC himself, my father was keen that I should follow in his footsteps. Curiously, however, we never discussed this choice at all before the necessity to make a decision about it was landed on me suddenly at school one day in late October. Because the boy I sat next to and knocked around with – his name was Gary Watkins – was choosing St Leo's, which was the conduit to De La Salle College, Malvern, where Gary's older brother, Max, was already a student, I chose St Leo's too. It was only when I announced this at home that night that I glimpsed my father's disappointment. He made no effort to alter my decision, though, and so I started at St Leo's in February 1949, intent on a junior government scholarship in November of that year.

Apart from his preference for CBC on sentimental grounds, it does not seem to have occurred to my father that the choices available might have been worth a closer look. For me personally, looking back, it scarcely matters. In later years, I would meet and in some cases become very good friends with blokes who went to St Thomas Aquinas or Kostka Hall. The story was always the same. Beltings, force feeding, rote learning, favouritism on the basis of class, intensity of demonstrated family Catholicity and size of family; with amelioration of the stringency of these criteria being achieved only by sporting or scholarly elitism. St Leo's was no more and no less of a hellhole than any of the others. You got belted for every mistake, had the flesh of your arm pinched until you wanted to scream, and were regarded as a nonentity (literally – I was 'Matthews' for months after the favoured ones were 'Gerry' and 'Brendan' and 'Johnny') unless you demonstrated Einsteinian brilliance, were a champion sportsman or had brothers already at the school.

The only time that I was ever called Brian was by

Brother Joseph about midway through that scarifying year of 1949 at St Leo's. 'Joe' was a barbarian, a savage assaulter of the hands, upper arms (by pinching) and legs, upon no matter what provocation. He had some 'pet' names for people, but mostly one was identified by a pointing finger, a snarl or a surname. I was invariably Matthews or a snarl. But one week in second term we were visited and observed by inspectors from the state Education Department. Joe was on incredibly good, indeed unrecognisable, behaviour. When he asked a question and in a gently modulated voice full of interest and encouragement invited 'Brian' to answer, I looked around with all the other kids to see who he meant. Everything reverted to type, however, as soon as the inspectorate had left, which showed, I suppose, two things: Joe was content with his basic methods and he was beyond embarrassment.

Many of my contemporaries fulfilled enough of the three criteria – especially having brothers go before them – to ensure that their time at the half-way house of St Leo's was tolerable. The only student in my year who easily fulfilled all three was Bernard Teague, now Justice Teague. Had there been a further benchmark requiring you to be a good bloke and a decent human being, Bernard Teague would have passed that one as easily as he did the others. In my own case, failure on the first and third of these criteria was beyond dispute. As for the second, I failed that pretty conclusively too, though I wasn't at all without sporting ability or aspiration.

Neither the school nor the culture of which it was a part, however, was interested in chronically late developers, whether intellectually or physically. I spent my entire time at St Leo's, and afterwards at De La Salle, wishing I was smarter, better at sport, had six brothers and an obviously Celtic name.

My second term report at St Leo's was gruesome and had tomato-canning factory written all over it. It ended with the words, over Brother Joseph's signature, *Perhaps this will be a lesson to him.* I worked very hard in third term, won the English prize and looked good. But I knew I had never at any stage of that year come anywhere near to coping. I was immature, wide-eyed, out of my depth.

When we finally emerged from the junior government scholarship examination room – it was an all-day affair – two of my friends were marvelling at how easy it had all been, especially the maths. I quickly learned and sang this tune, though I knew deep down that I had not found it easy.

At some time a little later, I visited Sacred Heart School, like a condescending and successful alumnus, and, when asked by Sister Burkman what I had thought of the exam, I said, 'It was a pushover,' parroting the exact words of my friends for whom it really had been a pushover. What a naïve fool she must have thought me, though she merely smiled and changed the subject.

I was not surprised when, in February of 1950 – it took that long for the results to come out, which meant we were all back at school and we St Leo's veterans had graduated to the first year of secondary education in De La Salle College proper – my name was not among the hundreds of winners. There was a 'B.A. Mayhew' on the list, and I remember, with a cringing chagrin that the years do not erase, going to a public phone in High Street in what must have been a terminal stage of desperation and ringing the number that was handling queries on the results, in order to wonder to some irascible and harried bureaucrat if there had been some mistake. Having scarcely ever made a phone call in my life (a phone was, of course, unheard of at Havelock Street and at Noel Street there was no phone until 1955), I remember beginning my plea with the deathless announcement, 'I'm a boy.'

Too much has been written about Catholic school experiences already and I have neither justification nor desire to add to the record. Suffice to say, I disliked most of it intensely while recognising that I undoubtedly bore at least half the blame for that failure, through investing so little in it. Three of my teachers, though, illuminated something of the world for me.

Brother Paul – 'Pauly', we were not imaginative with our nicknames – taught me English in leaving and matriculation. He was an unpredictable, tortured, unhappy man as far as I saw at the time, and he played favourites outrageously. I was not one of his favourites, though I drifted in and out of 'the suburbs of his good pleasure' because I was from time to time capable at English, especially in matriculation. But while his interest in me fluctuated, I was fascinated by him, partly because he was so visibly a misfit in the religious organisation, but mostly because of his profound and knowledgeable enthusiasm for literature, especially poetry. He was a truly great teacher of poetry, and he launched me – and, I am sure many others – into its excitements and passions and hair-raising moments of recognition with a momentum that for me at least never abated. It remained for later even more brilliant and complex mentors, like Vincent Buckley, to make more of this momentum, to my great advantage and eternal gratitude.

Brother Frederick – inevitably, 'Freddy' – was in

charge of my class in the year after I failed to win the junior government scholarship, Year 9, as we would say now. During that year, I had to complete the normal curriculum like everyone else but at the same time prepare myself for a second shot at the scholarship, the conditions and substance of which, wouldn't you know, had been radically changed. Freddy was a humane, intelligent and gentle man, too gentle for the barbarians he taught, including me. But he always maintained our respect and his own authority despite being disinclined to use the strap or other coercive measures that were taken for granted in other classes and by most of the other brothers. He restored my confidence in myself by judicious attention that fell short of the kind of favouritism I was already, rightly or wrongly, so conscious of, and by giving me a glimmering of the truth that it was an intellectual project we were engaged upon at school, even if for the moment only in a very preliminary way. He was one of those rare teachers who made you realise that teaching is one of the great intellectual and human arts, something to aspire to and not something you did because you were second rate.

And finally, Brother Stanislaus – 'Stanny' of course! Again, I was not someone much in his orbit, although he didn't have favourites in any particularly overt or objectionable way that I can remember. Stanny was saturnine, brilliantly witty, irascible (though he played up his irritability – it was part of his style), a fine teacher. I was no good at his subject, sciences, and didn't come across him all that much after junior classes. But Stanny was a St Kilda supporter. He had taught the great John Coffee, St Kilda's star half-forward flanker in the early fifties, and other St Kilda players. And so he broke the

De La Salle Brothers mould of following Collingwood – of course they would, wouldn't they – and could regularly be found on the terrace in front of the members stand at the Junction Oval watching the Saints crash to this or that ignominy. This was where I got to know him. It was never an easy relationship. I suppose the last thing he wanted was to be accosted by one of his pupils when he was trying to relax at the footy. But he was often on his own and in 1952 and 1953 so was I. He was kind, pleasant and very good fun and, in the absence of my over-working father at these games, helped to take the bitter edge off the experience of following the Saints.

After winning the coveted scholarship at my second attempt in November 1950, I embarked on three further years of schooling at De La Salle – intermediate, leaving and matriculation. In each of these years, I won the prize for English literature but did nothing else much of note except for being expelled from the school Cadets for insubordination. This expulsion involved my convincing my father to write a formal note confirming my desire to end my association with the school military organisation. I managed to convince him that this was a reasonable course of action, given my inability to take seriously the posturing, megalomania and absurd mimicries of the cadet officer elite. He was a reluctant collaborator in this, but I suppose he could see little point in forcing me to continue. I remember being uncharacteristically inflexible about it.

I was in general a very compliant school student. I didn't get in to much trouble. I was probably regarded by the brothers as rather boringly bland. But there must have been a healthy streak of anti-authoritarianism in me (I certainly developed one later on) – a combination perhaps of my untrammelled, rough St Kilda days and my sturdily irredentist upbringing. In the bigger picture of the school, though, bailing out of the Cadets almost certainly did me no good at all. Added to my indifferent sporting and academic performance and the pronounced absence of any brothers preceding or succeeding me, rejection of the Cadets was probably the act of defiance that finished off my dwindling chances of being regarded as a true-blue DLS product.

I did well only in matriculation and then my strongest motivation was that I wanted to please my father. A good result would be my ticket out of school forever and I would get into university and attain the 'piece of paper' – in my case, on my father's strong recommendation, a piece of paper that said I had a BA and a teaching qualification. I might have felt differently if my six (imagined) elder brothers had already passed through the school with sporting and academic distinction, and if I had had the wit to explain and demonstrate that I was a Celt, like it or not, whatever way you looked at it. I had a little Irish grandmother and a little Scots mother and a flotilla of church-going, formidable Celtic aunts all of whom had maintained *the* faith and their own spirits against odds undreamed of by most of the De La Salle parents on whom the brothers so doted. What more did they want? Much more, apparently.

My days at De La Salle ended on the note of farce that had always been threatening (given among other things my obsession with fictional brothers and my failed military career). As I had done in the previous three years at the College, I won the prize for English Literature in matriculation. Speech nights at De La Salle were big, ceremonious occasions. The venue was the Malvern

Town Hall and parents were very strongly encouraged to attend. Because I had been a regular prizewinner, my parents had always turned up despite my father's growing objection to large scale, self-congratulatory Catholic events presented and organised by 'bloody pillars of the church'.

Apart from my appearances on the stage to receive my prize from Brother Peter, the school principal, known universally to students and alumni as 'The Brute', the highlight of these occasions for my father had been the evening when raucous and arcane ceremonial chanting from the Masonic Lodge next door to the Town Hall had threatened to drown out the speeches and prize giving. My father loathed the Masons, at whose hands, he was convinced – probably rightly – he had suffered professionally because he was a Catholic. But he regarded the general run of middle-class Catholics as people who used their flaunted religion to justify smugness, self-satisfaction and easy ignorance of a rougher world of disappointment, bone weariness and hardship. When it came to a contest between them and the reviled Masons, it was in some ways a close call.

One of the ceremonial aspects of these speech nights was that parents were presented with their copy of *Blue and Gold*, the school annual. This was a sumptuously produced, well-illustrated volume full of class photographs, reports, sporting and academic accolades, and so on. As soon as we picked up our copy in the foyer on that night of my last appearance, I turned to the list of prizewinners at the back. There I read that the winner of the English Literature Prize for 1952 was not Brian Matthews but Ron Cullen.

Cullen, whom I knew very well (we had started

together at St Leo's) and liked a great deal, did not have the requisite older or younger siblings at the school, but he was a brilliant student, a fine athlete and had been, through his entire De La Salle career, the focus of an almost mysteriously intense attention and intermittent favouritism from the brothers. I quickly found Cullen in the crowded foyer and pointed out to him the mistake in the prizewinners, thinking that we should perhaps see The Brute and get some quick reorganisation arranged, especially as he habitually used the list in the back of the current *Blue and Gold* to call up the winners to the stage. But Cullen, who was also named, correctly, as the winner of the Religious Knowledge prize, seemed curiously unwilling to rectify the mistake. I told my parents what had happened, but by this time we were filing into the hall.

After the usual tedium of speeches and concert performances of one kind or another, Brother Peter took the spotlight first to deliver his annual report, then to distribute the prizes. Sure enough, he produced a copy of *Blue and Gold* for the latter task. As it happened, the English Literature prizewinner was next on the list after Religious Knowledge. So Cullen, having received his legitimate prize, had to half run across the front of the stage in order to reappear and collect *my* English Literature prize. For this inconvenience, caused after all by his demonstrated scholarly versatility, he received a ripple of sympathetic applause and affectionate laughter from the audience. My father looked dark and said to my mother, 'Time to go.'

That was in December. I heard absolutely nothing from the school about this event, Cullen did not volunteer to give me his prize (which, in any case, had his name on it) and I made no attempt at contact myself. My sights now were on enrolling at Melbourne University. In early February, a good friend of mine from the matriculation year brought me my belated prize, Eleanor Dark's *The Timeless Land*. He explained that he had been to the school in order to re-enrol for second year matriculation and one of the brothers had given him the prize to pass on 'when he saw me'. There was no formal or informal note included, no apology, no reference of any kind to the unfortunate mistake, no wish for the future or for anything else. As my mother would say, not even a 'kiss my foot'.

Thirty-five years later, I ran into a former classmate, Vin Pilkington, who had kept up a connection with the school. He told me that someone had begun making an effort to get the archives and the school history into some sort of order. Vin had volunteered to check the details of our matriculation year and also of the football team (for which we had both played, though he was a star while the security of my place fluctuated a good deal). He discovered, and pointed out, that there was no record of me whatsoever. There was a *Barry* Matthews but no information could be found about him. This was because he didn't exist. When I wasn't being called Matthews, I was frequently mis-named 'Barry' in class by some of the brothers, because there was a pupil of similar colouring to me and similar build named Barry in one of the parallel classes. He was a sporting star and had several brothers beneath and above him at the school. This confusion persisted right up to my last year. So all those years later I discovered that in a way I had actually been expunged from the records. Like Barry Matthews, I did not exist.

I don't know what became of any of my teachers (being a backslider in the matter of the duties of an alumnus), except for Pauly. He left the order, not surprisingly, shortly after the matriculation class of 1953. I would meet him once more, in Sydney where, with my mate, Ray Tynan, always a favourite of Pauly, we drank a lot of beer and talked well into the hot night. Not too long after, he had a heart attack and died. He must have been in his early fifties.

After that prize was delivered, I never heard from the school again except, years later, when I received an invitation to make a donation to the building fund.

CHAPTER 13

The Battler and the Death of Santa Claus

I was sad to leave the grime and greyness of St Kilda for East Brighton. I had come to consciousness there and had little awareness of alternatives. In my twelve years living in Havelock Street and roaming the surrounding areas, I had never heard a rooster crow or a kookaburra laugh, although I knew what they sounded like from films and newsreels. There were not many birds round our part of St Kilda, only the lecherous sparrows cheeping and bustling; and the doves tossing their haunting messages to each other across the network of lamp posts and wires in the rainy stillness of a winter Sunday. I remembered how the dust spun down the column of moonbeam from the skylight in the passage at 54. And the rhythm of Jim's limping, heavy footfall as he arrived home. And my mother singing a song that always sounded to me like 'Amapola, My

Pretty Amapola' as she mopped the kitchen floor. And the day a biplane swooped so low over Barkly Street near Rollason's, from which I had just emerged with 'messages', that you could see the pilot's goggled face. And the boom of the barrels of beer as they rolled down a plank from the truck and into the trapdoor outside the Prince Charles. And the green buses cocooned in fumes, battling up Barkly Street hill at the other end of which was exotic, forbidden Fitzroy Street and the Junction Oval, home of the mighty Saints. I remembered all this and much more and I was sad.

Once the move had been made, my school life was complicated by travel. I was one of two kids who were allowed to leave school a little early in order to catch transport before the peak hour started. The other one in this category was the ubiquitous and intrepid Darmody, who took a green bus over the hill towards Fitzroy Street and then to parts never precisely known or detailed even for the nuns. So, each day, a little before the official school bell announced the end of the day's work, I walked down Inkerman Street and waited outside the post office in High Street for the Number 64 tram and travelled almost to the terminus. I would get off the tram at Davie Avenue, walk down Alexander Avenue to Elizabeth Street, then along to the bridge over the canal where I would take a short cut into the paddock on the weed-waving expanses of which our house was the sole man-made intrusion.

Although parts of East Brighton in those days were already quite salubrious and would become more so in a couple of decades, including our 'paddock' and our S-bend street that none of the locals believed was there, the immediate surrounds, the streets that I traversed once

I jumped from the tram, were run down and on the edge of looking squalid.

This was not old colonial Brighton. You had to go down nearer the beach for that. This was old falling-down Brighton, and most of the houses I passed would in the years to come be demolished and replaced by an assortment of fashionable edifices ranging from the elegant and understated to expressions of, or variations on, contemporary architectural fashion of the kind that drove Robin Boyd to write his book, *The Australian Ugliness*.

Our house was simple but appealing – spare of line, weather-boarded, unfussy, airy and sunny looking, very Australian. My old man was far too good at design and had far too good a nose for the Australian ambience to scar the landscape with something that looked like a drug baron's last statement. He designed, built, foundationed, wired, plumbed, roofed, glazed and painted as much of the job as an almost criminally liberal interpretation of council regulations would allow him to do on his own. The house stood in vulnerable isolation, unfenced and surrounded by languid weeds, in the middle of a vast paddock. There was no sign of a road and, now that the house was irrevocably looking west and staring at the corrugated-iron fence of the Drill Hall and had the Elster Canal as its eastern boundary, everyone in the neighbourhood thought they could afford to laugh. The bugger's built it the wrong way round, Alf Davis, the Carter and Wood Merchant from the old area in nearby Alexandra Street, was reputed to have announced in the Brighton Club Hotel.

Cooking on the open fire in the lounge room, teetering across still-unfloored joists (by candlelight, for the first few weeks) along the passageway to the bedrooms, we lived in fear of the irregular visits of the Council Building Inspector, Mr Weekes. He particularly terrorised my mother. In her a Celtic spirit of hair-triggered anti-authoritarianism wavered a little when she contemplated, at the most vulnerable time of a long, hot and lonely afternoon, the expanse of empty, skeleton-grey grass in which our scarcely built house incongruously squatted, its only neighbour the outside, corrugated-iron, thunder-box dunny. Even she allowed a shadow of doubt to darken her faith in my father's oft-reiterated assurances, that there would one day be a street and nearby houses, when she saw the grey-dustcoated figure of Mr Weekes manifesting itself suddenly in the wilderness with an uncanniness that belonged to the Old Testament and seemed just as implacable.

But even Mr Weekes' insatiable appetite for manifest and citable instances susceptible only to the strict and honed razor-edge letter of the law eventually waned. His spectral figure appeared less and less often and that threat at least receded, leaving us to cope with the more graspable problems of no floors, no refrigerator, no stove, and attenuated plumbing.

A path ran right across the paddock of which our block was a part, roughly paralleling the canal, joining it at the bridge and offering a short cut for people going to the tram in Hawthorn Road or, on Saturdays – as we soon discovered – for those bound for the SP bookie. This path, well established, concave and brick-hard from the trudge of immemorial boots and shoes, ran for its last sixty feet right across the bottom of our 'backyard'. For a year or so, since we had no fence whatsoever, no one really noticed. We would see the passing parade from our kitchen window. We came to realise that the most inveterate of the path walkers were either oblivious of or undeterred by the proximity of our house, dunny and gradually accumulating paraphernalia – garden tools, kids' stuff, stacks of bricks, sand, and so on. We would be in the 'yard' doing this and that, and they would stomp by at the bottom of the block, gazing neither to left nor right.

My father's theory about this rather uncharacteristic unfriendliness was that they were embarrassed to trespass, knew they were technically trespassing, but were reluctant to go round the long way. So they braved what they took to be our mute disapproval by never making eye contact with any of us.

Eventually the old man built the fence, but it was a long drawn out business. For one thing, there was a lot of it – 354 feet of rails, palings and posts. And there was the cost – 500 palings, a plinth all round, 100 odd redgum posts, twice the length of the fence in rails. He worked it all out in his meticulous way – I have the pencilled figures and sketches before me as I write – costing it down to the last penny and getting a special deal from Ruoake Timbers of Alexandra, almost certainly a contact provided by Eric whose wife, Annette, came from that district.

And then there were the neighbours. By law, the owners of the adjoining blocks were to pay half the cost of the shared fence. Since there was not another structure to be seen anywhere on the weedy expanse of which our block was a part, my father had to find out who the owners were and write to them. During October and November of 1947, he carried on polite correspondence with Moule, Hamilton and Derham, solicitors for the owners on the northern side, and W.G. Batkin, the owner of the adjoining southern block; (the sixty-eight feet long, slightly dog-legged back fence followed the curving course of the Elster Canal and although, as we would discover, the canal regularly flooded in summer storms, undermining the fence, the Council acknowledged no responsibility). After many letters of the kind that begin *We are in receipt of yours of the 27th ult.*, he had secured, by Christmas 1947 pledges of nineteen pounds seventeen and fourpence and fifteen pounds twelve shillings from Moule, Hamilton and Derham and W.G. Batkin respectively, though the latter expressed his preference for a redgum plinth *as I have found hardwood most unsatisfactory in ground level situations.* I don't know what my father replied to this but it was a hardwood plinth that graced our ground level situation when the fence went up.

My mother and I fetched and carried and dug a bit, but essentially he did the whole job on his own. Each summer night when he came home from work, he would dig one posthole, make up the post and its footing, and line it up in position, shovelling the earth back – one of the jobs I could help with – then tamping and hammering the surrounding soil with the top end of a crowbar to set it all solid. Once all the posts were in, he started to nail on the rails, one near the top, one midway and the plinth along the bottom. This unmistakable sign of demarcation spreadeagled the trespassers, all of whom began to pick their way around instead of through our boundary.

Except for one bloke who every Saturday would make six or seven return trips to the SP. He used to wear dark trousers and an old black blazer-like coat. A cigarette drooped perennially from his grimly slitted mouth and the *Sun* form guide stuck out of his coat pocket. He walked with a sort of slouching limp and he looked as if every horse he had ever bet on had done him like a dinner. This bloke marched between the posts when they were standing up discrete and silent and he ducked down and climbed through the rails when they were nailed on – through the rails on one side, across the bottom of our yard and through the rails on the other side. On the Saturday when the old man was nailing on the palings, he waited for the bloke to arrive and said, 'Would you like me to put in a couple of gates, mate?' But the bloke was impervious to irony or deaf or too desperately in hock to the SP to be even touched by such saturnine sallies.

So, that same afternoon, after the bloke had climbed into, walked across and then clambered out of our yard for perhaps the fourth time that day – with the palings like a suburban Berlin Wall inching towards his Checkpoint Charlie to close it off forever – the old man slapped on a burst of speed and closed the remainder of the fence. Now you could not see out, so we posted a watch – me – on the new fence and I warned everyone with a shout when he came into sight, the slouching, defeated, black-clad figure looking like some medieval forerunner of the coming plague. We watched the return of the punter and cheered when, without breaking stride, he capitulated and walked round the back perimeter of the new fence. He didn't ever come that way again – but maybe he gave up betting.

Before ever the first fence post had gone in, when the backyard was simply an open bit of the paddock and the convoy of passers-by was still snaking across the path at the bottom of our block, an odd little drama occurred.

It was one of those moments that could have gone down in family legend as heart-warming and inspiring, but was mismanaged in a way that in the end seemed inevitable. 'Real life' versus romance.

A Saturday it was, and I was messing about in the pile of sand the old man used when he was mixing concrete, and trying to stop my toddler sister from destroying everything I built. My mother was hanging out the washing, a task she had grown to hate at the new house because it meant the entire neighbourhood could watch, not to mention the users of the track busily hurrying back and forth within thirty yards or so of her line. And the old man was bent over his saw-stools cutting lengths of timber for some purpose or other. We were all suddenly aware of a clattering, clop-clopping, creaking contraption shambling towards us over the paddock. We all knew who this was – Alf Davis, who drove this very horse and cart back and forth along Elizabeth Street across the other side of the canal a couple of times every day. He carted old iron and timber usually, but today he had a teetering load of kindling. The cart had one of those high-up chairs shaped like a saddle and Davis would flick a long whip at his old horse and say, 'Get a move on, yer bastard,' and splendidly survey the terrain from this battered and leaning eyrie.

It was Davis, along with his neighbours-across-the-road, the Coppers, who were loudest in their assurance that the old man had built the house round the wrong way. The Coppers would cannonade along Elizabeth Street every weekday and Saturday afternoon in their old red Ford truck on their way to the Brighton Club Hotel with their younger children squeezed into the cabin and the other four or five asprawl on the tray. At the pub,

Mr Copper would ferry beers out to his wife and lemonade to the kids and, in the intervals between these sallies, retreat to the gloom of the front bar to get a swift several into himself. Without any doubt, 'the silly bastard near us who's buildin' his fuckin' house round the wrong fuckin' way' would have featured occasionally in his anecdotes.

So . . . Alf Davis' rickety rig jolts to a halt and the old man stands up at his saw-bench and says, 'Gooday, what can I do for you?'

'I've brought you some wood,' says Alf Davis, 'for the fire. Thought y'might have some use for it, anyway.'

The old man looks from Davis to the load and back but says nothing. The horse shakes the harness, breathes out a great snuffling sigh and stamps one front hoof. Then Alf Davis says, as if the silence will throttle him, 'I brought it because I admire a battler,' and the old man says, 'Thanks mate, but I don't believe in Santa Claus.'

Alf Davis climbs back onto his cart without a word, turns it round in a tight circle – dragging the nag a bit hard – and goes creaking and clunking back to the road.

When he recalled this incident years later, my father said he had never stopped regretting it. In a very rare revelation of his inner self, he told me something had forced him to take refuge in a half-ironic remark – pride, of course, partly – but something else too, fending off what was, when you got down to it, an admiring, even affectionate gesture. He regretted looking nakedly ungrateful but had been keeping the lid on his feelings for so long during the war that he scarcely knew how to react without caution, could not help himself. He had to live with the damage unreconciled, though, because Alf Davis never spoke to him again.

CHAPTER 14

Australia versus England

When we began living in the new house, I spent the first several weeks nervously looking out for the boy I had hit with the stone. I never could remember how far back down the canal it was that I tangled with him and Bo, and I wasn't game to retrace my steps to find out. In any case, I was equally terrified of running into the man who had been fucking the girl. I hadn't told anyone about that, either, not even Darmody. In the week following that famous journey inland, I'd had every intention of regaling Darmody and any of the other boys interested with my sensational findings. But when it came to the point, I somehow couldn't get the words out. For one thing, the sentences I began to prepare in my mind as a way of beginning my story sounded utterly unbelievable. And even when I seemed to get around that problem, I found myself reluctant to reveal what these two totally unknown people had been doing. It seemed unfair somehow. I could not understand this reluctance myself, any more than I could understand the strange, totally unidentifiable tremor of exhilaration I felt when I recalled the incident. Perhaps I was having vague, unarticulated premonitions of what intimacy meant and how difficult it was to characterise it. Anyway, all I could detect in myself was an almost frightening resistance to allowing the story to come out. So, it stayed where I stored it, as one more addition to a growing, gloomy and guilt-ridden archive of taboos, evil memories and monsters.

I was pretty sure the boy I had hit with the stone was not dead, because diligent scanning of the *Age*, the *Sun* and the *Herald* in the weeks following my trip upstream had not revealed any unsolved juvenile murders. So, he was probably scarred for life and intent on revenge. I expected him to come lurching out of the canal one gloomy dusk, like the horror figure in the W.W. Jacobs story, 'The Monkey's Paw', which I read at just about that time, and claim me for the grave. So, guarding my secret, I had an extra reason for wanting our fence to close us off from the open view of the entire neighbourhood. If that boy came along the canal, upstream as I had done, there was some chance he would miss me and my signature red hair if I was behind walls. No chance if we were still out in the open.

Then, one day, for about thirty awful seconds, I thought it had happened. I was in our still unfenced backyard digging the vegetable patch. Every day after school I had to dig one row and every Saturday six rows. This was a Saturday and I was about half way through when, from the corner of my eye, I became aware of a disturbance at the canal bank. The tall grass and wild fennel growing at the top of the bank had begun waving and tossing violently for no apparent reason. At the same time, I heard an extraordinary shouting and howling. I pulled the shovel from the ground and held it across my body like a rifle. The grass parted and a blond-haired boy marched through it like Moses parting the Red Sea, swinging a piece of bamboo and shouting, 'Only one more mile and we're through the killer ants. C'mon, run! Run!'

He saw me and stopped. We stared at each other. Though he had haunted my dreams, I was never able to 'see' the boy from the canal clearly. Every memory of him that threatened to reveal details of his features always dissolved in rivers of blood. But for all that, I felt sure, after a moment's sheer panic, that this was not him.

'Gooday,' said the blond boy.

'Gooday,' I said warily.

He advanced into our backyard. Like everyone else, he seemed oblivious to the possibility of a boundary, the idea of territory.

'Do you read *Champion*?' he said.

'Yes.'

'I'll swap you some. I've missed a few. Did you read that story about the killer ants?'

'No – I don't think so.'

'From Argentina. This bloke, Lenehan or Lineahan or something like that. He tries to stop them with canals that he surrounds his house with. And the ants, they push leaves and things in and float over. And he pours petrol on the water and makes this wall of fire, but they get through as soon as the fire goes down in different spots. Because he can't keep it going, see. He does lots of things, but in the end he just has to try to run for it. They can strip a man's body of all the flesh in a few minutes.'

He lashed his bamboo stick at the ground where he stood as the ants surrounded him. The more adventurous of them were already milling round his feet, swarming on to his dusty, battered black boots.

'Like piranhas,' I said.

'Fish,' he said. 'Piranhas are fish.'

'I know but they can . . .'

'Yes but you don't *have* to get in the water, do you? If you don't get in the water, piranhas can't hurt you. But ants, well they're on land. They can chase you. Do you play cricket?

'Yes. I bat. I'm a left-handed bat.'

'Like Neil Harvey.'

'Yes,' I said, pleased with the comparison, which was one I liked to make myself, especially as I had recently become the proud owner of a Gray Nicholls bat autographed by Neil Harvey. 'I've got a bat autographed by him,' I said.

'We could play Tests,' he said. 'I'll be Australia and you be England.'

'We can toss to see who's Australia,' I said.

'Righto! Let's start on the first day of the school holidays. We can make a pitch out in front of your place. I've had a look at it. It's a good spot. My father says that your father thinks there'll be a road there.'

'There will be,' I said.

He whipped the bamboo stick through the air making a whooshing noise, and began to walk away, not towards the canal but across our yard, seeming to regard this as a legitimate short cut.

'I live round the corner,' he said over his shoulder, 'where it really is a road.'

'It will be here, too,' I said, loyally, 'in a few years.'

'I'll bring a ball and three stumps,' he said. 'We can use your bat.'

His name was Tod. He was a chunky, not so much blond as frankly white-haired scrapper, about my age, carefree and easygoing, pretty much unconstrained by a family who, I would come to understand, were recognised around the place as being a bit weird. Above all, though, the evidence seemed pretty conclusive that he was not the kid I had sconed with the rock a mile or two downstream. He didn't *look* like that malevolent young bloke, as far as I could put a face to the evil memory, and he certainly didn't act like someone who would turn his savage dog on you. Moreover, he didn't mention the incident or give the slightest indication that he vaguely recognised me. And though he had a dog, which burst out of the canal-side fennel as we chatted, it was not called Bo and its shambling, tongue-lolling, good-natured slant on the world quite obviously owed absolutely nothing to Alsatian bloodlines even if it was in debt to just about every other breed known to canine genealogy. So, in that offhand way characteristic of small boys – perhaps the earliest indication of Australian male resistance to emotional show – Tod and I became friends.

It was my turn to be Australia and I had won the toss and decided to bat. While I strapped on the single pad that constituted the entire stock of our available equipment beyond the bare necessities of bat, stumps and ball – Tod, whom we both saw as bearing an uncanny resemblance to Alex Bedser – warmed up at the other end. I would face 'Bedser's' first ball in my guise as Arthur Morris and as soon as I picked up a sharp single or leg-glanced a three with the peculiar nonchalance that left-handers often bring to that shot, I would become Jim Burke.

Padded up and twirling my Gray Nicholls bat autographed by Neil Harvey, I gazed around the field – at the boxthorn bush at square leg, the stunted and decaying apple orchard at deep mid-wicket, the potato patch that would become my family's front lawn at point. Then I checked the exercise book lying open immediately behind the stumps, in which was recorded in a large round, schoolboy hand my batting order: *Morris, Burke, Hassett, Harvey, Miller* ... Quite a handy team.

I carefully took block, settled into my stance and watched Tod Bedser come rolling in to bowl. The first ball of the second Test for season 1949–50 pitched just short of a length and on middle stump, which it knocked out of the ground after not bouncing even an inch and skidding through like a lawn bowl. Sensation! Morris out first ball. Obviously, despite assiduous sweeping with my mother's best kitchen broom, some small pieces of gravel must have eluded our attention. The packed dirt track was a tough surface for bounce at the best of times; sabotaged by gravel, it sapped the best deliveries of all resilience. As I recorded *nought* next to Morris's name and prepared to face up in the guise of Lindsay Hassett, I reflected that if my mother hadn't caught us using her broom and taken it away, the team might have got off to a much stronger start.

These England–Australia encounters went on interminably throughout the long summer. Their longevity was exaggerated by the fact that, unlike the real thing, our days were not necessarily consecutive. Play in a given Test might open on Thursday, continue Friday but then go into abeyance until the following Wednesday, when hostilities would be resumed. The reasons for these adjournments ranged from causes as satisfyingly realistic as a thunderstorm, to decidedly embarrassing interventions like a peremptory recall home for one or other of us; or long detention-like chores such as digging the potato patch or cleaning out the chook pens; or actual house arrest for some misdemeanour or other; or a request to 'do the messages'. Because the latter, unlike the St Kilda days, meant a bicycle trip, it was an interruption doubly dreaded: it took up valuable time, as much as a couple of hours, but it also meant that the courier returned to the crease weary, hot, sweating and generally not focused.

Tod and I were convinced we had invented this Test match extravaganza (though reminiscence years later would reveal the fragility of that claim). None of our other friends indulged in it and attempts to expand the personnel always ended in disputes and walk-offs uncharacteristic of the game of cricket. So we spent hours and hours together, bowling at each other, filling in the scores, enacting dusty mimicries of first-class cricket's timeless and arcane rituals – the toss, inspecting the strip of unmade track that was the 'wicket', announcing and setting a phantom field, sometimes even intoning a commentary in a voice we imagined was a dead ringer for the rich, basso profundo of Alan McGilvray – and then, for an hour or so after 'stumps', discussing the cut and thrust of the day's play and where the advantage for the moment rested. I don't think either of us ever cheated, despite the readily available opportunities to do so. (When, a couple of years later, Tod's family, who were always a bit strange and vaguely criminal, suddenly decamped to other, northern climes, a new partner lasted only one Test with me because I caught him doctoring his score during the tense second innings.)

Aside from cricket, Tod and I shared a rabid interest in reading *Champion*, *Rover* and the *William* books. We would discuss the exploits of Rockfist Rogan and other luminaries of those 'boys' weeklies'. And, when not engaged in our Test Match rivalry, we would model our lives as nearly as possible on the ethos and activities endlessly elaborated upon in the adventures of William and his Outlaws and embroider this stereotype with evidence from the school stories in *Champion* and *Rover*. We brewed, manfully drank, but actually detested versions of both the licorice water and the ginger beer to which William was so addicted, and we ranged through the nearby, dilapidated orchard with catapults constructed along lines we understood to be the Outlaws' preferred model.

We inhabited a fragile cocoon of romance and fantasy that was always on the verge of cracking apart if concentration flagged or disbelief became suddenly unsuspended. It was all packed up, tamped down and temporarily forgotten when we returned to our families at the end of each arduous day's play or hunting or roaming. To gaze at the pitch, for instance, in the intense heat of a January afternoon, perhaps after the England openers had weathered Lindwall and Miller's exhausting opening spell, and to see not the slightly yellowing consistency of a three-day-old Test wicket but the ruts made by Mr Davis's wood cart and the stones and rubble deployed by the council in response to my father's vigorous complaints, and to *admit* that's what you were seeing, was death to the whole make-believe construction. And very bad for line and length.

But sometimes reality was irresistible. On one of our hunting trips, during which we fired volleys of wildly inaccurate stones from our catapults at the local bird life with an apparently murderous abandon and in true and fond imitation of the Outlaws, I took aim at a rosella – a bird of glorious, riotous colours not often seen down our way – and wiped it off its high, song-strung perch with an unprecedented and totally fluky direct hit. It was stone dead before it began to topple over and when I picked it up I saw that blood had spoiled the elegantly merging miracle of hues on its chest. I was shocked, appalled. Vaguely I recognised that this was not in the script. Somehow, we had strayed off the stage and wandered outside into the harsh light, where there was no green sward, no neatly marked white creases; where our unvarnished and scarred stumps were stuck in the middle of an unmade roadway; and where birds died in agony if your aim was 'lucky' enough.

That harshly lit world outside the theatre of our dreams was also populated with people who did not understand our drama or wilfully refused to. Traffic was rare along the back track where our titanic struggles took place. But every so often a car or a delivery van, their drivers almost invariably lost and looking like it, would trundle round the bend at the bowler's end (we didn't change ends – the pitch had only one usable section and, anyway, we had only three stumps) and bear down on us. We adopted the habit of getting out of the way and off the road with an ostentatious show of speed, goodwill and co-operation designed to make up for the fact that we had left the stumps in the ground.

Every now and then, and to our utter stupefaction, a motorist would respond to this manoeuvre by running our stumps over. One driver actually broke two of them and signalled his satisfaction through the open window as he departed. Such occasions placed the whole fantasy under critical stress. Untutored though we both were in the ways of international cricket, having scarcely seen a game and not being able to fall back on television to provide us with insights, we nevertheless were pretty certain that vehicular traffic was not one of the problems the teams encountered out in the middle – no matter where they were playing.

For just those two summers of 1948–49 and 1949–50, when Tod and I advanced from age twelve to thirteen, doing so in a veritable welter of cricket and British boys' weeklies liberally embellished with *William*, I think we became rather imperial in our views and attitudes. Though to 'be' Australia in our regular Ashes jousts was naturally the preferred and valued option, 'being' England was an honourable – indeed, a more and more honourable – fate. If it had not become so, what would have been the point in persisting? You had to feel all right about yourself as you ran in to bowl in the guise of Brown or Bailey or Bedser; otherwise, you wouldn't bowl and bat well and you'd be thrashed. There were, after all, only two boys out on that track, not the two immaculately flannelled teams we saw in our imagination's gaze as we played. There were certain realities, certain facts that our cocoon of imagining, for all its elaborate fabric and strength, could never distort or blur. Neither of us, for example, was in the slightest doubt that when England, say (represented by Tod), gave Australia the father of a hiding by an innings and a hundred and forty runs (in the interests of verisimilitude, incidentally, all our scores ended in nought as each run counted for ten), it actually meant that Tod had made a terrible mess of *me*. Symbiosis between imagined team and the small boy carrying its entire burden of personality, performance and aspiration tightened ineluctably. So that, while an Australian bias in each of us was a given, we both with insidiously gradual effect came to respect, have exhaustive knowledge about, and even in certain ways admire – *the Poms*.

Aided by our diet of reading, an obsessive immersion in the game we thought we had invented and a school curriculum that almost never recognised the existence of Australian writers, Australian history or the Australian vernacular, we very nearly attained in those two summers a condition above nationalism. We were cricketers. We represented 'our country'. But our country was sometimes England. Although, needless to say, we did not give the matter a thought, the entire structure and ambience of our Test match series, with its transformation of national distinctions into the sporty 'old enemy' formula and its code of manly conduct derived from the twin sources of cricket folk lore and boys' weeklies, was actually in close accord with the Anglophile attitude of 1950s Australia at large. And, though we did not realise this either, the drama of our games was heavily underwritten by a sense, an acceptance, of the then established and settled Australia–Britain relationship. Our dutiful attempts to stage occasional one-off 'Tests' with South Africa, India or the West Indies – in line with what sometimes happened in the 'real world' – were at best perfunctory and, in one case if I remember rightly, suffered the unprecedented fate of being abandoned through waning interest.

Looking back, I think this must have been because we found it difficult to achieve the necessary identification with either the teams, the individuals or – though again this would not have been our conscious thought – the cultures of those other cricket-playing nations. South Africa, India and the West Indies were just about as rare occurrences in the school curriculum as Australia itself. But England was everywhere. Some of our politicians still referred to it as 'home'; our Prime Minister, Sir Robert Menzies, declared himself 'British to the bootstraps' and of the new Queen, Elizabeth II, he would proclaim (to even *her* embarrassment), 'I did but see her passing by / And yet I love her till I die.'

It is easy to overstate the impact of some of these influences and occasions in reminiscence. But I do not think there is much doubt about the fact that our attitude to cricket – the jewel in the crown of imperial games – was significantly shaped by the intensely Anglophile world in which we grew up and in which we actually played the game, even if only on a rough, outer suburban track. It was an attitude that combined an over-developed reverence for the game's character-building capacities, with exaggerated respect for its English provenance. That there was no televised cricket (until 1956) against which we could measure our attitudes and intuitions was also immensely important. I remember seeing a brief newsreel snippet of Bradman's 1948 team practising shortly after their arrival in England. They were in the nets, but because I had never seen players practising in six or seven nets at once, I became very confused – there seemed to be bowlers and batsmen everywhere and I somehow got the impression that this was how it must look in the middle, during a game. I was not prepared to show my ignorance and had to wait some months before I finally nutted it all out.

'Being' Australia, 'being' England against Australia: taking block against that lone figure limbering up at the other end – the two of you carrying throughout the long, hot day the burden of the entire antipodean or English strategy – that was our world of cricket. We were, of course, when it came to the point, larrikin supporters of the Aussies, but our games, as much as the real stuff, were played in a lingering imperial rather than incipiently nationalist atmosphere. If the Empire was already burning, we didn't notice, but kept our Neronian heads down and played forward – the only way to survive on our pitch.

Curiously enough, during the time that these rituals were being played out in our summer lives, our winters were probably intensifying the ambivalent, attenuated nature of our youthful nationalism. It was in winter that we became totally absorbed with football, but it was the Australian invention, Australian Rules football. 'Aussie Rules' had no international competitive outlet or counterpart; it thus encouraged us to ignore the world. We even overlooked the other states of the Australian Commonwealth, in some of which the game was thriving. As far as we were concerned, footy was a Melbourne phenomenon: not only did it not focus you out to the world, on the contrary, it turned your gaze inwards, usually to one of Melbourne's inner suburbs. My loyalty to the gangster-ridden, smoky, cosmopolitan purlieus of St Kilda and its football team contrasted sharply with Tod's, to me, rather bizarre preference for Geelong, the only provincial team in the league. He did not have relatives in the west, as far as I knew, so I would be inclined to say, at this distance, that Tod was simply going for the gun team of the time. But in fact Geelong finished ninth in 1948 (St Kilda were last) and eighth in 1949 (St Kilda were second last, so both teams improved one place). It was only in 1950 that Geelong began a triumphant run that took them as far as the Preliminary Final (St Kilda finished ninth), before going on to win successive Premierships in 1951–52 (St Kilda: tenth and last) – so perhaps Tod was just prescient.

Far from playing upon national feelings, football in Melbourne engendered the fiercest and most irrational parochialism. It was so divorced from national sentiment as to make that sentiment look redundant. On a cold, misty July Saturday in Melbourne, as the siren sounded and the ball was bounced to start yet another clash between the suburban titans, the long glaring days of summer and the idea of Australia being engaged in international contest seemed only a dream.

But, as the Test Matches between Tod and me drew to a close towards the end of the summer, and the 1950 school year stretched out its dead hand to usher us into another round of exciting education, an epochal decision occurred that was to make 1950 an important year for my father and me. Since we had moved to Brighton, my father had worked five days a week at Fishermans Bend and every weekend and most evenings at home, continuing to build the house around us. We *followed* the footy, certainly, but we had not been to a game for ages, since long before we left St Kilda. It was as if leaving the district had meant abandoning the team. As the place and the team were inextricably confused for me, the absence of much footy in our lives deepened my sense of loss, my nostalgia for those harum-scarum days round the depressed St Kilda streets: the crowds from the Junction Oval getting off the buses and trams after another probably losing Saturday, the paperboys yelling 'Eearda sportingglobeherald' under the rain-streaked street lamps, fish and chips on Friday bought in bustling Acland Street followed by the pictures at the Palais, sausages with lots of sauce for lunch on Saturdays because nobody noticed how much sauce you took when the form guides were spread all over the kitchen table and the pencils were out and poised for the betting systems.

Brighton was not like that, never would be, did not aspire to be.

In March of 1950, observing my father's exhausting regime, his brother, Eric, whose much more considering, weigh-all-the-options approach to life was sometimes construed, especially by his wife, as bone idleness, persuaded him to take at least Saturday afternoon off each week for the next six months and go to the footy ('Otherwise you'll kill yourself, y'silly bugger'). My father bought us membership tickets (I still have mine, with wins and losses marked by ticks and crosses) and we planned on going to every game.

And so the start of the season saw us journeying in Eric's Essex out to the Western Oval to see the Saints line up against Footscray in Round One. This was always a more or less doomed trip for St Kilda and one that Eric and my father had made only rarely. As for me, I had never set eyes on the Western Oval, or Footscray itself for that matter. The Saints had finished on a fair note in 1949, winning three out of their last five games against, in order, Richmond, Geelong and Collingwood. But they still ended up second last with four wins and fifteen losses, so it was difficult to be especially optimistic as we edged our way into the gloom, tawdriness and grey depression of the early 1950s western suburbs. That day, though, the Saints got up, by nine points, aided by some prodigally misdirected kicking from the Scraggers, as Footscray were often known in those days.

The following week, the Saints were at home at the Junction Oval to Hawthorn, the chopping block of the competition in those years when St Kilda relinquished this unwanted honour, and won handsomely by 109 points. Even against Hawthorn this was significant, this was how *good* teams dispensed with weak opposition. Two wins out of two was a raging start for the lads from the seaside, though influential scribes like Alf Brown in the *Herald* and the *Sporting Globe*, and Hugh Buggy in the *Argus*, to the extent that they took any notice at all, pointed out that 'they'd beaten nobody yet'.

Their third opponent was South Melbourne, the 'Blood Stained Angels' on their home patch at the other end of Albert Park Lake from the Junction Oval – a 'Lake Premiership'. South could not be regarded as *nobody*, but their record over the past several years had been patchy. The Saints got themselves into a hole in the first half, struggled valiantly in the third quarter, but entered the last five minutes of the game looking beaten, though constantly in attack. We were standing behind the outer goal and I remember the St Kilda rover, Keith Rosewarne – stringy, diminutive, older-looking-than-his-years, brilliant on his day – being tripped as he was about to break clear with the ball only twenty yards from goal. 'A trip! A trip!' my father yelled out and then, as the umpire blew the whistle, 'He's seen it, too.' Rosewarne goaled to bring the Saints within a point and they went on to win by nearly four goals with an impressive avalanche of scoring in the last minutes.

St Kilda were now verging on being a sensation. The Cinderella side was getting round to trying on the glass shoe and had forgotten even the existence of rats and pumpkins.

While the Saints were winning three out of three, Collingwood, divided by a power struggle in the club, lost two of them, a statistic which my old man greeted with dignified though admittedly vindictive pleasure.

Going each week to the footy with his brother and his son would have been a shot in the arm for my wearying father no matter what the Saints had done. The great *élan*, energy and innovation with which he had begun to lay and then realise his plans had worn thin after five solid years of struggle, hard physical work and apparently endless cliff-edge financing. Even the sight of the house, well built, four square and growing, with a garden slowly budding around it and a garage planned in which, at last, he would have a workshop comparable with the one in the big shed at Matthews and Sons Builders, was scarcely enough to allay the sense of being trapped by work and contingency at every point and on every new day. So Eric was right to drag him out to the footy. That the Saints then turned on an unprecedented show for the first three weeks was simply bonus.

In Round Four, the Saints were back at the Junction Oval, their usual knot of long-suffering supporters now massively augmented by St Kilda dwellers of less durable tolerance for defeat but with their residual faith readily re-ignited by success. If there had been any doubt about the quality of their first three opponents, there was absolutely no question about number four. North Melbourne, themselves one of the underdogs of the League, had won two of their first three, suffering defeat only at the hands of the always dominant Carlton. North were regarded as up-and-comers for 1950, a fair tip at that early stage because they would in fact play off in, but lose, the Grand Final that year. They were led by the footballing genius of the day, Les Foote, and the general consensus was that North would be the sharp, precise and merciless needle that would prick St Kilda's bubble.

When my father and Eric and I arrived that Saturday at the Junction Oval, we could tell something had changed. There were long queues into the car park and the Essex, to Eric's utter consternation because it was always in impeccable running order, boiled while we inched our way in. The Members' reserve and the old, slatternly grandstand were nearly full when we entered the ground and the atmosphere was crackling with loud talk and brittle laughter.

By the time the game started, the ground was packed and the bounce of the ball was greeted with an almost hysterical roar, such a relief was it to have proceedings under way. The Saints murdered North in the first quarter, kept up the pressure in the second and went in at half time six goals in front. After the break, North began a slow, error-ridden but ominous fightback, not only holding St Kilda to two points in the third quarter, while kicking three goals six themselves, but hitting so hard and often that the St Kilda players were cut down all over the ground. With only seventeen men standing and John Coffee, a star of the first half, parked in the forward pocket with a sprained ankle, the Saints hung on while North sprayed shots all across the goal front. They kicked three goals seven to St Kilda's one goal two for the last quarter. With everyone dwelling on the sound of the old bell which, in those days, signalled the end of the quarter and which, at times like these, was often inaudible, North was attacking again when the game ended with St Kilda two points in front. Apparently the bell rang for long seconds before the umpire heard it.

As we shuffled slowly with the huge and uproarious mob towards the exits, buoyed with euphoria and wrung with excitement, someone near us shouted out, a voice stark and incisive above the babble of relief, triumphalism and sheer joy. There had been a very controversial local government election in the St Kilda Ward that day and this bloke had obviously managed to pick up an early edition *Herald* from one of the paperboys threaded through the crowd. 'Michaelis won the election,' he announced as if reading the news on the radio but at fifty times the normal volume. 'Fuck the election,' shouted a bloke nearby and his motion was carried by roars of approbation, not the least strident of which came from my father and Eric.

St Kilda were now truly the sensation of the competition. They commanded attention. Scribes and pundits who routinely and automatically assigned them the same phrases of defeat and hopelessness almost regardless of what they did (though admittedly this was usually a safe bet as they rarely did much), now competed for the adjectival ground. The Saints had *come of age*; they were *no longer the Cinderella team of the League*, they were a *Premiership prospect*, they had *learned how to win*, they had *the killer instinct*, and so on. It did not do to get too caught up in this kind of language that the sports writers could trot out in vast quantities to deadline then, when ensuing games proved them 100 per cent wrong, not only retract without a blush but go on to suggest persuasively that they had seen the slump coming. *I* was caught up in it, though. And so was the old man, in his circumspect way. We bought the *Age*, *Herald* and *Argus* every day of the ensuing week and the *Sporting Globe* that Saturday night and on the Wednesday to read all about the mighty Saints. One of my father's great pleasures was to read Alf Brown, imagining him being forced not only to devote space to the Saints, against whom in my father's opinion, Brown was determinedly and irredeemably biased, but also to praise them.

The *Argus* in those days had some of the earliest colour photographs in Australian newspapers. St Kilda were not the kind of team that very often figured in these, but now things were different. On the Monday after the North Melbourne game (no Sunday papers then), there was one of my heroes, Jim Ross, flying spectacularly above a pack of players to take a huge mark, his red, white and black guernsey blazing brilliantly from the back page.

My other heroes in that team were the mercurial John Coffee; the inscrutable, brilliant Harold Bray, whose St Kilda-style luck saw him runner-up for the Brownlow Medal, the League's highest award, in 1947 and third in 1949; Peter Bennett, the full forward (who was also an Australian Olympic water polo player);

and the nonchalantly dazzling Bruce Phillips, who would come third in the 1950 Brownlow count. He was tall, athletic, blond and utterly spectacular – the kind of full back, not all that common in those days, who backed his judgement with charging runs down the ground, flew for and generally grabbed towering marks instead of punching the ball away, and emerged amazingly from packs seeming to have any amount of time to choose his option. That he was a flawed human being – his kicking varied between prodigious and erratic and you held your breath when he kicked out from goal – only endeared him more to his acolytes. These players were also my father's heroes, a demonstration of that blurring of the adult/child boundaries in the heat of the St Kilda obsession, which only struck me when I looked back, and he could scarcely stop talking footy all week.

This was hard on my mother who was as much in need of a break from strain and hardship as he was. But it was typical of her to join in with and enjoy our excitement, though she did not understand either the game or the passions it aroused, especially when the team in question was St Kilda. After all, she had *lived* there. She knew what they were like, the Saints, without ever having to set eyes on them. She had heard the sad sympathy of people purporting to support them. But she didn't understand the crucial difference between St Kilda *people*, like herself, who lent generalised but uncomprehending sympathy simply because they lived in the place, and true supporters, who knew profoundly what it was like to follow the Saints, who knew that something about the *place* – its beaten-up raggedness, its pinched streets and dusty gloom, its atmosphere of illegitimacy, smiling defeat – had entered into the team psyche and had to be exorcised by the coming of THE YEAR.

On the eve of Round Five, with the Saints on four wins out of four and sitting second to Essendon on the ladder, 1950 was looking like THE YEAR. But Round Five, according to all sane judgements and objective assessment, was definitely going to be the Saints' nemesis. They were playing Carlton at the Junction Oval. Carlton regarded themselves then, and they still do, as the team born to rule. Perennially dominant, affluent, never having suffered the ignominy of a 'Wooden Spoon', winner of innumerable premierships, and defeated grand finalists in the previous year, Carlton was the sort of club that only tolerated the existence of other clubs because there could not otherwise be a competition. If a means had been invented, then or now, whereby Carlton could maintain its reputation without the tiresome necessity of having to share an arena with other, lesser clubs, they would have jumped at it.

Alerted by our experiences of the previous week, we arrived early. Just as well. By the time the game started, 46,973 people had squeezed into the Junction Oval, the largest crowd ever at that ground. The Saints started nervously and were two goals behind at quarter time. But after that, they cruised home, answering every Carlton challenge. I remember during the last quarter worrying in my anxious, juvenile way that Carlton were embarked upon a resurgence which the Saints would not be able to resist and my father answering me with memorable serenity, 'No, they're done for, my boy. See how many of them have their hands on their hips. Look how they've slowed up. They've had enough.' And they had.

But there the story ends. Down to Kardinia Park we went the following week, the Essex enjoying a good, long, purring hit-out through the flat, rocky western landscape, out of which eventually, as we neared Geelong, the You Yangs rose mysteriously away to our right. I had never seen them before. Their suddenness, the massive presumption of their precipitous uprearing above that spare, flush terrain shocked me. It was easy to understand why, as my father explained, the Aborigines had named and revered the range as a holy place. But then we were past and closing in on the provincial city of Geelong. St Kilda were in the Match of the Day for the second week in succession – a dangerous accolade for a team that specialised in failing to live up to the occasion.

And sure enough, they failed to. Geelong annihilated them by ninety-four points.

You did not need to buy a paper to know what the headline would be. The pundits had it all worked up and set out, just awaiting its inevitable hour: *Saints' Bubble Bursts*, exulted the billboards, and even the scribes who had tipped them to win seemed to find relief in recording this apparent return to normality.

Kardinia Park had been the graveyard of many another good team – it was something to do with the sixty-mile bus trip, so one theory went. (Years later, when Les Foote coached the Saints, he actually got the players to pile out of the bus at the half-way mark and jog for a mile, to counteract the malign influence of the 'trip to Geelong'. They were slaughtered.) When you went to Kardinia Park, you would be members of a pitiably small band of opposition supporters. Your team's goals would be greeted with silence, their skilful or brilliant feats with derision and their transgressions with truly frightening aggression. At least at Victoria Park you were usually among a substantial band of your own supporters, even if the snarling, spittle-spraying Collingwood army was always massively in the majority. All in all, a loss at Geelong could be regarded as an aberration if you worked hard enough at it.

We worked hard all the next week to attain this state of delusion so that, by the time we set out for Essendon – 'Windy Hill', as that repugnant ground was justly known – our equilibrium was more or less restored. As we neared our destination and the footpaths on either side of the road filled with Essendon supporters wound in their red and black scarves streaming towards the ground, I asked my father if he truly thought the Saints could win, Essendon being on top, after all. My father pointed out that Essendon had won five and lost one, like St Kilda. This was another Match of the Day. He said he was 'quietly confident'. That day was when I realised that being 'quietly confident' was the adult way of saying you expected the worst.

Essendon had a huge following partly because they always did and partly because they had the most sensational full forward ever seen since the days of the great Bob Pratt. John Coleman had topped the League goal kicking in his first year, 1949, kicking the round 100, and was continuing in that vein in 1950 (he would head the list again with 120). Bruce Phillips held Coleman to one point up to half time. In the second half, Coleman kicked 11, Essendon ran all over St Kilda and so, the fragments of the already burst bubble were swept across the floor and out the door.

*

We continued to go, Saturday after Saturday, but the Saints never recovered the magic of those first five weeks. We all took defeat hard and our homeward trips after a thrashing or a near miss were glum, monosyllabic affairs. I used to feel sorry for the players and futilely resentful of the fate that seemed, as I wrongly construed it, to have claimed St Kilda for its own while smiling on such arrogant and unworthy sides as – well, most of the others. My father and Eric tended to greet defeat with an 'It's only what you might expect' attitude. While never conspiracy theorists like Mannie and Mr Armstrong – psychologically they were both too intrinsically dynamic to concede that everything came down to a dastardly plot and that therefore you might just as well stop worrying – they nevertheless accepted that they were the kind of people to whom nothing would come easily, not occasionally, not even once.

The record of the Saints' evil fortunes, looked at philosophically, seemed to prove this proposition by virtue of its very triviality. What did it matter, a team losing? But, from another point of view (or as Jim would have said, 'By the same token'), was it too much to ask that at least your *football team* could have a win? If you triumphed nowhere else in life, couldn't you at least have a winning team? It wasn't as if they were expecting to win Tatts – just a first ever premiership would do, or even merely a respectable season well endowed with wins.

This was the essence of what I have to admit is a peculiarly Matthewsian quality of gloom. It is always laced with irony and humour. It is always therefore surmountable, but it does start from the premise that there isn't much bloody hope really and that all you can do is the best you can – an occupation which, as Damon Runyon's Nicely-Nicely Johnson remarked, is very overcrowded in this town.

After that Essendon debacle, St Kilda won only three of the next eleven games. They finished ninth – two rungs of the ladder and four wins better than in 1949.

Sometimes I think it must have been the nature of St Kilda itself, the very essence of the suburb, that somehow put a curse on the team bearing its name. Perhaps, the dark cast of failure and despair that had haunted the denizens of that raging, rocky and unforgiving island in the Hebrides, forcing them at last to give up and leave, had clung mysteriously to the actual name, the very words, to blight all who laboured under its signature. *St Kilda*. St Kilda's early cosmopolitanism, most evident in the crowds and shops of Acland Street even then, was a disadvantage for the footy team in the days when the locality was important both as recruiting ground and support base. Many St Kilda people scarcely knew the team existed, others had a benign, distant connection – the kind of disengaged, essentially superficial interest that helps to feed, by well-intentioned ignorance, stereotypes of failure and catastrophe.

St Kilda was too scatty a place to have a football team, too distracted by beach and coastal pleasure domes, by some of the earliest manifestations in the country of ethnic diversity; too European to be seduced by the intricacies of Australia's unique game. And too divided. The much posher East St Kilda would scarcely tolerate a failing and incurably raffish team and inclined to follow

Melbourne. So that the club's rare periods of success would evoke indulgent, vague pride in the throngs living close to and immediately inland from Luna Park and Acland Street, and their much more familiar runs of disaster would be met with equally indulgent, even more vague nods of what-can-you-expect. Failure and the nature of the place dictated that the St Kilda Football Club would always have only a small band of truly loyal, fierce, knowing supporters. There was none of the obsessive, manic, unified addiction that one encountered in Collingwood, Richmond and Fitzroy, where distractions were few, life was more uniformly and more palpably grim, geography was more sharply delineating and Saturday was the one day in the week offering an unambiguous, untrammelled opportunity to give yourself wholeheartedly, in sympathetic company and without fear, to the truly common cause.

The St Kilda Football Club, any serious connection with which provides training in stoicism and endurance of disappointment, endows its acolytes with a touching, undying faith in the miracle of NEXT YEAR.

It was probably like that back in 1897 when, as far as the Saints were concerned, it all started.

'The Saints didn't win a single game in the nineteenth century,' David, my eldest son said to me one day. Of course, it sounds worse than it was. There wasn't much of the century left when they joined the new Victorian Football League. But they went forty-eight games without a win before breaking the drought in Round One of 1900.

Even then – typically – it was not straightforward. The match, against Melbourne, ended in a draw, but St Kilda protested that one of the opposition behinds was kicked after the three-quarter time bell and the encounter eventually went down as a Saints win – their first ever.

Our team had already blazed their way into the record book, however. In the match immediately preceding their first win, that is, in the last round of 1899, the Saints met Geelong at Corio Oval. Storming forward from the first bounce, they immediately scored a behind. They did not score again, while the Pivotonians, as they were then known, kicked goals at will. The final score line, 23.24 (162) to 0.1 (1) stood for twenty years as the biggest winning margin, while the Saints' score of one point was – and remains – the record low score in the VFL/AFL.

These are sobering statistics, the more so when you go on to recall that, despite their winning start to 1900, the Saints did not win another game that season. They did not trouble the scorer in 1902. But, after losing to Geelong by fifty-two points in the first round of 1903 – which completed their first hundred League games with a record of two wins and ninety-eight losses – they began a striking form reversal and finished the year in fifth place. It was an improvement, a palpable improvement.

Probably that is when the scribes started to say, *The Saints have come of age*. It is a process of development that has defied medical knowledge and gene theory by continuing for ninety-five years with only fleetingly visible signs that it might lead on to wise middle age or settled and successful maturity.

What difference would it have made to the club and its ragtag suburban base if their first Premiership had come in 1913, when Fitzroy beat them in a 'challenge' final, instead of fifty-three years later? What other team can boast the sort of success-drought that could accommodate two world wars, one of history's biggest revolutions, the world's worst financial collapse, the rise of the super powers, and the inventions of jet flight and nuclear weaponry?

It is true that Hawthorn, North Melbourne and Footscray supporters all had to wait a long time for their first premiership. But their patience was not tried by such miserable depths, thrashings, sensations, club coups, splits and barneys; nor are they burdened by a long-standing assumption of inferiority and inadequacy so ingrained in the club's psyche that it has proved almost impossible to mitigate, let alone banish.

New Hawthorn supporters, for example, whom you might expect to be a little sobered by their club's dog days of doom and desperation that preceded its recent dominance, do not espouse the team in the knowledge of a tawdry past. On the contrary, they are full of talk about the family club, the caring club, the tough, durable club. But new Saints supporters take on the patina of failure with a smile and a tolerant nod. Of course that's what it's about – failure and the adrenaline hope of a future in which, suddenly, the sun begins to shine and the saints come marching in. 'When The Saints Go Marchin' In' is an appropriate club song because you have to have a streak of evangelism, the hope that defies judgement, belief in occult intervention, to be and remain truly involved with the 'mighty Saints'.

Some memories stand alone. You see yourself as an actor in them, you know with certainty that the events really happened, but you have no sense of what went before or what came after. Some memories exist, like dreams that wake you up perspiring and disorientated, without apparent cause or effect; they are simply there – and they do not ever fade, the mysterious narrative of which they are a tantalising moment remaining forever incomplete.

So, there I am, some time in the early forties, running across the Junction Oval with O'Gorman. It must have been 1944 because in that year the Saints returned to their St Kilda Junction home ground when it became available again after several years of wartime requisition. We are small boys, too small to be at the footy on our own, so there must be some guardian or other in the background and it was not my father because he was 'away at the war'. Probably it was O'Gorman's father. We run and run, criss-crossing with other kids and with adults until we catch up with the teams leaving the ground. St Kilda has just been thrashed by Carlton – near enough to ten goals between the two sides at the final bell. I did not know at the time that I was a St Kilda supporter, but my father was, or at least had been before he went away, and his father and brother were St Kilda men.

I don't know if, in later years, I have simply endowed this small, running figure with misgivings about what he was doing. But my memory tells me stridently that, as we arrive, puffing, at our objective – the beanpole figure of a Carlton hero jogging triumphantly from the ground – and stretch up to pat his sweaty, blue-clad back (managing to reach not much higher than his waist), I am troubled with a sense of treachery. O'Gorman barracks for Carlton because his father does, but I do not. I am just stringing along, taking the easy way out, failing to face the St Kilda players who straggle off in their more or less usual state of amiable humiliation. That is how I remember it, anyway, and perhaps my feelings of betrayal on that day explain the deep and changeless loathing I have always entertained, very unjustly no doubt, for the Carlton Football Club and all its activities, aspirations and affairs.

No one enters upon the first game of any season with the lunatic fervour, the blind exclusion of rationality and evidence, the pumping of blood, the half-sob of sheer emotion that sticks embarrassingly in the throat, that St Kilda supporters carry with them through the turnstiles on the day of Round One. And few are more frequently, more routinely, more anti-climactically brought back to earth. Almost any first game will do ...

It is, let us say, 29 March 1997 and, curiously enough, this just might be THE YEAR.

'God, I hate Waverley,' I say to my mate as we leave the ground, having lost to Hawthorn, the 'happy club', by a goal, and head for the outer wildernesses of that infamous and now abandoned car park, in which the miracle of actually finding your car was eclipsed only by the greater wonder of getting out of it in under an hour and a half.

Like every one of the hundred that preceded it, 1997 was going to be THE YEAR but unlike most of the others it went very close. By means of the most difficult route – from stone motherless last to minor premiers in the space of the home-and-away season – the Saints arrived at the last Saturday in September staring the Flag in the face. Carrying the expectations of the entire state of Victoria, they succumbed to the dreaded Adelaide Crows and, once again, that was that. Except for ... NEXT YEAR. But another giant roller-coaster left them well short in 1998 and, in 1999, with one chance left to double their premiership record over the hundred years, they finished nowhere. So it was all over for the twentieth century. No wins in the nineteenth century, one Premiership in the twentieth. That was progress of a sort.

Cannon fodder! Sister Minogue was prescient in one way. I was cannon fodder all right, not hostage to world wars and revolutions but to the admirably consistent capitulations of the St Kilda Football Club. Or, perhaps the cannon for which I would be fodder was the whole St Kilda district itself, the very idea of St Kilda, which, taking its name from that evil group of God-forgotten rocks in the Hebrides, was cursed from the start, doomed forever to be the creature of storms and turbulence, real, imagined and psychological.

Despite the change of fortunes as the season lengthened, they were lovely, those Saturday afternoons stretching through the autumn, winter and early spring of 1950. Sitting in the wide, comfortable back seat of the Essex, I listened to the two brothers chatting and joking and joined in the football talk that gradually suffused their conversation as we neared our destination. Usually, my father and I would drive from Brighton to Caulfield in the Chev and go on from Eric's house in the Essex.

On that short part of the afternoon's travelling, my father and I would talk footy and prospects more or less without stint. Barracking for an Australian Rules football team in Melbourne is such an intensely irrational matter that it brings adults and children closer together intellectually, so to speak, than they really are or would normally be. My father's habitually sage and deeply considered judgement often went out the window when he talked of the Saints, especially during that winning streak. He thought he was being his commonsense self as he canvassed the team's rise and progress, but he was conceding to all kinds of mad possibilities, half-conscious bias, mostly non-existent or rapidly diminishing potential, and the vague, baseless resentment every supporter feels towards other teams, especially other more successful teams.

This was precisely what I was doing too, and more so, but as a thirteen-year-old boy I had the excuse of inexperience, naivety and an inability common to my age and stage of maturity to distinguish sheer bias from fancied logic. So we happily communed in a cocoon of temporary equality engendered partly by our love for one another and partly by my father's desperate need for the Saints to go marching in.

Eric, when we arrived at his Caulfield house – the family home that had once borne the sign, *Matthews and Sons Builders* – would be sometimes in great spirits and sometimes rather cast down. Even I could see that he was distinctly mercurial in his moods and phases. If he seemed a bit depressed, this would most often be because he had 'copped an earful' from Annette, whose attitude to his going to the footy was variable and unpredictable. So there would be days when Eric would travel *to* the game looking as if we had already lost. If, as happened with accelerating frequency, we then *did* lose, the whole afternoon took on such funereal proportions that my father would breathe with relief and swear in exasperation when, having arrived back at Caulfield, we transferred to the privacy of the Chev to go home. This in turn would make him feel guilty for entertaining such disloyal thoughts about his brother and our homecoming would be grim and spare.

You would hear in those days of Collingwood wives being belted by their returning husbands if the 'Woods failed to get up. My mother was never in any danger of such barbarity, needless to say. It was a possibility that never even entered her head, nor should it have done. Still, she knew when to serve the dinner and shut up.

What that football season also did for me was to reconnect me to St Kilda, the place, and allay the sense of loss I had felt when we moved to Brighton. At least every second Saturday, we would drive to the Junction Oval, often passing by the beach end of Havelock Street, or cruising round the Esplanade or through Albert Park or, after a game, whizzing straight up Barkly Street. Sometimes, heading for Marine Parade, we would even take a short cut along Havelock Street and run across the bottom of Acland Street, past Luna Park and round by the Peanut Farm. Somehow, these fugitive glimpses, caught while we were pursuing the St Kilda district's own team, settled the whole move in my mind. We had left St Kilda behind, but it remained deeply familiar, it was in my blood and heart. Every week this indissoluble bond, that comforting familiarity, re-manifested themselves. All the well-remembered excitement, unpredictability, wonderful joys and dreary let-downs, all the rag-taggery and second-rateness mixed with a sense that here really beat a heart, were re-embodied when the Saints, St Kilda's team, burst on to some oval somewhere, full of hope, scorned by the rest of Melbourne, yet somehow also envied for a spark, a verve, a maverick flair that deepest and respectable suburbia longed for but was never game to seek.

*

Towards the end of that football season, I went round one Sunday evening to see if Tod was home. One way and another, I had not seen much of him over those footballing months. We had swapped a few *Champions* and he had come around after the Geelong thrashing to do a bit of crowing, but overall there had been unusually little contact. It was not only football and school that had caused this. Tod was a bloke who liked to read, but he seemed to have no books and never to be given any. I, on the other hand, had a lot of books. A book was a standard gift at Christmas and on birthdays and for special events or achievements. So Tod had been busily reading through my *William* books.

Round about the time we finished our last Test match for the 1949–50 season, I lent him *William the Conqueror*. Months went by. I rarely saw him and the book was never returned, though I asked him about it several times. In the end, with great embarrassment, he handed it back – bent, ripped, ruined. His father had been reading it, he said, and had fallen asleep and rolled on it. Because it was a gift from my father, I was very distressed to hear this and see the sorry state of my book. I didn't blame Tod – I fully believed him – but I couldn't laugh it off either. My father shrugged and said I would just have to leave it at that. Tod had apologised and there was not much more to be done, though perhaps I should put more stringent conditions on future loans.

It was not the first time I had been quite shattered by having a treasured gift mistreated or undervalued. For some reason, I was already developing a sensitivity to the idea of gratitude. It shocked me to see my mother being scarcely grateful for a small gift my father gave her, on one occasion, for example, when things were going badly between them. This possibly overblown idea about how to be duly grateful as a receiver of presents, good offices and good intentions sharpened further as I grew up and it remains absurdly acute.

But all that was months in the past the day I walked round to Tod's ramshackle house on what he always persisted in calling the 'real' part of Noel Street. In all the time I knew him, I had never been invited in and had never seen his mother or his father. I had met both his elder brothers, one of whom was a pleasant but retarded young man of about eighteen or so. He spent a lot of time with the fluidly fragmenting and re-combining circle of kids in the district – boys and girls years younger than him – all of whom treated him with marvellous kindness and tolerance. There was some giggling at his odd ways, his disjunction, somehow, from the rhythm of things around him, his occasional amazing statements. But essentially, he was looked after and was made happy by the group. He would often be out in the front garden when I called on Tod, but this time neither he nor anyone else was around. I knocked on the front door but I could see already that something had changed. There was nothing lying around, the old sofa on the front verandah had gone, Tod's dog, usually an ecstatic greeter of visitors, was nowhere to be seen. They had gone. The whole family had disappeared.

I saw Tod once more, thirteen years later. It was outside my parents' Noel Street house. I was loading my old FX Holden with the multifarious stuff you think you need to carry everywhere when you have your first child. My wife and I and my parents were about to leave for St Finbar's Church where our firstborn, David, was to be baptised. As I struggled with the carrycot, and God knows what else, I became conscious of someone standing just behind me. I looked round. It was Tod. He was instantly recognisable, not much changed at all. The same shock of white hair, the same slightly round-shouldered burliness. He grinned and I had the insane premonition that he was going to produce a ball and bat and suggest we get on with a game. I realised – and I saw in his genial gaze the same thought fleetingly surfacing – that we were standing at about silly point on the old pitch, now transformed, of course, by asphalt and kerbs, while the 'outfield', the shaggy, curly-leaf-ridden orchard and weedy paddock, had disappeared under houses and double garages and a cul-de-sac and prim nature strips.

'Gooday,' he said, and we shook hands.

I explained haltingly why I was there and what we were doing and apologised that I couldn't stick around – we were already ten minutes late. He nodded, grinned again, said we must try to meet some time. I agreed, knowing as you do on those occasions that we would not. The family began to emerge from the house, ready to leave. Tod looked awkwardly down at his shoes and then began to walk away.

'Watch out for those killer ants,' I said.

He smiled, waved and walked on. At the corner he waved again. This time, he really did disappear forever.

CHAPTER 15

Going Bush

One way and another, 1950 was a big year. Not only did we go to the footy, but also Eric's insistence that my father build some leisure into his punishing schedule apparently made an important, if slowly cumulative, impression on him. Whatever the thinking behind it, he rented a house in the Dandenong Ranges for one week of the second-term school holidays (though who knows what might have become of this September idyll if the Saints' early form had continued and they had marched into the finals?). The house was near Belgrave, at a little dot on the map called Selby.

This first holiday was an insight into my mother's disinclination to move too far from whatever she saw as her centre, her physical and spiritual base. She was not at all keen on the idea of a holiday in the bush – for Selby in those days was definitely 'the bush'. Belgrave itself, the nearest 'town', with its high footpaths and Puffing Billy train, was utterly exotic. It was one of those occasions, and there were several others, when what my father had regarded as an important and exciting family announcement fell flat – as far as my mother was concerned, anyway. This was one of those times when my mother most clearly betrayed her St Kilda loyalties. She was delighted to have the freedom and space and privacy of her own house and was gradually reconciling herself to its apparent isolation, the long distances to shops, the walks in the heat with shopping bags.

But my mother was an inner city animal, comfortable among shops and traffic and close-crowding neighbours. When she left St Kilda, she did not realise that the days of striding off into the January heat or the mid-winter southerly wearing sensible flatties and dragging a shopping trolley were already numbered, even in 'convenient' St Kilda, where the Village Belle beckoned a mere five-minute walk away.

In the suburbs, especially those suburban edges where new houses were sprouting and new Avenues, Terraces, Closes and Courts were jigsaw-puzzling their way across formerly bland paddocks, women were beginning to get behind the wheel, conceding to distance and fashion, but just as often determined to share in the new mobility. True to the general but rapidly eroding custom of the day, my mother did not drive. Later, when women drivers were becoming numerous and accepted, she still hesitated. My father, it has to be said, did not help. Protected from decision at first by the self-evident fact that the Chev was a very difficult car to handle – double de-clutching, for example, was indispensable – and not suitable for a small, probably nervous woman driver, he had greater difficulty fending off her indecisive bursts of interest when in later years he became the owner of a second-hand Morris Minor in very good nick. He was reluctant to let her at it, though he desperately tried to convey exactly the opposite impression.

This advance and retreat impasse lasted through several cars, including the only new car they ever owned, a Volkswagen (my father would not consider a Japanese car), and eventually, by sheer effluxion of time and absence of decisive moves on either side, the whole issue disappeared and my mother never drove.

For a non-driving, one-time St Kilda dweller, the idea of swapping the spare comforts of the house in Noel Street for some half-baked hut in Selby, wherever that was, seemed lunacy. She thought it was too far. She wondered 'what on earth' we would *do* there (the answer was: walk, go to Sherbrooke Forest and see the lyre-birds, go for drives round the little hills settlements – all of which sounded wonderful to me). Above all, how would we *get* there? The answer to that one – the only answer possible – was in the Chev.

The Chev, even as we spoke, was undergoing yet another transformation. Its days as a ute had come to an end because my father no longer had to transport materials, timber, and so on. He did have a great need, however, for a sedan. The trip to Fishermans Bend, which had been relatively painless from Havelock Street – in my father's case, an easy bike-ride – was a major undertaking from East Brighton and not really possible by public transport. Not 'if you wanted to get there on the same bloody day', as he put it. So, he joined in with two workmates, both of whom came from the Brighton area, who used to take it in turns to do the drive to work. My father contributed to the cost of the petrol but was embarrassed that he couldn't actually do his share of the driving.

So my father and Eric got to work on the Chev over several weekends and converted it into a kind of station wagon. You had to climb in the back end, but once you were in, it was quite as comfortable as any modern car. It was in this hybrid that my father began taking his turn to do the drive to Fishermans Bend, and it was in this that we set off for Selby.

To get to the Dandenongs, you just went to the intersection of Hawthorn Road and North Road, where the paper shop was that we would walk to each Saturday night for the *Globe* and the late *Herald*. Then you turned right and drove with the long redbrick wall of the Brighton Cemetery on your left straight up North Road. It became Wellington Road some distance up, but you just kept on going. The Chev chugged into the unknown, turning eventually towards Ferntree Gully, itself a mere township and regarded as a sort of gateway to the distant ranges, but turning again, short of Ferntree Gully, to wind tortuously up through wonderful, sleepy towns – Upwey, Tecoma, Belgrave – each with its sign: the town name followed by *Slow Down Here*. This was an injunction the Chev had no difficulty obeying.

As the miles unwound beneath its thin, wooden-spoked wheels, the anxiety of the passengers deepened. My mother became tense because we were getting further and further away from 'civilisation' and she had not agreed with this trip in the first place. My sister, catching the mood, became agitated and irritable. She was at that time eight years old, a vivacious, curly-headed, laughing child, much put upon by my endless heavy-handed practical jokes and already beginning to show the vestigial first signs of a sturdy independence that combined glimpses of her mother's spectacular but short-lived temper with her father's mild, amiable eccentricity.

With each passing mile, my father and I listened with deepening anxiety to the stentorian rhythms of the motor, noting how the steepening climbs were taxing it just a little more each time. I, of course, had no idea what I was listening for and my premonitions of imminent breakdown were exaggerated and based on little or misconstrued evidence. With each successive curve rounded and each long haul accomplished, my father would visibly relax and wave a brown arm at the magnificent tree-fern-fronded countryside, the sudden sweeping prospects, the cold tunnels of overhanging eucalypts.

'Look at that! Bloody beautiful. If we'd lost the war, that'd be all rice,' he said.

No one believed this, but who were we to argue? In any case, we had to watch the road, willing the Chev to stay put while my father, to the eyes of us non-drivers, appeared to be devoting alarmingly little attention to steering.

Selby at that time consisted of a General Store and Post Office which was on the corner of the main road and a vertiginous track that plunged down recklessly into the bush and out of sight. My mother looked at this 'goat track' and said, 'My God.' She must have had a premonition. Enquiry in the Post Office established that our holiday shack was just down the hill. Down *that* hill. We descended in first gear and even my father's optimism was dented, not because the steep drop worried him but because he foresaw real trouble getting the Chev back up. The 'house', the only one on that track that we could see as we wound into the depths, was a rectangular, weatherboard structure with a corrugated-iron roof that swept down past the eaves to form a verandah along three sides. A redbrick chimney rose from the fireplace tacked on to and protruding from the timber wall at the verandah-less end. That characteristic chimney structure, my father cheerfully informed us, was always the one bit left standing after a bushfire.

Already feeling dwarfed by the canopy of tall mountain ash and claustrophobic at the bottom of that far valley, my mother heard these incautious words with stony gloom.

But gloom was not what I was feeling. The Chev bumped to a stop at the front gate and the engine noise gratefully died. No one spoke. Two kookaburras, visible on a low branch overhanging the tangled loops of wire that passed for a fence, regarded us, their heads cocked for better vision, before bursting into a cackle of derision. They, it seemed, had never seen anything so mad. And I, for my part, came suddenly and embarrassingly near to tears as that wonderful cacophony – which I had never heard 'in the flesh' – rang through the echoing chambers of the bush. As if signalled, magpies began their glottal ululations and bellbirds from hidden boughs struck up a running, ringing echo, a sound that explored the meeting point between half-chime and purest whistle. Behind and above and amid all this, the huge forest sighed and stretched and the rushing of water rose from somewhere very deep in the valley and the sun flickered down in shafts and fragments of light through the great roof of patterning leaves and arching, gnarled limbs. I had never seen or heard anything like it in my whole life.

As we began unloading the Chev, a bloke appeared from the scrub beyond our house, where the track curved into the gloom of the forest and began to ascend again. He was wearing blue overalls, army boots and a digger's hat and he had a cigarette in his mouth which he would speak through rather than remove, so that his words came out in short smoke- and cough-shaped bursts. Over his shoulder he carried an axe with a gleaming edge to it. As he approached, I realised that part of the enchantment of those first minutes of sound in the sudden silence after the engine, had been the clean smack of an axe somewhere down among the ferns and the fall of water, biting at wood hard enough to resonate like a cello. Somehow, he seemed to carry with him a fragrance of woodsmoke – as if his clothes were impregnated with the drifting tang of a hundred campfires.

My father said, 'Gooday,' and the bloke nodded. Then, taking in the Chev and the slant of the slope with a sweeping, smoky glance, he said, 'Hope y'like it down here, mate. The old Chevy might not make it out again, eh?' My father laughed. 'Well,' he said, 'I think we'll be right, but I might have to back out.' They both laughed, though this conversation remained inexplicable to me until later in the day when I learned that reverse is the lowest gear. 'You'll be right,' said the axeman, 'they're a great car, better than most of this modern shit.' He waved and headed off up the track. The axe blade caught a flash of sun down through the spangling leaves and a magpie chortled from a fence post.

On the morning after our arrival, I woke early, when my bedroom window was a just visible grey shape in the gloom of the unfamiliar room. I had been roused by a ridiculously proud, thoroughly dramatic alarm – a single, distant salute belonging to the first glimmer of light, to those few moments when the silhouetted gum trees stand statue-still, when a fugitive magpie slips from its night-time branch and angles to earth like a shaft of black light.

I lay as the bright day broke over the bush and listened to this untuneful and anarchic chorister haranguing his scattered and echoing acolytes, as I had so often lain in my room in St Kilda, watching the dust swirl in the skylight dawn and listening to the comfortable doves. Scarcely understanding why, I thought I might burst with joy. It was a sound as new and as exciting to me as the hooting, chiming and chortling amazement of the kookaburras, bellbirds and magpies that had marked our arrival the previous day.

Running down through the trees at the back of our shack, I soon caught sight of him – angry-eyed, bristling with ludicrous aggression, ginger-and-velvet feathers fluffing and rustling. A Rhode Island Red rooster. As soon as he saw me, he stretched his shining plumed neck, flapped wide wings and crowed raucously. This display merged into a sudden, dancing, stiff-legged rush at the nearest of his busy, scratching hens. He came at her in a detouring curve, as if to deny his intention, leapt upon her and copulated vigorously, undeterred by outraged squawks of what appeared to be profound reluctance. This ceremony over, he strutted among his brood, turning up seeds and other prizes for them under his murderously spurred feet, presiding over their meal with absurd pomp and throaty mutterings.

How silly it all looks now – a small, nondescript boy standing among the heedless trees, almost weeping to hear a rooster. But that triumphant, jolly crowing meant, for me, farms and bush and the drift of woodsmoke and cows gazing from big, bitten-down paddocks and pencil lines of dusty sunlight through nail holes in the corrugated iron and spiderwebs glittering with dew strung on wire fences. It was all in my head; I had never actually known any of it. That morning, it seemed as if the rooster had awakened me to another world.

And so he had, as surely as the old Chev had made it all possible by doggedly, if with the occasional falter, carrying us there and back.

Begun experimentally and, from my mother's point of view, looking bad from the start, the Selby holiday ended up a great success. None of us, including my mother, wanted to leave. For myself, I had wept with joy when we arrived. I was ashamed to be fighting a tear of sadness when we left, being vaguely – though wrongly, I am glad to say – convinced that I would never again be so close to and in tune with such wonders of nature.

It was one of the happiest and most important weeks of my life. Out of it grew my life-long love of the Australian bush – its orchestra of sounds, its 'weird melancholy', its massive indifference, its undemonstrative, yet heart-stopping beauties. A strange fate for the boy who thought he would scarcely survive the abandonment of Havelock Street, with its emigrant lost doves and dusty sparrows, its cramped spaces, its rage and seethe of humanity, its dubious fortunes flowing and fluctuating from smoky dawn to shouting, noisy dusk and on into the troubled, shadow-filled night.

As they walked back into the Noel Street house, where ubiquitous smells of paint, sawdust, putty and varnish had intensified during a locked-up week of silence and scarcely ruffled air, my parents were about to face the most testing, the worst time of their life together. It was not that they had no inkling of this, though they could scarcely have predicted it would be as bad as it turned out. So perhaps the timing of the holiday and my mother's slowness to accept its mute offer of relaxation and quiet healing were all influenced by the knowledge of what would quickly follow.

The trials they were about to face had their origin in the mistakes and manoeuvrings that accompanied Pop Matthews's death.

Ma Matthews was a difficult, perhaps disappointed woman. All the other strands in our extended family went back to Scotland, or Ireland, to poverty and possibly criminality; or, in Pop's case, to Devonian, skilled working class respectability. But Ma Matthews came from a squatter family who, to the best of my knowledge, traced their ancestry at least as far back as the 1820s in New South Wales. Somewhere or other along their trek through the centuries they'd fallen on hard times. There was one story of someone's uncle (at least the lore on that side of the family broke the regime of the aunts) making a fortune on the Ballarat goldfields, and blowing the lot on booze and women during a brief and inglorious return to Melbourne, but the authorised version had more to do with vast tracts of land, drought, incautious investment, and so on. Ma Matthews had the memories, some ancestral relics, the pedigree, but none of the wherewithal. She married a builder from Devon and seemed to settle into a state of neurotic regret for much of her remaining long life.

She was in many ways, though, the archetypal grandmother. My maternal grandmother, Annie Murray, was large, big-bosomed and mercurial; fond of a drop, a dedicated gambler, a tough taskmistress, full of love in a life that had almost never allowed much time for it. Ma Matthews was slim, almost ascetic, fastidious to the point of misanthropy. Yet, in her own way she was an interesting if slightly distant grandmother and her house was a paradise for a small child. Cool and dim in summer, the high-ceilinged rooms would be sibilant with their own hush and shoosh of silence, or resonant and sonorous with the *tock, tock, tock* of a grandfather clock, and bristling with amazing oddities, like the beautiful, mottled nautilus shells in which, when you clamped them to your ears, you would hear the roar and crash of the ocean; or the music box that tinkled with tunes from opera. On tables and sideboards there were flowers in vases and fruit in bowls; and from packed drawers, Ma Matthews would produce sepia pictures of another life in another time – up the country. A skilled, innovative and dedicated gardener, she could make a stroll among her flowers and fruit trees and herbs absorbing and beautiful even for a heedless little kid. Order and stateliness and due precedence ruled her approach to things. When she said we would be allowed to do something 'directly', it didn't mean, curiously enough, straight away, it meant later on. It now seems to me, as I try to recall this vaguely mysterious figure, that 'later on' was mostly where she lived her life. Her gaze seemed often fixed on distances and she had the air of one who lived in an uncomprehended mist of deferral. She was too edgy and probably at heart too discontented to be a calming presence for her husband and grown sons, but for a grandson, trailing behind her round the garden or through the sanctuary of her quiet, dim rooms was always a subdued adventure. Coming from the riot of Havelock Street and environs to the ordered, ceremonious interiors at the Caulfield house was like leaving a disco to enter a cathedral.

After Pop's death, however, and under the regime that came into being in accordance with the will, the bulk of the old family house became Annette's province. For years Annette and Eric, childless and seemingly doomed to stay that way, had occupied a 'sleep-out' in the leafy, flowering back garden and Pop and Ma Matthews lived in the house. When Pop died, Eric and Annette moved into the main house and rebuilt the interior to provide Ma Matthews with a small, self-contained flat. Annette abused, bullied and insulted Ma Matthews until the old lady pleaded with her other son, my father, to take her in. The urgency of the situation was suddenly and sensationally relieved when Annette announced she was pregnant. Well into her forties, she produced a son. Everyone was happy; everyone mellowed. The halcyon days arrived and if it had been a novel or a saga it would have ended there. What actually happened, of course, was that, besotted though she was with her first and, as it turned out only child, Annette nevertheless resumed her campaign and Ma Matthews, reduced by the constant abrasion of acrimony and stress, pleaded to be rescued. Eric could not withstand his wife's guerilla-like campaigns and crumpled under the pressure. The writing had been on the wall for my father almost from the moment Pop Matthews died and now he had no choice but to succumb.

And so Ma Matthews moved in with us late in 1950. Our still raw East Brighton house, which had been designed and built for our family, could accommodate her only by having her share my sister Carol's room. Justifiably disgruntled with this arrangement that had plucked her room away before it was even finished and after the briefest of occupancy, Carol raised some protest. Since she was at that time in very early training (going on nine years old) to become a tumultuous teenager, her objections were formidable enough considering her age, and her juvenile sense of disenchantment would add its own sharp momentum to the acrimonies that lay ahead.

My father and mother had enjoyed barely two wonderful, if rigorous and less than comfortable, years under their very own roof with their two growing children when it all ground to a halt and they were living with in-laws again. It was a truly catastrophic decision.

Ma Matthews had been too long the mistress of all she surveyed, too long the princess who needed but to beck and call, to be an easy lodger, even with her son and daughter-in-law. My mother, with more than a streak of Annie's tough stubbornness and her capacity for incandescent flashes of rebellion, was not the right person to deal with her. The mix was made even more volatile by my mother's resentment at having undergone the huge disruption of the move to Brighton only to have the whole plan undermined within two years. They had left St Kilda because my father had preached endlessly that living with the in-laws was not the way of a good marriage, nor was it conducive to bringing up a happy family. But that principle, it now appeared, applied only to living with the Murrays. Sturdy independence and privacy crumbled immediately before pressure from the Matthews. The whole arrangement reeked of potential disaster and disaster duly followed.

The house at 11 Noel Street filled with tensions and unstated anxieties as poor old Ma Matthews tried honestly to flow with the tides and currents of each succeeding domestic day while at the same time, despite herself, frequently muscling her way on to the bridge and taking the helm. My father, so adept in so many ways, was not good at confrontations and certainly not when they occurred almost daily. Somehow, he and my mother could never get themselves on the same side in this deadly progress towards grief and disjunction. My mother – convinced, wrongly, that son and mother were ganging up on her, impatient with and intolerant of my father's doomed position, caught in the middle between son and mother – deteriorated visibly. She became depressed, as we would say today, desperate. This situation was probably already critical when fate, with the usual exquisite timing, made it worse.

The deepest springs of Ma Matthews's life had been closed off forever when she was forced out of the house she had built and shared with Tom. Always at least subconsciously resentful of having been 'brought down' in life, she now had little to live for. Her beautiful garden was lost to her, and ours, which would one day be as fine, was at that stage barely started. Removed from her haunts in Caulfield, she had few friends mobile enough to visit her. Naturally dominant, she seemed, as she saw it, scarcely able to utter without riling my mother and creating an 'incident'. She was down to a good book and cups of tea, to petulance and complaint when, suddenly afflicted by a slight stroke towards the end of 1952, she took gratefully to her bed. She would never leave it.

The strain of having an aged, bedridden patient requiring almost constant attention brought my parents to the precipice. My mother's health declined, she became pencil thin, unsmiling, bitter. My father, once so full of plans and excitements, was gloomy, strained and irritable. He lost interest in his garden, which he had looked forward so much to establishing, and in the house which, still requiring plenty of work, now became simply another burden.

He lost interest in footy, too, but on 2 June 1953 – a holiday to celebrate the Coronation – he and I began listening to an unusual event on the wireless. The VFL was running a knockout 'Lightning Premiership'. A series of shortened games between the League teams, starting around eleven o'clock and played all afternoon on the MCG, was to produce two finalists who would play off for the 'Premiership'. Expecting the Saints to be eliminated in the first round, we became interested when they not only survived that hurdle but triumphed in the next game and went on to enter the semi-final. In that sad house, with my mother wordlessly passing and re-passing on various domestic errands (which included doing her share of waiting on Ma Matthews), my father and I listened in an agony of pessimism as St Kilda won their semi-final. We then switched off the wireless and went for a walk in the cold, windy sleet, unable to submit ourselves to the ordeal of listening to them attempt to win an actual Premiership – even if it was only 'Lightning', it was something.

During that walk, my father guardedly tried to acquaint me with what was in his heart about the crisis they had come to. I was sixteen and desperate to help, but he was so careful not to seem to be taking sides against, or criticising my mother, and made so many qualifications to explain how Ma Matthews could not really be blamed for anything much that had happened, that the point, whatever it was, was lost. I had never seen him so inarticulate, so defeated.

When we returned home, my parents immediately had a tense, *sotto voce* set-to about something that had arisen concerning Ma Matthews. It seemed that spending a good deal of the afternoon having the football 'blaring' on the wireless, then going out in the rain for an hour, was not what we should have done. I was not sure then, and of course never have been since, whether this judgement emanated from my mother or my grandmother or whether, in a moment of rare congruence, the two women had agreed on it.

Whatever the truth, it electrified the atmosphere in which my father and I then switched on the wireless to learn that – the Saints had been murdered. With youthful insensitivity, I launched into a tirade of disappointment that included, I remember, the outburst, 'They never, never, never, *ever* rise to the occasion!' My father yelled at me, shouted to me to SHUT UP and not be so stupid, kicked me out of the room and told me not to show my face again till I could be sure of having some sense. It was an unprecedented outburst, delivered with totally uncharacteristic injustice and a never before glimpsed venom. I was not smart enough to see, while it was happening, that it was not me who was the trouble. With my ill-timed and self-indulgent complaint, I had made myself conveniently a symbol of, and target for, all the awful, directionless, desperate agony and sadness of his plight. I understood this only much later, just as I saw, with a wry inward smile, how apposite it was that another of St Kilda's many failures should have become associated with one of our life crises.

At the time, though, I was shocked and aggrieved. This comforting self-absorption turned to panic and despair when, a week or so later, my parents had a shouting, poisonous row while the rest of us cringed in our corners of the house. When it seemed to have abated, I crept to the closed kitchen door to listen, as I often did, in order to understand what was happening and to hope for good signs and sounds. What I heard was my mother say, 'If it wasn't for Carol, I'd leave you because of all this' (meaning, certainly, the life they were living with the bedridden patient overshadowing everything, physically destroying my mother especially, not being coped with by my father). To which my father replied, 'What about Brian?' 'He's capable of looking after himself,' she said – and, for the time being, broke my heart.

Throughout 1953, our domestic lives were dominated by the patient at the end of the long hall which led to my room and Carol's and which had so excited both of us when we first picked our way along it (there being no floorboards then, only the bearers) and imagined what it would be like to each 'own' a whole room at the far end of the house. My sister still slept in her room, but for all other purposes, it had become a hospital ward, a geriatric ward. Equipped with a bell to summon help, Ma Matthews – whose own psychological agonies my parents must have been aware of yet scarcely capable of assuaging – would dominate the days and nights, sometimes cheerfully (she had been not without a pleasant, kidding wit in her prime), sometimes plaintively, sometimes remorselessly.

I could not understand why two apparently similar conditions had produced such violently different results. At 54 Havelock Street, we had been crammed together in a small house and were living with my mother's family, above all with the matriarchal Annie. Yet, almost all my memories of that time were of noise, laughter, movement, risk, luck and the fascinating dance of life. In East Brighton, which should have been a kind of apotheosis of hopes and plans, especially for my parents, we were living only with my father's mother and – even to my untutored gaze – we were falling to pieces. Of course, I failed to account for many things in this assessment. My own rose-coloured view of life at St Kilda was one. It was an easy view to adopt and hold on to if you were a small boy in that absorbingly chaotic environment. Another was my parents' age. At Havelock Street, for all its trials, they were emerging from the war, revivifying their interrupted marriage; they were youthful, energetic, full of hope. At Noel Street nearly a decade later, despite the initial exhilaration of achievement, they were quickly knocked into shape by the no doubt expected brunt of mortgage, growing family, continued job insecurity and tightrope finances. The family machinations that gradually and relentlessly put Ma Matthews at the centre of everyone's concerns and made her my mother's helpless, demanding and implacable patient must have seemed the work of an unfair and uncontrollable fate. Seeking to take control of their lives and futures, my parents found themselves caught in a spiral of contingencies in which family ties, filial love and decency precluded complaint while offering not a vestige of hope or direction.

It was a bad house for mothers, our house at Brighton

in those hard days. My father, caught, in the time-honoured manner, between his mother and his wife, could only please one by hurting the other. He could only explain his position to each of them by resorting to a quality of patient, unyielding logic that exactly characterised the situation, its traps and labyrinths, but which neither of them remotely wanted to hear. Ma Matthews was impossible in her demands. Yet these represented the only way she could reach out of that room, mitigate her own powerlessness, carry on the guise of sequential and consequential existence while, above all, keeping at bay the sunny, garden-blooming world of her past that crowded her demented head and made her weep with loss and waste.

As for my mother, she had little time for her own children and resented it. She looked after us as always but she scarcely had a smile or a song – so different from the natural ebullience of her St Kilda days. I put my own twist on this behaviour, of course. I knew she didn't want me, didn't care if I left or stayed.

Towards the end of 1953, Ma Matthews became incontinent. My sister went to stay with Jean and Mannie. As I was by then doing matriculation – engaged upon my big push towards the 'piece of paper' – I kept my head down, did my work, ate my meals, came and went. Eric and my father did several tours of hospices and old people's homes in Eric's Essex, trying to find one with a vacancy and which they could afford. On both scores the task was apparently difficult verging on impossible and the weeks dragged by. Eventually, they managed to have her admitted to a home that would take her for an emergency three weeks only. The move was made, and a blessed relief settled on our house. But there was little real slackening of the tension. Three weeks was not long and the prospects beyond them looked bleak.

One Sunday, a week before the emergency deadline, we set out in the Essex to visit all the possible places where Ma Matthews might be admitted and be well cared for and comfortable. Eric was behind the wheel, my father next to him, my mother, sister and me in the wide back seat. Our first stop was the Caritas Christi Hospice in Studley Park Road. My father and Eric had enquired here before, but now they returned, with my mother, to make another attempt. The three of them went in and when they came out again, the verdict was obvious from the men's glum expression – Eric had a particularly gloomy mien once he decided things were going badly – and from the blur of tears in my mother's eyes. The Mother Superior was sympathetic but adamant: Caritas Christi was bursting at the seams. We then ranged all over Kew and environs and further afield as well, but for one reason and another, there was nothing that combined suitability, availability and affordability.

In deep silence, stony-faced, with my sister and I having by now learnt well the lesson that you kept quiet through such times, we were winding back towards the city when it became evident that our route would take us past Caritas Christi again. As we approached, my mother said, 'Stop. Stop here.' The car wavered, as if the decision was being made somewhere beneath that long, capacious bonnet. My father said, 'It's pointless, you'll only upset yourself,' and Eric, as if reassured, speeded up again.

'Stop!' my mother said. 'I'm trying here again. I don't care what you think or what they think.' She opened the door before the car had properly parked. 'This could be our last chance,' she said and, as my father made to join her, she added, 'No, I'll go on my own.'

She was away a long time. While we waited, I could not help thinking of those happy days in the Essex when all that was on our minds was the fate of the mighty Saints and when our deepest glooms were caused by setbacks as ephemeral as a thrashing. At last, my mother appeared round the curve of the rosebush-lined pathway that led to the hospice entrance. She was walking very fast, but then she always did.

When she arrived at the car, she went to the passenger side door as my father opened it and said, 'I've got her in. They'll take her. We'll have to go back to the other place now and make the arrangements. She has to move tomorrow.' Then she fell into my father's arms and sobbed with such wrenching, naked misery that my sister and I were embarrassed. And Eric looked at the crowded instrument panel of the Essex as if it held somewhere among its shining dials and arcing needles the answers to great human mysteries, one of which was being enacted beside him.

My mother told me, years later, what had happened. She had asked to speak to the Mother Superior who, on seeing my mother again and recognising no doubt the depth of her desperation, took her into an office and listened to the whole story. A sad tale of compassion, guilt about the old woman's plight, revulsion at the tasks, advancing destruction of a family and a marriage, shamefaced resentments. When my mother's story ended, the nun said, 'Have her brought in here tomorrow. I'll find a place for her, even if we have to glass-in the verandah. And we'll look after her, don't worry. You've done your part, more than most would have even tried to.' Then she hugged my mother, gave her a clean handkerchief and said, 'We'll meet again tomorrow.'

Ma Matthews was as happy as her condition and state of mind allowed at Caritas Christi for nearly a year. Every Wednesday night, Eric and my father would visit her and we would all go, including after a while Annette, on Sundays. At each Sunday visit we would give her, among other things, a Cherry Ripe, which she would often though not always share with my sister and me. I have never since bought or tasted that confection, my detestation of which came to be equal only to my hatred of cards.

Ma Matthews died in 1954, bringing to an end at last a tortured life and an almost uniformly disastrous episode in the history of my parents and some of the extended family.

It is an old story. I often wondered why, back in the St Kilda days, my father didn't rent a house. As a matter of fact, I know they did rent briefly after their marriage, in Empress Road, East St Kilda. I presume they gave that up because it was cheaper to live with Annie, yet it cannot have been that much of a burden to rent a small house? I suspect that my father was deeply imbued with that ethic that said, 'Rent is money down the drain.' You lived with family till you could run your own show, trying, demeaning and often unpleasant though that arrangement might prove to be.

My father's massive effort to build and move his family into their own house at a time when everyone was advising against it (until postwar shortages and prices eased) took a lot out of him. When the whole dream was subjected to crisis and threatened to disintegrate amid acrimony and marital dissension, he had for the moment few resources left or in reserve to cope with such an oblique yet telling blow.

My mother was thrown badly off balance by the long drawn-out trauma of Ma Matthews's last years, but she was a tough woman when the chips were down. She would come up with scorched-earth solutions that appeared, and perhaps were, rather callous – such as deciding, in that terrible argument which I overheard through the kitchen door, that I could look after myself and that only Carol's needs stopped her from leaving. But if her response to the hard times was correspondingly hard (and by no means always wrong no matter how unpalatable it seemed), her natural mode was a kind of mild, contained *joie de vivre*. While there were so many ways in which she was unadventurous (for example, about leaving St Kilda, going to Selby, and so on) and therefore would risk a needless narrowing of her range of experiences, and while she remained broadly faithful all her life to the religion of her childhood, there was in her makeup a streak of mild hedonism. For all that the Church offered her solace beyond the grave, and for all that she by and large accepted the offer, there was that in her which found the price too high, the grave too final, too private. Under a different dispensation from fate, she would have danced and sung and laughed and gathered together her friends to entertain them, and she would have done all these things often and with great gusto. But her life took a different shape and she was happy with it.

In some ways, though, she was much more adventurous than her husband. When I started at the university, she announced that she would read through the literature course with me. She had always been a keen reader but had essayed little more than romance and mystery. To my shame, I know that I privately doubted her capacity to carry out this intention and I think my willing concession to it was spiced with the condescension that is the often unwitting trademark of the newly intellectualised young. Not only did she embark on this journey with signal success – *Crime and Punishment*, *Pilgrim's Progress*, *Tom Jones*, *Middlemarch*, *The Tree of Man*, *Heart of Darkness*, *Don Quixote* all fell before her voluminous attention – but she also soon began to engage me in sophisticated discussions about them. Why shouldn't she? This was a woman with not a moment's training in or experience of the world of literature and learning. But she came to it like an old hand, causing her to realise yet again, no doubt, what might have been, though she never whinged on that score and scarcely ever mentioned it.

As he grew older, my father became in some ways narrower than the lateral-thinking maverick who had come back from the war with a head full of plans and designs and ideas. He would not join my mother in her literary saga because, he said, he preferred Australian books! Accordingly, he read *The Tree of Man*, which I recommended to them both with enormous excitement. My mother loved this book as much as I did. My father loved it until he came to the episode in which Amy commits adultery with Leo. This, he said, was not true to the character of Amy; it just 'wouldn't happen'. Though he finished the book, he dismissed it. My mother, already familiar with how the larger-than-life world of art can throw probing light on even the most suburban of dilemmas, had no difficulty at all with Amy's treachery. On the contrary, as I discovered in our discussion of the book, she understood what my father refused to countenance: that Amy's actions were governed not by any diminution of her feeling for her husband, Stan Parker, but by undifferentiated, half-understood longings within herself, by a desire to possess totally. The last book she read, battling through despite rapidly failing sight, was Vikram Seth's *A Suitable Boy*, of which she said, 'It's a wonderful story beautifully told, but I don't think he needed so much Indian politics.'

Though I never forgot my mother's dismissal of me in the heat of argument, I never raised it with her and she went to the grave not knowing I had overheard. It was in the end a trivial matter. It just seemed catastrophic to me at the time, when our whole life together was overwrought, a prey to unpredictable sensitivities and renewed crises. Nothing evil came of it. If anything, my mother and I became closer as we read through the great works of literature during my university years and somehow she herself developed an intuitive understanding of and tolerance for the sometimes self-indulgent, sometimes hard-pressed, sometimes unbearably tense, sometimes thoroughly chaotic life of the student. She became my confidante and occasional wry adviser as I began the agonising business of working out how to 'meet girls'. More so than my father, she glimpsed the loosening of time-honoured social bonds, the almost imperceptible shuddering of hitherto impregnable moral edifices that were about to collapse.

It was one of her triumphs in her long years of

widowhood that she would enter with ease and dignity each age of change and fashion, and she encountered with aplomb revolutions in her own extended family of a kind she could scarcely have imagined back in the secure days of home-building in East Brighton. She lived on into a world which many women of her age and experience found impossibly alien – the world of massive social change, moral upheaval, the questioning of everything she had been brought up to revere, including her religious faith. She was able to accept, as many of her peers could not, changes in moral and social behaviour which reached even into her own immediate family. She found herself in the fullness of her age to be mother, mother-in-law, grandmother, great-grandmother, step-grandmother, confidante, family icon, matriarch . . . In her last years she secretly enjoyed her eminence in this diverse family.

She also enjoyed her friendships. She and her sister, Aunty Jean, became legendary for their late afternoon shandy and smoke and a yarn with old mates and family dropping in. She had five cigarettes a day and decided it was far too late to worry about it. When the doctor at one stage told her to take a walk each morning for her low blood pressure, she rang me and said, 'That's all very well, but I walk into town once a week, play bowls three times a week and go swimming on Fridays – I haven't got time to go for a walk!' Her friends included all the residents of her block of flats – Ukrainians, Poles, Russians and a Jewish survivor of Auschwitz; she organised the block's finances, rostered them to sweep and weed the garden, arbitrated inter-flat rivalries and arguments and counselled their pubescent children. She never expected to, but she'd entered multicultural Australia with a vengeance and she handled it with serenity.

But if my mother and father's trials back in the 1950s amounted to 'an old story' it was also, in this case, a happy one after all. My mother's resilience had helped them through the terrible period with Ma Matthews. She now turned her energies back to rebuilding their lives and bringing up their family in the house they had made for themselves. She and my father returned to the closeness they had enjoyed in the precarious St Kilda days and for the first wild, makeshift year at Brighton. They enjoyed themselves and each other for more than a decade. Their garden flowered and became famous in the district. The enigmatic Noel Street turned out to run just where my father always said it would and became a leafy, pleasant suburban backwater. Through unremitting effort and brilliant gifts (which included studying Building Construction Parts I, II and III part time in his mid-fifties and coming top each year), my father finally both advanced in and secured his job in the aviation industry. It was no less busy and there was never much financial leeway, but it was a good time for them, with many joys and achievements. Until 1966.

But that is another story.

PART TWO

Another Story

[His] life had now become two lives. There was Version A and Version B, and both of them were his story. He had lived them both in equal measure . . .

PAUL AUSTER, *The Red Notebook*

CHAPTER 16

At the Footbridge

It is quarter past twelve on the afternoon of Saturday, 24 September 1966 and I am in a hurry. Just a week ago, the whole of Melbourne was cringing before lashing rain and a biting wind, but now the sun shines from a fluffy, cloud-scudding sky, the bright flags whip and snap in a pleasant breeze and, as if celebrating the benign weather, trams, trains, buses and family cars snake in from the suburbs bringing 101,655 people to the Melbourne Cricket Ground. I am in a hurry; so are the several thousand people bustling along behind and in front of me – no one is going anywhere very fast. But we are moving, step by step in good-natured tolerance, jostling and bumping, full of anticipation, excitement, dread, exquisite impatience. We are inching our way across the footbridge leading to the MCG.

Everybody meets everybody 'at the bottom of the footbridge', which is why that convergence of paths under the spreading elm trees is always packed before any football game or Test cricket match. And when we have managed to meet whoever we are meeting, we will all stream towards the gates and the ticket windows and rat-a-tat our way through the spinning, chattering turnstiles. And then it is up the stairs to the first view of the ground, that breathtaking sudden sight of the somehow impossibly green oval with its precision of white lines and the four stern white posts at each end and the thousands of dots that are the crowd, like a pointillist painting endowed with the voices of a safari full of hungry lions. And then we will rush on round the causeways and down aisles, to get ourselves the best view we can with standing-room tickets, to choose finally *our spot.*

That is why I am in a hurry. I am meeting my mate, Ted Fitzgerald, at the footbridge. He has managed to scrounge two standing-room tickets for this Grand Final between Collingwood and St Kilda and we must get in to the ground early to find the best possible position. Because 1966 could be THE YEAR.

As I reach the downward slope of the footbridge and begin craning to see Ted's blond head in the waiting mob, I am most certainly not thinking of the past, or at least nothing further back in the past than that same time the previous year when the Saints were again on my mind at Grand Final time. But if someone had been conducting a survey, as various institutions and groups frequently did in the fruitful fields outside the MCG gates before a game, I suppose I could have filled up their form. Not with anything extraordinary. Just the same old story – job, marriage, births; appearances, disappearances. I was a university graduate, for example, as my father had hoped I would be. But that, I discovered, did not look as special out in the unforgiving and dispassionate world as it had from Havelock Street or dusty Noel Street.

I was the first person in my entire family ever to set foot in a university. When I set my foot, though, I met many like me. The working class was on the move and one of its great stepping stones was an Education Department studentship and a career in teaching. My parents could not have afforded to give me a university education any other way, and there were many like them. So I had my *piece of paper*, as the old man had counselled, and I was a teacher, as he had advised and hoped. As I walked across the footbridge on that day of days, I had a shoulder bag containing a packet of sandwiches, lovingly made by my wife, and several cans of beer lovingly provided by me (you could take cans into the ground in those innocent days). And if I had swung that bag in a random, wide arc through the bumping and pushing bodies around me, I would have hit at least one teacher.

Equipped with a degree and a Diploma of Education, an almost entirely worthless one-year, postgraduate course during which I, for my part, learned to drink, ride a motor bike and play a fair game of billiards, we were cast like biblical seeds across Victoria to fall upon what ground we would. Some of us discovered we could teach and some of us discovered we could not. Some of us endured, some did not. Some had breakdowns, some caused breakdowns. Some burrowed into the inner city. Some, like me, went bush. In my case, to Shepparton Technical School.

The world of the Technical School was exclusively, unashamedly and even aggressively male. At Shepparton all the staff and pupils were male and the only woman involved full time in the whole set-up was the Secretary. Staff membership of the VTU – the Victorian Teachers Union, an overwhelmingly male-run instrumentality – was solid and was made to seem more or less mandatory. The VTU in Shepparton, covering the high school, the tech and several primary schools, was heavily infiltrated by the Communist Party and involvement in it was an intensely political business. The fact that I had been finally deterred, while still a student, from joining the party by the Hungarian uprising and the Twentieth Party Congress of 1956, and was well read and opinionated in all these matters, was no advantage whatsoever. The other union organisation, the fledgling VSTA – Victorian Secondary Teachers Association – was spoken of at the Tech and among VTU members generally in the same way as one might describe the onset of the Black Plague or an outbreak of leprosy. My growing intuition that the VSTA was where I actually belonged constituted one of several causes of great angst for me in my first two years' teaching. Most of the other causes had to do with the daughters of the rich graziers in the district, any one of whom could have taken me away from all that but for some obscure reason chose not to.

My stint at Shepparton Technical School began in 1958. I went up on the train the day before school started and signed on for duty (and I mean signed on – this was in the days of the Time Book) at about eight-thirty on the first morning. I wore my charcoal-grey suit, in the inside pocket of which was my new Parker fountain pen – a Christmas gift from my parents which, by the end of the day, had completely disappeared. I never saw it again.

Not much happened on that first day, at the end of which I found myself waiting on the front verandah of the main building for the only other person I knew on the whole staff – a fellow Dip. Ed. student newly appointed like me. While I stood there amidst quite a crowd of chatting and often raucously laughing teachers, a bloke came up and said, 'Gooday.' He wore the ubiquitous grey dustcoat that was the uniform of all the teachers at Shepparton Tech except those engaged in non-dusty subjects like literature and social studies. Aged about thirty, he was one of the more senior men in the school. After affable introductions, he said, 'Up from Melbourne Uni are you?'

'Yes,' I replied, immediately suspecting trouble. The Techs were not over impressed by arty types, or universities for that matter.

'BA Dip. Ed?'

I said, 'Yes,' in a voice deepened by wariness.

'Mind if I give you a bit of advice?' he said.

'No, go ahead.'

'Be a cunt till Easter and kill your own snakes.'

Inelegant maybe, but it wasn't bad advice at that, more succinct, more accurate and far more tuned in to the truth of the world I had entered than anything I'd learnt formally in the Dip. Ed. What was also interesting about this exchange, I realised later, apart from its deadly pertinence, was his amiable and certainly respectful assumption that my teacher training, as distinct from whatever might have been my intellectual training, would scarcely have come near preparing me for the realities of the classroom. Though a bit on the harsh side, this assumption was largely correct. My new mentor's name was Don Walker. It was the start of a lifelong friendship and I owed a great deal to him and to another senior teacher, Jack Hennessy, for not only showing me how to survive at the Tech but also how to thrive there, how to be a teacher.

The Tech teachers were very well versed in their particular disciplines and by and large adequately trained for the task of teaching, though there were gaps and exceptions of some significance. Wherever inadequate or insufficient pedagogical skill became a problem, however, they simply became enforcers. Straps and canes were freely used at the tech (hence the advice about killing your own snakes – dealing with your own discipline problems on your own and in your characteristic way), and it was very difficult for a new, young teacher to resist that culture.

I ran with it uneasily for a while but gave up corporal punishment forever after I overheard, from an office at the back of the classroom where I was spending a free period, the following scene involving one of my colleagues, a maths teacher, who was regularly slaughtered by every class he confronted:

Having encountered yet again a widespread outbreak of intransigence, he advances down the aisle, strap at the ready, towards the ringleader, a tough little Caledonian delinquent from Dhurrungile, a nearby home for youthful Scottish outcasts.

'Put your hand out!' says the teacher.

'No!' says this grinning and recalcitrant Pict.

'*Put your hand out!*'

'No!'

'This is your last chance – put your hand out!'

'No!'

'All right – all right – ' a long, sinister pause ' – *don't* then!'

Huge uproar, whistles, hoots of triumph, applause and murderously accurate mimicry ('*Don't* then, *Don't* then, *Don't* then . . .').

I felt sorry for the teacher, but determined not to let the same thing happen to me. I decided that if I could not win the kids over by being interesting and humane (assuming I could manage to achieve or counterfeit both these challenging characteristics), then the game was not worth the candle. I began to ponder then and continued to do so for the whole time that I was a teacher, whether you could ever truly train a teacher to do the job of teaching children. I wanted to prove that it could be done, but time and time again I was confounded by the question of innate natural talent. Some people seemed naturally to be teachers; others, no matter how heavily invested with training and incentive, seemed inevitably not to be. Failure to resolve this issue was one of the influences, I decided, which continually prevented teaching from assuming its rightful place as a profession alongside medicine and the law.

Ted emerges from the restless ranks thronging at the bottom of the footbridge and we join the long, multicoloured columns of hopefuls heading towards the fabled stadium, the 'home of footy'. A roar swells from the grandstands and terraces – some minor sensation has stirred those of the crowd already inside and paying intermittent attention to the preliminary game between the junior teams. We quicken our pace. We need to get in there. We have, after all, only standing-room tickets.

CHAPTER 17

The First Quarter

As I watch the Saints take the ball away from the first bounce of that 1966 Grand Final and head for goal, I have a lightning vision, almost a feeling more than a mind's eye shot, of all those times I had seen them fail, or heard of them failing, or knew with dread that they were going to fail. I think briefly of that ghastly Lightning Premiership day as Collingwood repel the Saints' opening sally and attack in their turn, and then . . .

Nineteen fifty-five flickers an instant in my head, uninvited exemplar of one of the Saints' truly awful years. I was tackling my second year at university following an undistinguished scrape-through in the first. My analysis of my academic position was that I would have to work even harder. Hours and hours of obviously ineffective study had brought me to the brink of ruin in 1954 so the obvious answer was to put in even more hours. It did not occur to me that another equally obvious answer was that I might need, by some means or other, to deepen my actual understanding of the pages blurring before my midnight eyes. My only recreation throughout that year of 'harder work' was to follow the Saints on Saturdays. I would go on my own, because my father was still working weekends on our house or helping his mates build theirs, but would often meet Stanny at the Junction Oval and, anyway, there were various hapless *habitués* of St Kilda games whom one came to know in rain or shine and serial, uninterrupted defeat. So I was rarely lonely – just disappointed.

That season consisted of eighteen games, of which I saw seventeen. St Kilda lost seventeen and won one – the only one I couldn't go to.

I enjoyed university, but the figure I see as I look back at myself now looks a bit dogged, unimaginative, immured in the library or stuck at my desk at home – a desk my father had built for me by converting an old table he came across somewhere – not taking much advantage of freedoms and diversities I thought I had been longing for during my last year at De La Salle. But perhaps it had something to do with performance.

After another stagger-through result at the end of 1955, I suddenly went berserk in 1956, my final degree-year. For some reason, no doubt hormonal or something, I felt and in fact was thoroughly on top of everything. I must have become uncharacteristically cocky if the incident I recall most of all from that year is anything to go by.

One cold May afternoon, I was walking along the top floor corridor of the Old Arts Building at the University of Melbourne (which was then the only university in

Melbourne). The Old Arts Building was called 'The Old Arts Building' even though there was at the time no *new* Arts Building. This is known as 'university tradition'. Anyway, there I was, a final-year Arts student, meandering along the corridor between its railway-station-brown walls, past a succession of nineteenth-century classrooms and fusty, small staff offices – small offices, fusty staff. As I walked along, I was whistling, and rather tunefully too because I am one of those people who can really whistle. I was whistling a tune from the musical *Kismet*, which was playing in Melbourne at the time with Hayes Gordon in the leading role. The reason I was favouring *Kismet* was that I had recently, at ruinous expense, taken a girl of my acquaintance, a fellow student, to see this show. Her name was Marie. Against evidence to the contrary that anyone else would have perceived instantly and without even a ghost of indecision, I entertained high hopes for this relationship – to use a word we *never* used then. In the second half of the 1950s, having high hopes of a relationship meant that we would have endless cups of coffee together, go out a bit, and eventually, tentatively and with a massive restraint that cannot have been good for us, fleetingly kiss. After which I would be emboldened to take her to yet another cripplingly expensive extravaganza and thus conduct the affair into its next stage. Ah! They were the good old days.

Although it is not important for this story, I can record that I did get a little bit further before disaster struck. The object of my passion daringly suggested that, for some celebratory reason I now forget, we should have dinner at the Windsor Hotel. It was and probably in certain establishment ways still is Melbourne's poshest hotel, the haunt of prime ministers and other notorieties. This fabulous experience was wasted on me, a working-class boy from St Kilda. Most of the time I was worrying about which of the several dozen pieces of cutlery I should choose, to prod, scoop or carve the mysterious platefuls of flora and fauna in front of me – some of which I discovered, too late, were mere decorations not meant for human consumption. When I was not worrying about that, I was mentally trying to guess the price of our choices since the Windsor Hotel menu delicately refrained from mentioning anything so undignified as money.

Imagine my distress when, some weeks later, after these dedicated efforts to demonstrate both my ardour and urbanity, Marie suddenly announced her engagement to a League footballer – from the Melbourne Football Club, to make matters worse. In a blinding flash I realised why she had only ever been able to see me on Tuesdays and Thursdays. They were the football training nights in the good old days.

Anyway, still innocent of all this, and having taken her to the theatre the night before, I was whistling the tune from *Kismet* on that fateful day in September as I walked along the top corridor of the Old Arts Building at Melbourne University. Suddenly, my tunefulness was interrupted by a deep, gruff voice.

'Stop that whistling,' it said.

The speaker was a very tall bloke, scruffily dressed, with tightly crinkled grey hair. Recovering from my surprise, I said, 'Why? Why should I?'

'Because,' he said, 'it disturbs people doing their university work.'

I told him with a vigour I would regret that I thought

this was the most arrant nonsense; it wasn't disturbing anybody and in any case this was a university not a high school. Who did he think he was anyway?

'I am the Dean of the Faculty of Arts,' he said, going a rather deep reddish-purple colour.

'And I'm President Eisenhower,' I replied wittily, naming the American leader of the day.

There is an explanation for the confidence – cockiness? – with which I was handling this apparently academic encounter. I reckoned I knew exactly who – or rather what – this bloke was. Every now and then in those days, old lags, derelicts, drunks and tramps would wander into the grounds of Melbourne University from the surrounding parks and drink their port on the lawns from bottles wrapped in brown paper bags. Many of them were articulate and educated but had fallen on bad times. My mate Ray Tynan and I had actually arranged for one of these nomads to give a talk in the Public Lecture Theatre. Several conversations with him had established that he was obsessed with the Perón regime in Argentina, so we advertised a day and an hour and were pleased with the modest crowd that turned up. The talk itself was less pleasing, being a rambling but at times graphic account of how our man imagined the sex life of Eva Perón. There was a good deal of rich fantasy and it was less and less clear whether Eva Perón had actually done these things or whether they were activities he himself would have liked to try out on her, or on any woman who would hold still. It was a bit of a disaster and we narrowly escaped disciplinary action.

Here, I was sure, standing in front of me pretending to be the Dean, was one of those bibulous visitors. And that was another thing in my favour: I *knew* who the

Dean of Arts was. It was Professor A.R. Chisholm. Professor Chisholm had the depressing task of trying to teach me French, so I knew him well. And in any case, Chisholm, far from being tall, was a very short bloke. So no worries.

After I had said I was President Eisenhower, he had a sort of seizure before recovering himself and asking me my name. At this point I made what I later realised was a serious error: I told him.

An hour or so after this, I ran into Ray and described this strange encounter to him. Acting very casual and unconcerned, I checked with him that Professor Chisholm *was* still Dean of Arts. No, he wasn't, his term had ended and he had been replaced by Professor Hunt – a very good bloke, Ray added. Ray was a member of Professor Hunt's Latin class and knew him well. And then I asked with even greater casualness, so casual that I was practically falling asleep standing up, what Hunt looked like.

'Very tall,' said Ray remorselessly, glimpsing already where we were headed and loving it, 'deep rough voice, crinkly grey hair, dresses like a down-and-out.'

I then became so casual, I had to sit down and have one of the Craven A cigarettes which in those days I affected as a sign of sophistication and to solve the problem of what to do with the hands when under social stress.

A few days later, I received this letter:

Dear Mr Matthews

You are required to make an appointment to see me not later than next Wednesday, May 9.

Yours faithfully
H.A.K. Hunt
Dean of the Faculty of Arts

When I arrived at his office in a borrowed suit the secretaries all looked out to catch a glimpse of the madman who had made their boss speechless with rage.

'What's the matter?' I said to one of them. 'Am I *that* notorious?'

'Brother,' said his personal assistant, 'are you notorious! He's talked of no one else for days. You are *for* it.'

He had examined my record practically back to my baptism, and I of course did the only thing available to me: I apologised, assuring him that I was not in the habit of insulting Deans, though I did not go on to explain that I had mistaken him for a drunken derelict.

After which he gave me a sherry, we had a chat and parted with mutual expressions of friendly satisfaction.

When I graduated early the following year, I had to go up on the stage and receive my certificate from the Dean of the Faculty of Arts, Professor Hunt. As I took the scroll from him, he gave me a slow, uncharacteristic wink. Later, when I was having afternoon tea with my proud parents, along with all the other graduates and *their* proud parents, Professor Hunt came over to us and asked to be introduced. When the formalities were done, he said in those well-remembered deep tones: 'Congratulations, Mr Matthews. I must confess there was a time when I thought you wouldn't make it.'

It's 1966. Darryl Baldock, the St Kilda captain, and 'Cowboy' Neale goal in the first five minutes and the

Saints get the jump on Collingwood. But Waters and Kevin Rose are in commanding touch for the Pies and, when the quarter becomes an arm-wrestle, it is the Maggies who break the nexus with two goals. The tackling is ferocious, the kicking hurried and often off the mark, but the play rushes up and down the ground in surging sweeps of skill, luck and ricochet. The noise is deafening, the tension unendurable, a goal umpire is rolled over in a mêlée under the posts and has to receive attention, and then it is quarter time and the Saints are four points in front.

'They've let 'em back in,' Ted says, handing me a can with the expression of a Presbyterian elder about to pay out on an adulterer.

'No one's quarter,' I say, calm, philosophical, the sage among a surf of emotion. 'But Bingley's shut Tuddenham up.' It is all I can do not to add 'just as I told you he would' but from the suffering look of him, Ted would be hard to impress even if you predicted the imminent outbreak of the third world war. The siren sounds. The teams have changed ends. Umpire Geoff Crouch holds the ball up. There is something both tragic and ironic about the fact that St Kilda, who have never won a flag and whose visits to the MCG in September have been so rare, are playing in their second consecutive finals series and yet are haunted by a horrible loss in 1965. The siren sounds again and Umpire Crouch moves in to bounce the ball. Three quarters left in which to be made or broken, three quarters remaining to make up for last year.

CHAPTER 18

The Second Quarter

Last year. Towards the end of that season, 1965, the Saints were on top and looked like staying there.

'How would you like to go to the whole finals series,' my father said one day in early August. 'I reckon they'll go the distance this year. I'll shout you.' So we went, enjoying the cool objectivity with which we could observe, from the excellent reserved seats the old man had arranged for us, Essendon knock out Geelong in the first semi-final. Then dying a thousand deaths as the Saints scraped in by one point from Collingwood in the second semi and thus assured themselves of a shot at the Premiership.

There we were at last, the old man and me, together at a Saints Grand Final. There we were side by side at the game that could make it THE YEAR. All the false hopes of long ago – the run of wins in 1950, the spurts and brief triumphs that had come to nothing in season after season, the 'wooden spoons', my treachery that time I clapped a Carlton player on the back – all seemed about to be redeemed.

In a drab match, the Saints looked flat and clueless against a robotic, clinical opposition, and they lost by thirty-five points. As coach Allan Jeans later admitted, they hadn't really known how to go about the occasion – it was, after all, fifty-three years since their only other appearance in a grand final and the 'race memory' of that occasion had worn very thin. A team meeting at Allan Jeans' house on the eve of the game was, he himself admitted, a serious error. Full of anticipation, nerves, dread, elation and adrenalin, they went over and over how the Grand Final afternoon might go until their heads were full of it. That intense session, added to a disturbed or, for some players, sleepless night, meant that by the time they ran on to the field they were, as Baldock observed, so mentally tired they could hardly wait to get the whole thing over with. And they looked like it.

All of Melbourne (apart from Essendon) grieved. And so did I. And so did my old man. Which made it the more puzzling that he had shown no interest now the Saints were back in contention in 1966. Because when Ted produced his two standing-room tickets in the pub a few days before the game, he was planning a master stroke.

'Where did you come by those?' I asked him in some awe.

'We have our methods,' he said, tapping his right nostril with the right index finger. 'One's for you and one's for your old man.'

From long association with me and my family, Ted understood the place occupied in the Matthews psyche by St Kilda and its notorious football team. This handing over of a ticket he could have kept for himself was an act of extraordinary and touching philanthropy.

But, to my amazement, when I phoned my father with the news, he knocked back the offer. Rather ungraciously, I thought. He said he didn't want to stand for the whole afternoon being buffeted by a huge crowd.

'You've spent half your life standing at St Kilda games,' I said, incredulous. 'And they might *win* this one. This might be THE YEAR.' But he was unmoved. There was a depressed note, a resigned quality to his refusal of the ticket that vaguely disturbed me at the time. Much later, when I eventually understood what was going on, what lay behind his refusal, I would deeply regret not having paid more attention. But I wouldn't work that out for some time.

'You're not letting last year put you off, are you?' I said. A last ditch effort. No, he was not letting last year put him off. He did not wish to stand all afternoon at the MCG. That was that.

He was fifty-six years old, lean, muscular, a veteran of years of tough, demanding hours on his feet. Why didn't he want to stand?

One minute thirty-one seconds into the second quarter the Saints score their third goal. Gabelich quickly gets one back for the Pies, Griffiths scores again for St Kilda – and so it goes, a wonderful point-counterpoint unfolding, more fluid and purposeful than in the nervous opening quarter, with advantage bestowed now on one now on the other, slender margins become dangerous breaks only to be erased again in minutes, players float into the air, smash through defences, rake the arena with long kicks and move the crowd to gusty gasps with mis-kicks. St Kilda's Ian Stewart out-generals everyone in the centre, but Terry Waters is impassable on the Collingwood back line. And when the half-way mark arrives and the players walk off the ground puffing, heads bowed, hands on hips, there is only one point in it – Collingwood's way.

'This is not going to be an easy afternoon,' says Ted. I for my part am, for the moment, speechless. We have a beer. The old bloke next to me, whose afternoon has been a mixture of anguished agitation and alcoholic exhilaration, says to me, 'I think it's goin' ter be the same old story, mate. The same old story.'

'You never know,' I say to him, with much more of an amiable smile in my voice than I really feel, 'you just never know.'

The half-time crowd begins its ponderous advances and retreats and pincer movements in search of pies, beer, toilets and general relief, and we turn, the three of us, as if under direction from some orchestral conductor, to stare at the scoreboard towering up behind us.

	Goals	Behinds	Points
Collingwood	5	7	37
St Kilda	5	6	36

Which, all things considered, tells us nothing.

CHAPTER 19

Half-Time

A few years before these epochal events at the MCG, the political and professional tumult in the secondary education system in Victoria was not only fostering in me career misgivings that I was for the time being vigorously suppressing, it was also convincing me that I should at least equip myself to do something else. This was in itself a monstrous and radical thought for me, because part of the acceptance of 'the piece of paper' and its lifetime of security was that you did not change your job like a flibbertigibbet, you stayed on, advanced, prospered and retired.

I had not been able to take up any of the postgraduate offers at the triumphant end of my Arts degree because I was bonded to the Education Department and committed to take the hapless Diploma of Education and then to teach for three years. But it had occurred to me, round about 1964, that the offers or some of them might still be open. So I rang Vincent Buckley, whose last words to me before I disappeared into the maw of the Education Department, had been, 'If you ever decide to have a shot at an MA, come and have a yarn.' Buckley was a charismatic teacher, an exciting intellectual, a fine poet and a great nurturer of diffident or hesitant student talent. Controversial for his political, literary and religious stances, he had a large circle of loyal friends and a further penumbra of solid supporters. His denigrators, however, were probably almost equal in number, though a lot of them tended to be of the pop-out-of-the-woodwork variety, according to whatever issue was in contention. As an undergraduate, I had admired his meticulous preparation and brilliant expositions as well as his obvious dedication to the profession of university teacher. I had also admired, in so far as I had been able to glimpse them, his larrikin tendencies and anarchic informality on selected occasions. These characteristics amounted to much more than, but certainly included, his reputation, in the 1960s, as a significant drinker when moved to it. In any case, he always gave me the impression that he had thought out what it was he was doing in a university and why he was doing it. This appealed to someone who was endlessly and without resolution rehearsing the problems in schools of training versus natural talent, of whether true professionalism could ever be achieved without rigorous qualification standards.

So, with much trepidation and a telephone style that took me all the way back to that day when I announced to some bureaucrat on the other end of the line, 'I am a boy,' I rang him and made an appointment. 'Think about two or three topics you're interested in, mate,' he said, 'and we'll see where that gets us.'

At the appointed time, I wavered outside Buckley's door in the Old Arts Building, not too far away from the corridor in which I had affronted Professor Hunt nearly a decade earlier, and finally knocked.

'Have a seat, mate. Good to see you.'

As I sat down opposite him, I was enveloped briefly by the silence of books. Packed and unruly shelves of them more or less surrounded us, and where there were no books there were paintings – an extraordinary Dali *Crucifixion*, a Leonard French mandala. I thought to myself how pleasant and inspiriting it would be to have an office with books.

We chatted a bit and then he asked me what topics I had brought along for discussion. I had approached this task with deadly seriousness, believing that the fields I evinced interest in would need to be pukka, beyond reproach as serious, proper literary endeavours. So I started with my interest in the early Tennyson. This was a genuine preoccupation which I had developed years earlier during my undergraduate degree and had pursued in a dilettantish way since. When I was reasonably well launched on my spiel about the early Tennyson and what hypotheses I might consider in relation to him, Buckley interrupted.

'I wouldn't worry about Tennyson, mate.'

'No?'

'No. What's your next one?'

My next provisional topic, somewhat less genuinely of interest to me, was the influence of Darwinian theory on certain nineteenth-century poets. As I began to expand on the influences and the poets in question, Buckley said, 'I wouldn't worry about Darwinism, mate.'

'No?'

'No. What else have you got?'

'Well,' I paused as if in thought but in fact consumed by advancing embarrassment – I had gambled on our never arriving at this moment. 'Well, you said to work out three topics, but actually I've really only thought of two.'

'Very good,' Buckley said, sitting back in his chair and looking as if I'd just passed some test with honours and accolades. 'I reckon you ought to write on Henry Lawson.'

I was staggered – and delighted. Nothing would suit me better, but I had assumed Lawson was absolutely beyond the pale – vernacular, untutored, *Australian*. This episode was typical of Buckley. He was a wonderful mentor and staunch friend to many students but certainly to working-class, Celtic-looking kids who wandered round the university in their early undergraduate years clearly unable to differentiate their arse from their elbow and yet having something or other to offer the intellectual community if given the merest glance of encouragement. It was also typical in another way. He was one of the pioneers of Australian literature study in the university. To suggest Lawson as the proper focus for an MA was maverick, courageous and exciting.

It was, anyway, a big moment which changed the direction, quality and purpose of my life ever after. It was also the start of a marvellous, occasionally stormy but always close and inspiring friendship. We argued and disagreed and agreed about many things, but on one point we were beyond any dream of reconciliation: Vin barracked for Collingwood.

CHAPTER 20

The Third Quarter

The Pies look disturbingly fresh and ready as they bound back on to the arena after half time in the 1966 Grand Final. Are the Saints looking a little stunned? Dispirited? Have they given their best already – or is that just the gloomy insight of someone who has seen generations of their supporters streaming away grim-faced from the old Junction Oval, heading back into the labyrinths of St Kilda with another loss under their belt and a deeper conviction that St Kilda – its team, the place, the idea, its history and the saint himself whoever he was – was the subject of an unshakable curse?

But not in that third quarter on 24 September 1966. It is a blinder. It is the Premiership quarter, as the cliché has it. Both sides make a furious attempt to steal the game. The Saints do it brilliantly for most of the quarter, despite some atrocious kicking. In the bright afternoon sun under a cloudless sky, the no-nonsense black and white of the Magpies and the red, white and black of the Saints strobe up and down the ground and round the flanks taunted by the gleaming reddish football – its float, its rebound, its languorous wafting when you least expect it, its pestilential bounce now true now defying physics, its agonising out-of-reach-ness, its torpedoing range. Such a simple game: we have the ball, or they have the ball, or there it is running free. Yet such exhausting gyrations, bursts of speed, sudden stops and reversings, desperate fingertip lungings for the simple aim of possession. The Saints do it all, they never let up, they hammer at the goals and repulse the 'Woods, who glide back through the defenders and refuse to be dominated and sitting shots are missed and impossible goals kicked. But after all that, at three-quarter time, there are only four points in it – St Kilda's way.

A hundred-thousand-strong sigh rolls round the stadium as the players sink to the grass in their team groups to be addressed for the last time in 1966 by their coaches. Allan Jeans looks grim, but he usually does. He is clutching a rolled-up sheaf of paper, which he waves to emphasise and to point at one goal or the other. Bob Rose, the iconic, favoured-son Collingwood coach, bends to talk now to this one now to that one before straightening up and calling all the players close in. Papers and streamers swirl across the goal fronts. A buzz like an anger of bees drifts from the bars where the state of the game is being canvassed, weighed, questioned and above all imbibed. I realise I have completely forgotten my sandwiches. I offer Ted one.

'Specially made and packed,' I tell him. 'I don't think

it would be a good idea to take them home unopened. Wives aren't keen on that.'

We met, my wife and I, at a party in 1961, just after I had returned from Shepparton to work in the city. In the crowd, most of whom I didn't know, she drew my attention. She was slim, dark, very tanned, slightly taller than average. Her hair was pulled too severely back from her forehead and beneath unplucked, black arching brows she had the most haunting eyes I had ever seen. I saw her laugh often, yet it struck me that there was something inherently sad about her, certainly something mysterious. At about the three and a half hour mark of the evening, I noticed she was on the periphery of a small, animated group but not for the moment taking much part. I joined them then, circling round, I stood so that she was between me and the others.

'I'll come round here to include you,' I said.

'Thank you.'

Within fifteen minutes, we had established that we were the same age, give or take a month or two; that she was from England and was working in the operating theatre of the Albury Base Hospital and was in Melbourne for a holiday; that we both liked jazz and the Goon Show and Tchaikovsky; that she would be prepared to consider Sibelius, but had her doubts; that, yes, it would be nice to go out for dinner before she returned to New South Wales; and that, yes, she could make it on the following Thursday.

This smiling, mysterious stranger was from East Anglia and she was born in a place called March in the month of March, an extraordinary omen of beneficent congruence if ever I had heard one. Good old East Anglia. Blessed month of March. Wonderful *town* of March (in reality, much less than wonderful, its only distinction being the size of its railway marshalling yards). Fenlands forever.

I rang her every day until we met again to go out to dinner. When she returned to Albury, I took her to Spencer Street Railway Station and farewelled her. We kissed for long minutes on the platform and it was I, not she, who finally gave in to convention and urged her on to the train. We wrote to each other every day until I could manage to visit her in Albury where we spent three agonising days on the edge of consummation. Then we wrote to each other every day until she resigned her Albury job and came to Melbourne where she worked in the operating theatre of the Jessie McPherson Hospital. We would meet most nights and every weekend and talk often on the phone. Until one night late in November, as we sat in my reconditioned FX Holden, I asked her with the minimum of elegance and eloquence if she would marry me and she said, 'Yes,' and then, as if giving it further thought, 'Oh, yes.'

And so, six months after we met, we were engaged; eight months later we married.

So, as I stood with Ted on that last Saturday of September 1966, bracing myself like the other hundred and one thousand people for what was clearly going to be a scarifying last quarter, I was the father of two children with a third due in November, a less and less convinced member of the teaching profession but studying my way out of it, and a Saints supporter from as far back as memory would take me, a supporter who on this afternoon might be on the brink of glory and illumination.

CHAPTER 21

The Year – At Last

Chasing glory, the Saints start the last quarter with a sensational running goal from Moran to take a ten-point lead then squander a succession of opportunities to put the whole thing out of Collingwood's reach. The Pies fight back, as we know with dread they will, and Tuddenham, the seven-goal *bête noire* of that earlier semi-final, bounces a long shot through. Another one from Collingwood forward, Ian Graham, and the difference is back to one point till 'Cowboy' Neale kicks his fifth and it's seven points again, with about fifteen minutes left. The old bloke next to me is riding every kick and tensing with every tackle so that we are bumping and shepherding each other as if we are out on the ground. Perhaps my old man was right to give this the miss, I think . . .

*

I had managed to arrange with the Education Department, notoriously parsimonious in matters involving intellectual improvement on the part of its teaching staff, a day off each week to work on Lawson for my MA. Every month or so, I would take a chapter to Vin Buckley and we would discuss it and plan the next move. Sometimes our planning session would be adjourned to University House where we would take in quantities of drink and go on somewhere into Carlton for the singing of Irish songs. In June 1966 I was awarded a university research grant to go to the Mitchell Library in Sydney and to Bourke and environs on the trail of Lawson's one substantial sojourn in the outback in 1892–93.

This was to be a trip of about ten days. My mother arranged to move in with my wife and the family while I was away. Since our disappointed assault on the 1965 footy finals, my old man and I had of course seen plenty of each other, but there was some restraint working even then that I did not quite understand. A distance, a coldness, the like of which I had never before encountered with him. I knew that this was partly to do with my political activities in the VSTA, and especially my support of strike action and my position as an organiser of the strike at my school. Relations between us were also beginning to feel the heat of the rapidly growing controversy over US policy in Vietnam and the attitude of the Australian government. Being much in contact with university circles, I was involved in these debates and vocal about where I stood. The old man had gone a bit to the right as his planned retirement, at sixty, came closer and his circumstances improved. He was on edge when he found himself disagreeing with me on the

Vietnam question and other issues that almost invariably arose now when we met.

For my part, I was slow to realise and then to accept that his views, his whole orientation, might have been undergoing a change as he and my mother, for the first time in more than thirty years, settled down to live their own lives with each other, free of debt, pressures and family. But even aside from argument and opposing views, even if these were for the moment ignored, he still seemed to me to have lost much more of his old dynamism than could be explained simply by being in his mid-fifties. And his geniality seemed to have evaporated to be replaced by a too often surfacing and too easily triggered irritability.

So when I told him about the research grant and where I was going with it, I think he expected me to say that I would invite Ted or Ray along. When I invited him, his delight was touching and then rather overwhelming.

'If you're sure . . .' he stumbled and, when convinced of my certainty and that I was not making some awful filial sacrifice, 'That would be bloody terrific, mate. Listen, we could drive, take the car, do a bit of a tour.'

I had actually never quite worked out exactly how I would make this trip. The grant would not run to airfares and I was vaguely thinking of the train. Lawson, after all, had been given five pounds and a rail ticket by Archibald, the editor of the Sydney *Bulletin*, when he made the journey I wanted now to duplicate. But travelling by car would be ideal, more pleasant, more flexible, cheaper. 'The car' in question was that only new one my father ever owned, a Volkswagen – he refused to have anything to do with Japanese cars and for some reason I don't remember he was not an admirer of the Holden.

It was a splendid coup, which brought us back very close together (although I think we both exaggerated the degree to which we might have been estranged).

Our swing through far western New South Wales was relaxing, dramatic and instructive all at once. We arrived in Bourke in the worst drought since the one that so appalled Lawson in 1892–93. Old timers there could speak of nothing else as they gazed hopelessly at the flawless blue sky where no cloud of any importance had been glimpsed in a couple of seasons. The sheep on the 'long paddock' were reduced to eating the roly-polies bowling along the dusty roads in the hot wind. Disaster was imminent and you could see why Lawson, in another and tougher age, would have been horrified.

We stayed in one of Bourke's several pubs and, after a day on the Lawson trail, we would have a beer in a different one each evening. On one of these visits we were in a riotous, rough-and-tumble sort of bar, standing out of the way at one end of it. My father was leaning against the brick wall and I was facing him, with the whole of the bar and its tumult behind me. Suddenly, I was whacked on the shoulder by what felt like a piece of railway sleeper and then swung round. Facing me was a bloke about two inches shorter than me but several feet wider and with no neck to speak of. Wearing shorts and a blue singlet and 'lastic-sided boots, he was several axe-handles across the chest and was in general built like the proverbial brick shithouse.

'Okay, Bluey,' he said, grinning with utter friendliness, 'you look like y'could go a bit. What about we find out?'

No need to explain that he would have ended the experiment with one blow, but his mate ambled over at this point and grabbed him by one huge arm.

'Come on, Charlie, for Chris' sake, just let's have a drink without the fight. Just this fuckin' once.'

He turned to me and the old man. 'Sorry boys, the bastard can't help himself when he's on the turps.'

And so I lived not to fight another day.

Then, back in Sydney, there were our hours in the sepulchral quiet of the old Mitchell Library, during which my father, under my instruction, would transcribe sections for me from various Lawsonian manuscripts, beautifully rendering the text in his own draughtsman's copperplate while faithfully reproducing various of Lawson's editorial quirks – the curlicues on certain letters, the full stop enclosed in a circle. In some transcriptions, he actually copied Lawson's handwriting, producing something that was often almost indistinguishable from the original, so that I took home with me vivid reminders of Lawson's laborious hand at a time when photocopying that material was not allowed.

In Sydney, we stayed in a much more salubrious place, a motel near the Cross, and we would walk to and from the Mitchell Library each day. One night, having stayed at the library quite late and then gone for a beer somewhere, we were walking back up the William Street hill towards the Cross when the old man stopped outside one of those car show rooms and peered in at – whatever they were, I can't remember now. But Jaguars, perhaps, or Mercedes, something of that elite order. I kept on walking, but he called out to me to 'hang on', so I went back.

'You can't afford 'em,' I said, scanning the polished sweep and curve of automobile luxury and extravagance. He muttered something, but kept looking. I became impatient and walked off again, but I had to wait several minutes until at last he turned away and slowly caught up.

'Since when have you been interested in that sort of stuff?'

He did not answer, and we walked on. It was a curious incident, though, and precisely because it was so odd, so out of character – usually he was corrosive about such cars and dismissive of their owners – it stuck, buried and out of reach in my mind . . .

Until the moment, three months later, when Collingwood's Max Pitt, with only minutes left in the game, kicks a monstrous goal from seventy yards out. This catastrophe causes the old bloke next to me to shirtfront me near enough in his anxiety and I think, fleetingly, in the midst of my own rampaging anxiety, how does this old codger, seventy if he's a day, stay on his pins in these conditions, if my father, younger and fitter, was worried about it?

And then I see it all. My father hadn't been interested in the cars that night in Sydney. He was stopping for a rest and he didn't want me to know because there was something wrong more serious than merely being a bit puffed. Other small incidents – his reference to taking a break on the park bench on his way from the station after work, for example, when he had been ordinarily a ferocious, tireless walker. His irritability. His apparent lack of interest in this 1966 Grand Final, the game he had been looking for all his St Kilda-following life. I cannot work it out further than that in the roaring, grandstand-bursting next few seconds during which Tuddenham cannonades out of the centre after Pitt's goal and has a long shot which rolls through for a behind. The scores are level, with a minute or so to go. 10-13 73 each. Dropping with exhaustion, every player on the ground, regardless of allegiance, looks horrified.

But later I would check on all this and confirm that he was ill and depressed about it, that he had arteriosclerosis, that it was serious and might worsen. He had to give up the smokes and this made him unbearable and anyway he didn't manage it. His legs hurt and, with that fate which is reserved for all of us when we are most vulnerable, he encountered at just this time a period of taxing stress and difficulty at work. Less than two years after that famous game that heralded THE YEAR, the game that he refused to attend because his legs hurt and he couldn't stand, my father had a stroke.

Collingwood attacks again and Hutchesson has a hurried shot but misses everything. The Saints struggle the ball round the wing. Payze rises into the air to take a phenomenal mark on the flank and kicks into the St Kilda forward line where a huge pack descends on the ball. From the bounce, Cooper's scrambled kick drops towards Collingwood's Potter but eight or nine players rush him and Crouch signals another bounce. This time the ball slews from the punching fists of the ruckmen and Barry Breen grabs it and slams it awkwardly on his boot. High in the air the ballooning kick floats towards the goals and the world stops. The erratically spinning ball bounces high from clear ground on which players converge from everywhere, but too late and the leather shines in the level sun before the ball drops again into the shadow, seeming to hang in defiance of gravity before – slipping in past the behind post.

The Saints are one point in front. There can't be more than a minute left.

After the kick-out, Waters marks (yet again), runs right across the goal (a radical manoeuvre almost unheard of in those days) to kick to the southern-stand side where Tuddenham – bloody Tuddenham – gathers in the ball with the whole outer wing empty in front of him. But he decides to kick instead of run. Perhaps he thought the clock would beat him if he tried to run, and perhaps it would have at that. There are only instants left when Bob Murray marks Tuddenham's typically enormous kick and sends it back. The ball is dropping towards players on the Collingwood forward flank when *the siren sounds.*

The Saints have won the 1966 Premiership by one point.

By the skin of its teeth, THE YEAR has arrived!

The old bloke grabs me in a hug. Says, 'By Christ, they've done it! They've done it and I saw it all!' Ted just stands there, beaming at the ground and the St Kilda players mobbing their coach, saying over and over, 'You fucking beauty!'

In a pub much later, I came across a drunk who was attempting to focus on the television replay. He was watching those last few minutes and, when Tuddenham swooped on Waters' kick and turned for home, the drunk said, 'Look at that, I reckon the 'Woods'll get up this time.'

All over Melbourne celebrations erupted, horns blew, people sang in the streets, pubs filled up and the drinkers swayed out on to footpaths and roadways. St Kilda itself was a blaze of light, flags and streamers. Those always apologetically lukewarm denizens, whose lives were too busy, complicated, criminal or cosmopolitan to endure the agony of a whole season's loyalty, now flocked into their sleazy byways and dark lanes and sinister streets to claim kin with the team that had broken a thousand hearts.

One of St Kilda's best players in the Grand Final had been Brian Sierakowski, son of the publican at the Brighton Club Hotel, to which my father had taken me for my first official and legal drink – that same pub to which the Coppers and the Davises had daily adjourned in the days when Noel Street was a Test match pitch and a roadway that went nowhere. On this night of nights, the whole team ended up at Sierakowski's and could scarcely be removed. Committed to playing in Adelaide on the following Saturday against the South Australian premiers, the Saints did not make it and poor, battered and disillusioned Collingwood did the right thing and filled in. Not a dignified thing for the Saints to do, but when you had waited as long as they had, well, to hell with Adelaide.

PART THREE

Recessional

We must act the play out and live
misfortune down . . .

CHARLES DICKENS, *David Copperfield*

CHAPTER 22

Getting It Wrong

Well, to hell with Adelaide, indeed, but what was good for the St Kilda football team was not this time also good for me. Rather than dismiss Adelaide, I was about to embrace it. With my MA well advanced, I managed to get a job at Flinders University. We were bound for South Australia early in 1967. To my 'pieces of paper' I was now about to add 'a room with books'.

But that final siren, which had at last rung in THE YEAR, brought nothing else that was good. Within weeks, I had the confrontation with my father that had been looming. Undoubtedly, it took momentum on his side from the fact that he just was not feeling well. He hated to be ill, had rarely lost a day through sickness and was magisterially impatient of constraints imposed by incapacity. And then there was tobacco. My father was and had been since his teens a serious addict of the weed. Rolling his own for years, especially during the war, smoking long and regularly on building sites and over drawing boards, which he would carefully shield from the ash, he had taken in just about every bit of balm, illusion, debris and evil on offer from nicotine, along with every known additive and byproduct. Small concessions made to health by resorting to various filters and other nostrums scarcely altered his average and in any case came far too late. So around the time of that Grand Final, he was off the smokes for the good of his arteries and hating it. That didn't help either.

Like most such altercations, ours began for ludicrous reasons – mostly because I became annoyed at his apparently offhand attitude to the great win of the century. It had been all very well for him to enthuse over the Saints in the past – in those heady first weeks of the 1950 season, for example – but, not consciously knowing he was so sick, I felt brushed aside by what I saw as his phony detachment about an event he had been obsessed by for decades. Because he had not been there, despite having been offered the chance, he wasn't interested.

All this was too hard of me, of course, and I was not being sensitive enough to the unadmitted knowledge that had grown already far beyond a suspicion that he was not merely off colour but perhaps quite seriously ill. But that is the way these things go. Within minutes, on this day, we were on to politics and after some fiery sallies and ripostes, our discussion petered out grumpily. But did not end.

In the following year, on a visit back from Adelaide, I found myself again arguing with him – this time about the looming catastrophe of the seventies – the Vietnam commitment. Inhabiting university circles as I then was, I was full of this debate and well versed in its evolving intricacies. I remember now using the expression, at one stage of our increasingly acrimonious encounter, 'There is intransigence on both sides,' that is, on both the American and the Viet Cong sides. I had parroted this lofty announcement from a speech given at the university by Gough Whitlam. The old man simply said, 'I can't talk in that kind of language,' and then, while I was struggling to reply to this arrant piece of strategic self-deprecation, he added, as if concluding the matter beyond any further need of discussion, 'Worst thing you ever did, going to that bloody university.' We both knew he did not mean Flinders, he meant Melbourne, all those years ago, in quest of the piece of paper. A narrative which had begun with the joyous hyperbole, 'The boy's a bloody genius,' was now ending on an opposite, equally inaccurate note of sad defeat. In ten words and one disastrous moment, he seemed to be intent on smashing to pieces a part of his life's philosophy, as it had been imbued in me and made manifest by my actions and achievements. It had all been wrong. And it had all gone wrong.

But fighting with my father, something unimaginable to me until it all began, was not by any means my main preoccupation in the months between the Grand Final and the end of 1966. We were preparing for two big events – the birth of our third baby and the move to Adelaide, which we were planning for early January.

Genevieve Frances began life on 6 November 1966 as a buxom, dark-haired baby with her mother's haunting eyes. She took a brief look at our world before dying of septicaemia and meningitis, within hours of her baptism, aged twenty-one days. And, though I would have derided such an idea had it been proposed to me, that was the last time I saw my beloved wife. The woman I married died as Genevieve Frances's small white coffin was lowered into the yellow earth, already dusty and hard in an early burst of summer heat.

> ... The funeral baked meats
> Did coldly furnish forth the marriage tables.

For my wife and me, it was rather like Hamlet's observation in reverse. On that sunny baptismal-Sunday afternoon in November we returned home from the church of Blessed Oliver Plunket and crammed our laughing friends into our small rented house. We drank champagne and ate the splendid spread, the 'baked meats', that she and my mother had prepared. And we toasted Genevieve, who was peculiarly sleepy and had refused almost all nourishment since waking.

Three days later, we were all back in the whispering gloom of Blessed Oliver Plunket's where the sight of such a pathetically small, white coffin silenced even a school party who were crocodiling in for confession. And then we were surrounding the grave, shortened but deep enough, and gazing dully at a half-interested priest whom none of us knew and who was on duty that morning and whose cassock cuffs, my wife noticed, were grubby. And the hot wind blew the yellow dust in our aching eyes as Genevieve Frances Matthews entered the earth from which, the intoning priest assured us nonchalantly, she had come – but how could such a jewel come from that arid and crusty waste and why, why should she be going there?

And then we all went back to the house, yet again, and drank whatever was around, some of it left over from Sunday, to replace the words we couldn't find and repress the tears we felt we shouldn't for some reason give way to. And afterwards we all went sadly to our beds and life, in its callous way, resumed. Dawn broke, alarms sounded, jobs and commitments and appointments called. As if she had never existed. And it seemed as if she scarcely had.

It was full of the sorts of things that we somehow imagine happening only to other people, that terrible Sunday in November 1966.

Genevieve wakes us just on dawn and her mother, as she often does, brings her into our bed to change and feed her. But instead of the lusty, demanding bellow that we have become accustomed to, she seems querulous, half drugged. She shows very little interest in either breast or bottle and, when returned to her cot, goes immediately to sleep.

Knowing that people like us don't have catastrophes, we go through the morning, my wife and I, reassuring each other that it is probably just the heat. Or 'a touch of wind', as my mother suggests when she and my father arrive later in the morning. Beyond the shimmering rooftops, the bright water of Port Phillip Bay flashes randomly in the hot sun. A dry northerly blows rubbish and dust through the blinding streets and the sound of traffic on nearby main roads intensifies as people head for the beaches.

My wife and my mother prepare salads and rolls and bake little pies and make cakes and desserts. Our two bigger children run excitedly from room to room. I sweep and vacuum and potter about. My father reads the paper, pats his pockets every now and then for cigarettes and matches and sighs when he doesn't find them. And Genevieve, checked on anxiously, almost apologetically by each one of us in turn, sleeps on, not in peace but with a little moan on each expelled breath. A 'sighing respiration' the doctor will call this – a phrase I won't ever forget.

At one o'clock we are all supposed to be ready and my wife is complaining that she looks a 'bloody mess'. She is slightly overweight still. Her brow is puckered with unease under the intermittent curtaining of her long hair. The unfathomable eyes are lambent, almost feverish. She looks anything but a mess. As so often, though, she is not a calming figure. There is about her too strong a sense of depths in unreachable tumult. I have been conscious of this before, but it is only now, needled by dread and the always imminent pessimism that is my unwanted Celtic legacy, that I can express it, grasp it as a reality and not merely as a fancied aura.

We are all cheered and relieved when Genevieve shows some interest in suckling and so we set off late for the church. The vinyl car seats burn through our summer clothes, the steering wheel is untouchable and has to be doused with a wet cloth, the burning north wind rasps in the overhead wires. A pall of black smoke rises above the distant hills as bushfires fan through the gum trees volatile in their oily aura of flammable eucalyptus. My mother nurses Genevieve and tells her in a cooing voice that she's got a touch of colic.

There are several candidates for baptism on this November Sunday, and the priest becomes confused between Genevieve Frances Matthews and Francis Eric Matheson but eventually this is sorted out and Genevieve Frances renounces the Devil and all his works and submits to a dash of cool water without seeming to notice. Her fortitude is praised by all the onlookers, but my wife and I exchange a troubled glance. We would rather she galvanised her small frame into loud and spontaneous complaint (as the young Matheson duly does when his turn comes, emitting a shriek that makes all of us jump as we mill around in the porch photographing and talking).

I am slightly soothed by champagne in the middle of the celebrations back at our house, when my wife takes me quietly aside and says she thinks we should find a doctor.

It is not easy on a summery Sunday in the suburbs, but eventually we track down a locum in a clinic a few miles away. He is a young, slightly hesitant man who, I realise with a contortion of panic in my stomach, is puzzled. While he is examining our baby, a door somewhere in the clinic slams with a cacophonous CRACK in the blustering wind. Genevieve leaps visibly on the examination bed, arms and legs briefly flailing. The young doctor smiles with relief.

'Well, that's a good sign. She is very sleepy but she reacted well to that sudden noise. I think it's probably a gastric thing that's knocking her about a bit.'

He tells us what to do about possible dehydration (which my wife knows anyway), says he thinks we'll find her coming quickly back to normal, but gives us a number where we can reach him again if we feel unsure.

We return to the party, which has gone on unabated, but now quickly breaks up as we admit to the strain of the day. We subside gratefully onto chairs on the verandah after the last guest departs. It is half past six. The wind has dropped, the heat is stifling. My mother fans the baby, whose rhythmic sighing begins to torture us all. It is the evident collapse of my mother's jaunty, homespun confidence, her weatherbeaten, pleasant face raised to me in pitiable mute anxiety that finally makes me face the unthinkable.

Within the hour we have sent the other kids home with my parents and we are back in that unfamiliar clinic. The doctor, obviously shocked by the baby's deterioration and her loud, sad, sighing sleep, drives my wife and Genevieve to the Children's Hospital ('It'll take too long to get an ambulance') and I try to follow. But he travels at tremendous speed. A motorcycle cop who draws alongside obviously looking for trouble becomes his escort after a brief conversation and they disappear from my sight. Lights flicker on in streets and shops as I race through the dangerous hot dusk. When I switch off the engine in the hospital car park, the pulsing inane scream of thousands of crickets in the gardens opposite fills my head, as if to prepare me for a larger madness, a more elemental scream.

I catch up with my wife and the doctor at the lift in the foyer. Her eyes glisten. In her cradling arms Genevieve sighs on and on.

'I have a very sick child coming up in Lift Four,' the doctor says into the lift intercom and we go all the way up without a stop. Genevieve is taken from us. We wait. Around us, the hospital gradually subsides into another uneasy night.

We wait. At eleven o'clock, a pleasant-voiced young nurse offers us coffee, which we accept, but, when asked, she knows nothing about Genevieve or what is happening to her.

We wait, holding hands now and then; once, unaccountably drawing close together and kissing for a moment passionately and then guiltily drawing apart. As if to comfort each other, by whatever means, was wrong, as if we already had accepted that we were for it, the full treatment, and that nothing could save Genevieve and nothing would save us.

At about 1 a.m., a youthful-looking doctor (how young they all seem in retrospect, yet we ourselves were young) tells us evasively that Genevieve is very ill but that everything possible is being done. He seems embarrassed and we are too tired and dispirited to give him a hard time.

Perhaps we dozed then woke again to the hospital's deepest night. The boom of traffic from far below had long since ceased. There were occasional human sounds – a child crying, an amplified voice. There was the clank of a lift somewhere, a creak now and then in the ceiling, the clatter of a trolley. Corridors echoed with footsteps but they always turned out to be going somewhere else. We waited. No one came near us. No one told us anything. I thought I heard Genevieve, her 'sighing respiration', but her mother couldn't hear it and I supposed I was imagining.

At half past three, when the hospital seemed – like the bodies it enclosed – to be at its lowest ebb, we heard the distant *clack-clack* of someone approaching. These were not nurse's shoes but high heels. *Clack-clack*, *clack-clack*. It was almost ludicrous amid such awful, potent silences. The sounds came right to our waiting-room. It was Margaret, Ted's wife. She had felt worried after leaving the afternoon party and had rung my mother. She came to share our vigil. We waited. All three.

At eight o'clock that morning, shortly after Margaret had reluctantly returned home to attend to her own family, a trim, severe-looking nurse approached with a white shawl bunched up in one hand. She thrust it at my wife.

'Is this yours?'

'It's . . . it's my baby's. How is . . . ?'

'Well, I'll leave it with you.'

She walked briskly off. That was how we were allowed to guess that Genevieve was dead. We sat paralysed with grief and fear, knowing yet not knowing.

It was half an hour before a doctor arrived, by accident, it seemed, to confirm our fears. And it was only when we asked to see her for the last time that we discovered a post-mortem had already been carried out and that, therefore, she was scarcely viewable.

Months later, after thinking about it often and feeling more and more disturbed for him, we wrote to the young locum who had driven Genevieve to the hospital. We wanted to tell him we held no grudge, harboured no sense of grievance. It was possible he had blamed himself for delaying. We were not absolutely certain of his name but felt we were close enough to ensure that the letter finally would reach him. Anyway, no one – not him, not anyone – ever replied. It was as if he had never existed, as if our letter, long delayed, had never been written after all.

The most dignified and memorable gesture of that sorry time was made by an old man clipping his cypress hedge. He must have glimpsed the funeral cortege approaching along his street. Though poised quite high up on a ladder, he turned awkwardly around, took off his grey felt hat, held it to his heart, and stood to a sort of attention on the rungs to salute the unknown and passing dead. He was portly, probably about seventy years old and looked not unlike Pop Matthews, even down to the smokeless pipe between his lips. I saw him only for seconds through the darkened glass of the funeral limousine, but the image has never faded.

One morning about a week after the funeral my wife and I woke early and clung together and sobbed. And she said, 'What on earth are we going to do?' I knew exactly what she meant. How could we go on? How could we survive? But that was the only time we wept together (she had been stony-faced and tearless at the funeral and I, with some mad 1950s version of masculine endurance stuck in my head, had remained *in control*) and this was probably the only time we really grieved together.

Genevieve was buried in what was called the Lawn Section of the cemetery. There was no plaque, no headstone, only a small disc with a number on it. Our plan was that, when we had thought about it and could bring ourselves to it, we would supply some form of simple identification, in keeping with the natural and unspoiled look of the sweeping lawns over which on cloudless afternoons crept the shadows of the sighing she-oaks. But we did not do it. We agreed that we would, that it was not urgent, but something to be done calmly, perhaps as much as a year later. On the anniversary even. But we didn't do it. We never went back, while constantly intending to; and, rarely mentioning it even to begin with, we gradually allowed the whole topic of her grave to die between us.

I often thought of it, with growing guilt but also heavy disinclination. And my wife, I know, must have thought of it with similar guilt. But we didn't confide in each other and we didn't go back together. Ever.

Most families visit the loved one's grave, at least for a few months or years: to read, over and over again, now streaked with rain, now glaring in a hot sun, now plucked at by some winter's withering wind, the same sad words, *Beloved husband of*, *Wife of*, *In memory of my Dearest*; to clear away the browned stalks of the previous visit and lay fresh, bright flowers . . .

It's all hopeless yet these rituals allow the lost one to fade rather than to be expunged. By never going back, by failing to foster each other's grief, we transformed poor little Genevieve's death into a disappearance. She was there. And then she was gone.

'She almost certainly would have been a – she wouldn't have been – normal. Even if she'd, if she'd survived.'

My wife said this one night, suddenly, without preamble, as we sat half-watching some television current affairs program.

'Genevieve,' she went on. 'The meningitis – it affects the brain. It's very unlikely that she would have . . .'

'I know,' I said gently. 'It's just not, it doesn't bear thinking about. You'll only upset yourself.'

I had thought of this myself, many times, but couldn't really decide what it meant. Would I have preferred her to live regardless? As a vegetable? Or was her death 'for the best', as people say? How could the death of any defenceless, powerless child be for the best? But my solicitude, I now realise, was comfortless. It was always, 'Don't think about it', or 'Don't cry' or 'Try not to be upset.' I was well-meaning and loving, God knows, but I didn't understand the nature of my wife's loss, even though in so many ways it was identical with mine. She needed to grieve and she didn't know how to. I should have somehow got her crying, sobbing; I should have carefully raised the matter often, until we both felt more easy with the words, the naked words of loss. I should have expressed my own desperate sense of emptiness and doom instead of remaining locked in that awkward, vaguely loving but inadequate toughness with which I had grown up and which had been impressed upon me, like it or not, as a value, a way of behaving which was superior to the alternative of emotional nakedness and revelation. So, we stiff-upper-lipped ourselves into two brave torture chambers from which we never escaped.

Though there was one thing I did at about that time, before the doors closed on us completely. For me it was a quite extraordinary notion to entertain and even more amazing that I should have carried it out. I wrote a poem. I knew that it was not a good poem and, as I look at it now – the much-folded, yellow-edged page with its three typewritten stanzas – I find no reason to change that judgement. Yet I can still see – and feel – the desperation, the longing, the dread that is locked into the uncertain and inexperienced discipline of those inadequate words, lines and rhymes. I should have gone on writing such poems, however bad, and I should have read them to my wife and got her to read them to me. Until at last we might have reached, through this harrowing and clumsy *in memoriam*, our own poor version of Tennyson's:

> Far off thou art, but ever nigh;
> I have thee still, and I rejoice;
> I prosper, circled with thy voice;
> I shall not lose thee tho' I die.

But we remained silent each in our prison, and only a bad poem, harboured for years afterwards among my wife's treasured photographs and cuttings, came anywhere near unveiling our deepest hurt to each other.

On the Death of My Baby Daughter

The mindless waves still navigate
the gulf; suburban beaches horde
the tide-gnawed shells (insensate
this flux, these nerveless actions –
pointless contraries, blind attractions).

And trees hug earth as greedily,
still cage street lamps in studious arms;
showers switch at lawns as readily,
and grudging breath that's rough with pain
will, paradoxically, sustain.

There was my worst mistake: her life
once gone, I thought all life must stop.
But the stars blazed and waned; the knife
slipped knowingly past bone and turned
with a skill forgotten, but re-learned.

This poem was written six months after Genevieve's funeral. By that time we were in Adelaide. Despite having many times decided to abandon the whole South Australian adventure, we did go after all, in early January 1967. So the poem when it was finally written took on the new context. Instead of the bare street of our northern-suburban rented house in Melbourne, there was the leafy, tree-canopied avenue in Adelaide's Myrtle Bank, where we bought our first house. Instead of the flat waters of Port Phillip Bay which, one way or another, had gleamed and flashed in the background of most of my life, there was the 'gulf', the green, translucent expanses of St Vincents Gulf.

Encountering this poem years later and knowing the circumstances, the painter Tom Gleghorn made it the subject of a splendid religious painting entitled *A Fragment of The Passion and The Death*. And so, in a way, the disastrous episode found at last an end and a resolution. But too late, too late.

CHAPTER 23

Luck, Coincidence, Fate

Early in 1968, my father came to Adelaide on business. He was designing control towers and operational buildings for outback airports, places like Leigh Creek and Alice Springs, and he would be working from the Department of Civil Aviation in Adelaide for a couple of weeks. On my way to pick him up at the airport, I had been to the State Library to collect the bound copies of my MA on Henry Lawson, which was finished and ready for the examiners. These were strewn across the back seat of the car, thick, bright navy-blue-covered volumes with gold lettering.

Whatever had been the distress and resentment of our clashes in the months before Genevieve's death, and even on my visits back after our move to Adelaide, most of the tension was gone by the time I ushered him out to the car on his arrival at Adelaide airport. And if a slight uneasiness remained, just a little strain or uncharacteristic formality, it was dissipated spectacularly when I said to him as we drove off, 'Take a look in the back.'

When he saw the books his face crinkled with pleasure and an uncontrollable grin (he'd been till then maintaining a rather patriarchal soberness of mien). He reached back and picked one of them up, hefting it in his large brown hands, then skipping through the white pages of neat black type.

'Good on you, my boy,' he said. 'Good on you.' And then, with an ironic, sidelong glance, 'I reckon you're a bloody genius.'

Neither of us knew then that the thesis would become a book called *The Receding Wave* and that its dedication page would read:

To the memory of my father
Owen Thomas Matthews

When it came time for him to return to Melbourne, we shook hands and then hugged each other at the airport departure gate and, even though he could not possibly have seen me, I waved him goodbye until he disappeared into the plane. It was the last time I saw him on his feet.

I flew to Melbourne when he had the stroke a month or two later and went straight to Prince Henry's Hospital in St Kilda Road (long since demolished). Though I was worried by what my mother had told me about his sudden collapse, I was looking forward to his pleased surprise when I walked in. But when he saw me, he said, with a coldness that verged on a sneer, 'What are *you* doing here?'

At the time, I thought instantly that he had regressed to the days of our falling out and had lost the memory of recent months. But later, I realised my sudden and unannounced arrival might very well have scared him, have convinced him that, as he was already suspecting from the rogue and remorseless nature of his trauma, he was dying and the death-bed tableau was assembling. He settled after a while and we chatted with the underlying note of desperation that afflicts hospital visitor and patient, the one knowing he will return to a world outside the ward, the other haunted for the first time in his life by visions of the shadow, poised to engulf, palpable and menacing in the lonely depths of the unreconciling nights.

I stayed with my mother and visited him each day. He said often that he had been 'very lucky', by which I thought he meant that the stroke which disabled him might well have killed him. But again, in retrospect, I suppose he was ranging more widely than that, perhaps reviewing his whole life. Beyond that and some idle small talk, however, he was incapable of concentrating for long or getting his tongue round the sentences he needed. The prognosis, though, was for a full recovery provided he could be shepherded through the danger period when another stroke might occur. Today, no doubt, this 'shepherding' process is highly sophisticated, but in 1968 it seemed to me a bit hit and miss. Still, we all had good hopes. After about a week, when I was thinking I would have to return to Adelaide and go back to work, there was a phone call from the hospital in the early hours. There had been, as they put it, 'another bleed' and he was in a coma.

For two weeks we sat with him, taking turns to watch,

whisper, stare, wait. He breathed on, a laborious, struggling rasp and sigh, hour after hour, far sunken from us in a world unreachable. One day, sitting with him alone, I took his hand in mine. The strong brown hand that had swung a tireless heavy hammer, that had wielded a straight-as-a-die saw, that had gentled pencils and pens across the waiting white paper making marvellous sketches or intricate technical designs. I willed him to squeeze my hand as a signal. After a while, I *told* him to.

'Squeeze my hand, Dad. Just a little squeeze, to show we're together, to show you're here.'

I thought he did, but I may have wanted it too badly. I have thought for a long time that he did squeeze my questing fingers, the barest flutter of muscle. But I was never sure.

Three days later, he died. He was buried in the North Brighton Cemetery under a gum tree and only a couple of drop kicks from the newsagents where he and I used to buy the *Sporting Globe* and read the reviled Alf Brown and the latest story on the mighty Saints. Outside the long, redbrick wall of the cemetery, North Road stretches on up to the Dandenongs and Selby, but 1928 Chevs are rarely spotted in the passing parade of traffic.

My mother, like hers before her, now began thirty years of widowhood. For a year or so after my father's death, she coped very badly. The family house, squatting comfortably on its quarter-acre of shrubs, flowers and fruit trees with the chook pen hidden in vines and creepers across the back fence, was too big and complicated for her. And so, in an agony of betrayal and guilt, she sold it and moved to a flat in Elwood not far from the beach end of the Elster Canal, where I had once set off upstream. Living alone for the first time in her life, she could scarcely write a cheque to pay a bill and was dismayed by the intricacies of domestic finance and banking, because my father had always made these his preserve. Dependent on everyone around her, she made little effort to break out of the prison of grief where she felt safe and indulged. After about a year of this and with the approval of my sister, I gave her a stern talking to. The transformation was swift. Within another year she was conducting her life with the old zest and energy, was working as a volunteer organiser for some charitable outfit in the Village Belle, running the affairs of the four flats in her block, had joined a bowling club and become a champion bowler and had resuscitated her betting career with some stunning early successes. She lived to eighty-nine, the matriarch of a broad, scattered, diverse and loving extended family, the likes of which she could never remotely have envisaged when she walked down the aisle with her Owen on 27 October 1934.

Sometime in the late 1980s, I went to Melbourne from Adelaide on some mission or other. My eldest son, David, who had been a postgraduate student at Melbourne University for several years, had offered to meet me and drive me into town. 'After you've done whatever you're doing,' he said, 'let's have lunch.'

He rolled up on time in a calamitous looking FJ Holden, borrowed from a friend. It was blowing thick, noisome fumes and the motor, missing on a cylinder among other complaints, sounded like a tractor in a railway tunnel.

'Get in, Dad,' he shouted, 'I'd rather not have to switch it off.'

Once on the move, the mechanicals seemed to settle a bit and so did David.

'Have a look in the back,' he said, with a quizzical expression I could not read.

I turned and scanned the peeling vinyl back seat. Arrayed across it were four thick, black-bound volumes with gold lettering.

'My PhD,' David said, with a triumphant flourish of one hand off the steering wheel. 'Just collected it on the way here. What do you reckon?'

I held one in both hands. It was chunky, smelling new and feeling svelte. I turned some pages, but the print dissolved in a mist of tears. I tried to rub them away and disguise them at the same time and managed neither. I did not attempt to tell him of the coincidence we were caught in, the outlandish, credibility-testing kind that no one would countenance in a fiction.

'What do you reckon?' David said again. He was enjoying himself and was choosing not to notice my confusion.

'I reckon you're a bloody genius,' I said.

*

London – Melbourne – Little River

1995–2000